SIGNED

SEALED

DEAD

CYNTHIA MURPHY

SIGNED
SEALED
DEAD

■SCHOLASTIC

Published in the UK by Scholastic, 2024
1 London Bridge, London, SE1 9BG
Scholastic Ireland, 89E Lagan Road, Dublin Industrial Estate,
Glasnevin, Dublin, D11 HP5F

Text © Cynthia Murphy, 2024

The right of Cynthia Murphy to be identified
as the author of this work has been asserted by them under
the Copyright, Designs and Patents Act 1988.

ISBN 978 0702 31852 8

A CIP catalogue record for this book
is available from the British Library.

Printed and bound in Great Britain by
Clays Ltd, Elcograf S.p.A
Paper made from wood grown in sustainable forests
and other controlled sources.

3 5 7 9 10 8 6 4

This is a work of fiction. Names, characters, places, incidents
and dialogues are products of the author's imagination or are used
fictitiously. Any resemblance to actual people, living or dead,
events or locales is entirely coincidental.

www.scholastic.co.uk

For everyone who endures cancer treatment.

For everyone who has to watch.

1

The house looked like it had been abandoned decades ago.

I pressed my forehead against the truck window as Dad manoeuvred us on to the drive and flung open his door in excitement. "We're home!" He yanked the back door open so fast I almost took a dive on to our new front yard. "What do you think, Paige?"

What did I think? I thought I was exhausted after a long journey and a trans-Atlantic flight. My brain was at capacity right now.

"It's perfect, Jake," Mum cooed, getting out of the car and walking around to join him. "I can't believe it's ours!"

I slipped off my glasses and slowly put them away, rubbing my dry eyes. Were they even looking at the same building as me?

"It's totally haunted," I snorted, trying to joke. Truth was, the place was so run down I wouldn't be surprised if a few ghosts were floating around in the rafters. I got out of the car, pushed my arms behind me and stretched, a loud yawn escaping.

"Oh, stop it." Dad grinned, flashing those perfect all-American teeth of his. "Come on, let's go in. Sarah, do you still have the keys?"

"Yep." Mum handed him a brown envelope and I watched my parents practically run up the path to the front door, giddy with excitement. I leaned back against the pick-up, yawning again as I watched my dad do the cheesiest thing imaginable and carry Mum across the threshold. Yuck.

"Oh, please," I grumbled, though a spark of excitement was kindling in my stomach. Despite my initial nerves at moving halfway around the world, seeing my parents so happy was kind of nice. Seemed I couldn't help getting caught up in the move after all.

This house was huge compared to the one I grew up in, back in England. I'd memorized the listing after Dad had approached us about moving to the US. I ran through the details in my head as I looked up at the peeling blue exterior. 407 Ocean View has five bedrooms, four bathrooms, a distant view of the Atlantic from the top floor (which I have already claimed) and a pool. A POOL. At home we'd lived in a terrace for as long as I could remember – two bedrooms, one bathroom and a view of the train tracks.

This might be a cool place to live after all.

"Paige? You OK?" Mum stuck her blonde head out of the front door. I touched my own hair, the once tight braid now coming apart at the nape of my neck. I hoped one of the four bathrooms had running water; I was in desperate need of a shower and my bed.

"Yeah, Mum. Coming." I grabbed my small carry-on case and headed up to the house, pausing only to test my weight on the porch steps, where the wood looked damp and spongy. "Are you sure this place is safe?"

"Of course it is!" Mum laughed, grabbing my hand and dragging me up the steps. "It's just been empty for a while, that's all. It's a good job your dad doesn't start his new job for a few weeks; this place needs some serious TLC."

"Yeah. It's a shame you have to go back to work so soon." We stood there for a second, still holding hands. She squeezed mine.

"I know, but we were lucky my company agreed to the move, so I have to jump through some hoops. You coming in, then?"

I looked at the tarnished numbers on the pillar next to the front door, my vision blurring slightly. It really had been a long trip. "Yeah," I repeated, letting go of Mum's hand and dragging the case over the threshold.

A shiver rolled over my shoulders. There was no going back now, not that there was much left at home anyway. Everyone had kind of drifted away from me over the last

3

twelve months. I took a deep breath, trying to channel positive thoughts. A fresh start was always good, wasn't it?

I parked my case and closed the door, gaping at the huge entrance hall.

"Wow."

"Right?" Mum grinned. "Go explore!"

"Sarah! In here!" Dad called from somewhere in the depths of the house. Mum gave me a nudge towards the stairs before following the sound of Dad's voice. I walked further into the hallway, my trainer-clad feet tapping softly on the wooden floor. A staircase climbed the wall on the right and curved around, sweeping up to the next floor where the thick banister disappeared in a curve of dark oak.

I had an overwhelming urge to follow it.

"Paige!" I blinked, putting my foot down on the step. I was partway up but didn't remember starting the climb. My eyes refocused, taking in the darker patches on the ancient wallpaper. Someone else's family photos had hung here once. Dad shouted again. "Come and see what you want to eat."

"One sec," I called back. I craned my neck but I couldn't see all the way up the stairs from here. My stomach growled at the thought of food that hadn't been cooked on an aeroplane and I turned around. My room could wait for a bit.

"Here she is!" Dad beamed as I entered the huge

open-plan kitchen. I knew from the listing this was all new – Mum had swooned hard over the white quartz worktops. Adults get excited over weird things. "Come and have a look at the takeaway menus the realtor left. I don't know about you, but I am starving."

"Yep, me too." My feet made a different noise this time, the white tiles more sterile, hollow compared to the wood in the entrance hall. "Jeez, this is like the whole downstairs of our old house. You could cook for an army in here!"

"Isn't it great?" Dad smiled, pushing a pile of colourful leaflets across the island. I pulled a tall stool out and settled down, resting my elbows on the cool stone as I flicked through menus. "What do you feel like?"

"Chinese food," Mum and I said it together and Dad rolled his eyes.

"Why did I even ask? You are both so predictable. Come on, we're in America! Look, this one used to make awesome burritos … or the burgers here were amazing … or Giuseppe's Pizzeria! We used to go here every Friday when I was a senior!" He stopped as Mum and I burst into laughter.

"Dad, you order. Get whatever you want. We'll have anything, right, Mum?"

"Anything," she agreed, pecking him on the cheek. "You know this place the best. We trust you. Paige, shall we go and check out the top floor? Get you settled?"

"Yep." I jumped off the stool as Dad tapped a number into his phone.

5

"Hello? Hey, Mr Bonucci, you're still there! It's me, Jacob Carmichael!" He paused. "Yeah, I'm home!"

"Oh, bless him." Mum sighed as we climbed the stairs. "He's so happy."

"What about you?" I asked, following her on to the landing.

It was dark up there, the doors all closed. Thick curtains covered a large picture window at the front of the house. Mum pulled them open in a puff of grey dust.

"Yuck," she spluttered. "God, I hate curtains. They'll be the first thing to go."

"You didn't answer me."

"I'm fine, I promise, excited even. If there's one thing us Carmichael women can do it's adapt. I'm just glad your dad is happy. He lived in the UK for so long, and now my mum and dad have gone…"

"I know." Silence fell between us. "I miss them too, but I'm glad he's happy. And it will be nice to see Gran and Gramps a bit more often now we're here."

"It will be. Your dad has missed them." Mum tried the doors until she found the right one. "Ah ha! Here you go, the third floor awaits."

"You mean second floor," I said, climbing the narrow steps.

"Nope. There's no ground floor in the US, just the first floor."

"What? Why? America's weird," I mumbled.

6

"At least Trump isn't president any more."

"Fair comment." I climbed the last step and emerged into the room, Mum behind me. "Oh, wow."

"'Oh, wow' indeed." Mum leaned over the rail. "Jake, get up here, we picked the wrong bedroom!"

"Haha, very funny." I walked over to the long window. It took up almost the whole wall and Shorehaven stretched out before us.

"That's pretty amazing," Mum said. "Makes it worth the move?"

"Almost." I leaned on her. "We were ready for it though, weren't we? The last year was … well, it was pretty awful."

"Yeah." She stroked my hair as we stared at the distant sea view of sparkling blue and white cresting waves. "It was. Did you hear from any of your friends? I thought the leaving card they made you was sweet."

"I've not turned my phone on yet," I said. Yes, the card was sweet, but it was an empty gesture. This time last year they would have thrown me a party, but between helping look after my grandparents and their new social lives in sixth form, I'd become a ghost to them over the last twelve months. I couldn't remember the last time I'd had a meaningful conversation with any of them.

"The food needs to be collected!" Dad called up the stairs, breaking the spell. "Who wants to come? Paige?"

"No, but let me grab stuff out of the car before you go," I shouted, jogging down the stairs. I barrelled to the bottom of the second flight and met him at the front door.

"All right, champ." He ruffled my hair. I let it slide for today. "Come on. I can't wait for you to taste this pizza; you've never had anything like it! They put cheese *and* sausage in the stuffed crust."

"Can't wait, Dad. Grab a fizzy drink too, will you?"

"We call it soda here, honey." He winked. "What do you need from the car?"

"Just my big suitcase; it's got the air bed in it. I'm shattered."

"Me too. Food and bed. It must almost be" – he checked his watch – "seven p.m." He chuckled. "Time difference still gets me, can you believe it?" He lifted my case out of the pick-up's massive, covered boot – trunk, I corrected myself – and plonked it on the pavement.

Sidewalk.

Dammit.

"Can you take your mom's too? She has pyjamas and toothpaste and stuff in there for all of us."

"Sure," I said. He dropped the second one down and ruffled my hair again.

"See you in twenty, kiddo. Tell Mom to call me if she needs anything."

"Will do." I waved him off and turned back to the house, wondering if I could drag both cases at once. I was not doing two trips if I could help it. I nudged my case in front of me and the wheels immediately got stuck in the uneven paving.

"Hey, need some help?"

I whipped my head around, heart in my mouth, to see a tall brunette girl. She was flanked by two boys and they were standing on the road where Dad's car had been. "Where the hell did you come from?" I blurted without thinking.

"Hey, I'm sorry! I didn't mean to scare you," the girl said, her cheeks flushing. She had thick, bouncy hair and was dressed – and I'm not even kidding – in a red-and-white cheerleading uniform. The boys were slightly more casual. One of them wore a tight-fitting beanie hat, even though the October air was still kind of warm. I tried not to think about what I must look like in my travelling sweats. My curly hair was probably poking out of the braid and starting to go wild.

"No, I'm sorry," I said, reprimanding myself. "I didn't mean to shout at you."

"That's OK. We didn't mean to creep up on you!" Wow, this girl was chirpy. She pointed to herself and then to the slightly taller boy in the hat. "I'm Madison and this is my brother, Carter. We live down the street."

"And I'm Josh," the other boy interrupted with a wave. He was slightly shorter than me but well-built, and he wore a red–and–white jacket that matched Madison's cheerleading uniform.

"We're all seniors at Westpoint High." Madison gestured at the large, embroidered W on her top and waited expectantly.

"Nice to meet you. Oh, sorry! I'm Paige, from Manchester. The one in England. I mean, we've just moved here. To Shorehaven." Duh, Paige. Stop talking.

"Well, Paige" – Josh took a step forward and leaned in, like he was whispering a secret – "did you know your new house is haunted?"

2

"Haunted?" I wanted to sound cool and collected, like I found the accusation ridiculous, but the word stuck in my throat, and I choked it out instead. "What do you mean?"

"Nothing." Madison shot Josh a sharp look. "He's just teasing." She glanced up the path to the house. "There just hasn't been anyone living there in a really long time."

"Oh? I thought there was an old couple who died?" I grabbed the handle of Mum's case and started to drag it. "Just give me a sec to take this in, I'll be back in a minute."

"We can help!" Madison said. Her brother made a move to grab the other case and she waved him away. "No, Carter. Josh will get it, won't you, Josh?"

"Sure." He sighed. I shrugged, too tired to argue as Madison bounced up the path behind me.

"So this place has been empty for ages?" I asked.

"Yeah, since we were in, like, eighth grade." She grabbed the handle on the side of the case and helped me lift it up the porch steps, her arm muscles strong and defined. "It was always kind of the … weird house on the block, if you know what I mean?"

"Great!" I laughed, pushing the front door open. "Hey, Mum!" I called. "Did you know our house is haunted?"

Madison paled. "Oh … no, I didn't mean…"

"She's joking, Mads." Carter appeared behind us, Josh puffing up the steps with my oversized case. "I think the new girl has a sense of humour."

"I will after I've slept. Thanks, Josh," I said as he peered around the doorway. "Come on in, then, you must all be dying to see the weird house, right?"

"Well, yeah, kind of," Carter admitted, a crooked grin lighting up his pale face. He rubbed the back of his neck, scratching the skin that was covered by the rim of his hat. Madison tapped his hand, making him stop. "Sorry," he said automatically.

"We really did just want to come and say hi, though," Madison chimed in. "Our moms went to school with your dad. I think he's been talking to them on Facebook or something. They knew you were arriving today."

"Oh, cool. Well, hey, that's really nice of you. I'm sorry I'm so out of it, I'm just jetlagged."

"Of course, sorry. We didn't think." Carter's face

12

flushed. "I know how being tired can make you out of it. Rain check?"

"That means we can do something another time, right?"

"Right." He smiled again and I felt a little flip-flop in my stomach. Beanie boy was cute.

"Why don't we take you out for coffee tomorrow?" Madison suggested. "We can show you the wild sights of Shorehaven on a Saturday." All three of them laughed. "OK, we can walk around town, at least. Maybe drive down to the water. What do you think?"

"Er, yeah, sure, why not. Do you guys drive, then?"

"Of course, everyone here does! I have practice in the morning but we can come and get you for lunchtime? Around twelve?"

"Perfect," I agreed, making a mental note to set eleven alarms so I'd be ready. Carter smiled shyly at me.

"Great. Hey." Madison glanced around the hallway. "Where's Josh gone?"

"I'm out here," he called from the porch. I pulled the front door open wide to see him hovering at the bottom of the stairs. "I just remembered I have to go."

"Uh, OK," I said. Josh was looking up at the house, not at us. "Sorry, I didn't even offer you a drink. Actually, I don't think we have anything to offer…"

"No, we're sorry for barging in." Madison shook out her hair and pulled Carter on to the porch as Josh practically

13

ran to the road ahead of them. "You need to get settled. But we'll see you tomorrow, right? I want to hear *all* about England."

"OK!" I laughed.

"Great, see you then." She bounced down the steps and for a second, I thought she was going to cartwheel across the lawn. "Sweet dreams!" she called, waving. I waved back and Carter held up a hand. Josh waited for them, standing stock still, staring at the house.

He looked scared.

I watched the trio wander down the road before the twins turned into a drive a few houses down and Josh climbed into a gleaming red SUV. They seemed decent. Well, Josh was a little off with all the "you live in a haunted house" stuff, but Madison and Carter seemed nice enough. Potential friends.

I hoped.

I was about to go back in when Dad pulled up from the opposite direction, beeping the horn and sticking his head out of the window as he parked on the drive. "Want to give me a hand here, kiddo?"

"Sure." I walked down the path to meet him, and he passed three huge pizza boxes through the window.

"I couldn't decide what to get, so I got us one each. You're cool with pizza for breakfast, I assume?"

"You assume correctly," I agreed. The cardboard was hot in my hands, so I put the boxes on the bonnet of the truck and pulled my sleeves down. When I went to pick them up again, a glint of light caught my eye and I looked back towards the house, just like Josh had.

He had been staring straight at my window.

"Well?"

"Delicious," I said around a mouthful of hot cheese. I swallowed and took a swig of cola. "Best pizza I've ever had."

"Told you." Dad grinned, picking up another slice. The molten cheese actually stretched up with it, just like in the movies. "Maybe we can try the burrito place tomorrow." Mum shook her head.

"No need. I'm going shopping tomorrow. I've been dreaming about going back to Target since the last time we visited your parents. They don't have shops like that in Manchester." She dabbed her lips with a napkin and took a sip of the beer that Dad had brought home. "What about you, Paige? Did I hear you making plans for tomorrow?"

"Oh, yeah. Madison and Carter invited me out for coffee, maybe show me around town."

"You've made friends already?" Dad smiled. "Good for you, P. Wait – Madison and Carter? The Garcia-Moore kids?"

"I don't know." I shrugged. "They didn't say. They did say you went to school with their mums, though?"

"Yeah, that's them. Mia and Emma," he said.

Mum nodded. "Of course, I didn't put two and two together. They seemed like nice kids. There was another boy too. Josh?"

"Yeah, he was … less friendly," I admitted.

"How so?" Mum finished her beer and started collecting up napkins and putting all of the leftover slices into one box.

"He – well, this is going to sound ridiculous– but he said the house was haunted."

"Did he now?" Mum raised an eyebrow. "And why would he say that?"

"To wind you up, honey," Dad chimed in, though I didn't miss the warning look he shot Mum. "Scare the new kid. There's no such thing as ghosts."

"I know, I know," I said. I chewed the crust of my pizza thoughtfully. "The house does look kind of spooky from the outside though, doesn't it? And they said it had been empty for a long time, like years. Is that why we got it so cheap?"

"That and the upstairs needs some work," Mum said, placing the empty boxes in front of me. "Right, I hate to break it to you, but bin duty extends to America. Can you see if they do recycling here? I think the bins are on the back porch."

"Fine." I sighed. "But if I see a raccoon, I'm keeping it."

Dad laughed. "Hey, check the mailbox too while you're outside. Do you remember what to do?"

"Make sure the little flag thing is down when I've emptied it?"

"That's the one. If there is anything in there it'll probably be junk, but bring it in, just in case I need to forward anything."

"OK." I grabbed the boxes, headed into the utility room and pushed open the back door, emerging on to the porch. It was dark now, but I could still see that none of the squat metal bins – trash cans, I heard my dad say – were labelled. I pulled the lids off to find them all empty, so picked one to shove the cardboard in. That would do for now.

The air had caught a chill since I'd been out earlier and I burrowed into my hoodie as I headed down the back porch steps and around to the front of the house. I smelled of pizza and aeroplanes. Yuck.

The mailbox was at the end of the driveway, next to the road, and the small metal flag on the side was already down. I never understood why mailboxes were outside in America – at home, every door had a letter box, so the post could be pushed straight inside. None of this having to leave the house to get your letters business.

I grabbed the little handle and flipped the door open, leaving it hanging from its hinge at the bottom. It was dark inside. I reached in and patted around, my hand closing around a thick wad of paper. I pulled the mail out and walked back around the house, leafing through it as I did. More takeout menus, a couple of local election leaflets, a flyer for the homecoming parade – that looked pretty good, actually, I'd keep hold of that one – and, at the bottom, a thick, cream-coloured envelope with one word scrawled on it.

Paige.

3

What the hell?

Goosebumps broke out on the back of my neck as I pushed open the door to the utility room. I spread the mail out on the counter and double-checked everything. It was still there, among several pieces of junk mail. An expensive-looking envelope, my name all jagged, carved into it as though the writer had wielded their pen like a weapon.

"Paige? All OK?" Dad stuck his head around the door. "We got mail after all, huh?"

"Yeah," I said, my throat dry. I pushed it all back together and held it up. "Just junk, menus and stuff."

"Bring it in anyway; I'll recycle what we don't need." He turned his back as I followed him into the kitchen, and I took the opportunity to slide the letter out of the pile and into the pouch pocket at the front of my hoodie. I don't know why, but I didn't want to show it to Dad yet.

There was something off about it that I couldn't quite put my finger on. I wanted to open it in private.

"There you go," I said, my voice loud in the big, empty kitchen. "I think I'll get ready for bed; I'm pooped."

"Yeah, us too. I'll bring your case up now, Mom's just unpacking hers… Oh, hey! The homecoming parade!" He passed me the flyer I'd meant to keep hold of before I got distracted. "I haven't been to this in forever. It's next Friday, before the football game. We should go."

"Sure," I said, taking it from him as the letter burned a hole in my pocket. "Sounds good."

"Oh, jeez, look at this. Chase Vickers and Chad Astor are campaigning for mayor." He shook his head, looking at the election campaign leaflet. "I played football with these guys. I can't believe either of them are mature enough to actually be the mayor of this town."

"Er, Dad? Will you help me with that suitcase?"

"Oh, yeah, sorry, honey." He dropped the leaflet. "You were right, just junk mail. Come on, let's get you settled."

We hefted the case up both flights of stairs and placed it in the middle of my empty room. Dusk was drawing in and my view had turned into a long expanse of black and navy blue, punctuated by twinkling streetlights.

"That's some view, Paige." Dad stared out. "I forgot how pretty it was here." He turned to look at me. "How are you doing, then? Really?"

"I'm OK," I promised, not even thinking about

20

whether that was true. I just wanted to open that bloody letter and find out what it was.

"And you're sure you want this room?"

I laughed then. "What, this whole top floor with its panoramic views and full-sized bathroom? Yeah, I'm sure."

"Just checking." He grinned. "OK, I'll send Mom up with the rest of your stuff." He squeezed my shoulders and pressed a kiss on to the top of my head. "G'night, Paige. And … thank you."

"You're welcome. Love you, Dad." I returned the squeeze and he headed towards the stairs.

"Love you too. Sweet dreams."

I waited until I couldn't hear his feet on the stairs any more and pulled the letter out. My name was still there, staring accusingly at me. There was no postmark, no return address. Someone had put this envelope into our mailbox by hand.

But who?

"Paige, are you decent? Coming up!" Mum started to climb the steps, so I shoved the envelope back into its hiding place and hurriedly unzipped my suitcase. I'd dragged out the air bed by the time she reached the top. "Do you need an adaptor for that?"

"Oh, yeah, please." She reached into the overnight bag she was holding and produced one, searching for a wall socket to plug the air bed into. I unfolded the bed as best as I could and we switched it on, allowing it to fill with air.

"This is all yours." Mum started to unpack the bag before she saw there was nowhere to put anything. Aside from us, the room was completely empty. "Guess we need to get you some furniture, hey? We could have a look tomorrow, after you meet your friends?"

"Yeah, that sounds good. Thanks."

"How's the bathroom situation?"

"Not looked yet." I crossed the room and pulled open the door, something brushing against my face. "Argh!"

"What is it?" Mum was at my side immediately, batting the offending item away. I focused my eyes and saw it was only a string pull for the light. I laughed weakly and pulled it.

"Oh, god, sorry. I'm so tired, I thought it was a cobweb or something." The light was dim and a whirring sound started up immediately, punctuated every few seconds with a rattle – an ancient extractor fan. "Wow."

"'Wow' is right," Mum echoed. The bathroom fittings were all a sickly shade of salmon pink, the toilet seat and edges of the sink scalloped, like a seashell. An age-spotted mirrored cabinet hung over the sink, and I opened it tentatively, but it was empty and seemed sturdy enough. I twisted each tap and breathed a sigh of relief when steam started to rise from the basin.

"It might be ugly, but it has hot water."

"And it's all yours," Mum agreed. "No sharing. Does the shower work?"

"I hope so." I glanced around. "It's not that bad … kind of vintage?"

"I'm glad you think so." Mum sighed. "It might take a while before we can renovate it."

"That's OK, I can make it work. And like you said, it's all mine, no sharing."

"Exactly. Here." She handed me the bag. "Towels, toiletries and tissues. Plus pyjamas and a bottle of water if you need it. Oh, and fluffy socks. And…"

"Thanks, Mum!" I laughed, gently pushing her out of the bathroom. "I'm going to see if this shower works."

"OK, honey. I'll unplug the air bed on my way down. Love you."

I gave her a peck on the cheek before closing the bathroom door. "Night, Mum, love you too."

The shower did work – in fact, it worked so well that I soaked the whole bathroom because I forgot to slide the shower door shut. Once I'd finished drying it off, the rattle from the extractor fan had given me a banging headache. I'd have to ask Dad for a screwdriver tomorrow, see if I could take it off the wall or something. I combed some leave-in conditioner into my curly hair, wrapped it in a towel and shimmied into the checked pyjamas Mum had packed for me. I pulled the light switch as I exited and the noise from the fan died immediately.

Silence.

Bliss.

Mum hadn't just unplugged the air bed, but she'd made it up with the duvet and sheets I'd insisted on bringing from home. The pillows still looked a bit flat from where they'd been vacuum-packed into my case, but they looked and smelled like home. I was glad I'd brought them. The air bed was against the main wall, facing the windows, and I climbed into it, shivering as my warm body met the cool surface. I wrapped myself in the duvet before looking down at the object I held in my hand.

The letter.

"Right, then," I whispered. I flipped the envelope over and hooked my finger under the bit near the top that hadn't sealed properly. The tearing sound of the paper seemed obscenely loud in the quiet room, even though my ears were still ringing from the extractor fan. It was heavy between my fingers, thick and obviously expensive. I tore it open all the way and pulled out a single sheet of paper that had been folded in half.

I held my breath as I opened it and read the chaotic black letters.

Hello, Paige.

Welcome home.

407 Ocean View has been waiting for you. You are the new blood it has been craving.

Are you ready to be a part of its story?

I dropped the page, my fingertips burning. What had I just read? The words swam on the page, hard enough to see without my glasses, but no matter how much I squinted they didn't change, didn't say anything different. Two words jumped out at me over and over again.

New blood.

New blood.

New blood.

What the hell did that mean?

4

"She has risen!" Dad cried as I entered the kitchen still dressed in the pyjamas and fluffy socks I'd worn to bed. He was way too chirpy for this time of the morning. I yawned widely. "How was your first night Chez Carmichael?"

"Good," I lied, pulling out a stool and climbing on to it. I had tossed and turned after reading the letter, but I didn't want to talk about it right now. I could barely function. The thick smells of coffee and cinnamon perked me up a little. "What's all this?"

"Your dad found a local coffee place for breakfast." Mum smiled across a steaming paper cup. "He's my hero."

"And mine!" I laughed, eyeing the box of pastries and doughnuts on the counter. "These look amazing!"

"They didn't have that cold brew stuff you drink, though," Dad said, handing me a cup, "so this was the best I could do." I sniffed it tentatively. A milky coffee.

"Smells good! Thanks, Dad."

He sat down with us and I selected a fat, fluffy cinnamon roll from the selection on the counter. My fingers sank into the thick white frosting and I took a bite, wondering if this was a good time to tell them about the note. Mum's eyes were still a bit glazed over and Dad was engrossed in what I assumed was the local newspaper. I took another bite and was washing it down with a swig of vaguely warm coffee when he let out a little gasp.

"What is it, Jake?" Mum asked.

"Nothing. Just, er, current events." He closed the paper and folded it in half, sliding it to the opposite end of the island. "I forgot how different some things are over here."

"Like what?" I asked. "Was it about guns?"

"No, no, nothing to worry about." He forced a smile before changing the subject. "What are your plans today, P?"

Suspicious.

"Madison said they'll collect me at twelve. I guess they want to show me around Shorehaven."

"That's exciting," Mum said, draining her cup. Her eyes glittered, much more alert after a double shot of caffeine. "Do you remember going there when you were little? It's such a pretty town."

"Not really," I admitted. Even though Dad had grown up here, my grandparents had moved out to another town called Seymour when he finished university, so we'd only been here once. "Are we talking Stars Hollow pretty?"

"Prettier." Mum smiled at the Gilmore Girls reference. "You'll love it. Oh, you'll need money! I have dollars upstairs, remind me before you go."

"Thanks. Actually, I need to sort my phone out. Do you think I can just buy a new SIM card?"

"Hopefully," Dad said. "I need to sort our contracts out, but I guess you can get a temporary one for now. No Wi-Fi until Monday though."

"Monday! That's forever away."

"Sorry, kiddo." He grinned at me. "You'll survive."

"When does the rest of our stuff get here?"

"Some of the stuff we sent a few weeks ago should arrive today. Your mom is going to go shopping and I'm waiting on the movers. Once we get unpacked this place should start to feel a lot more like home." Mum nodded in agreement and took a swig of her empty cup and frowned.

"Ugh. I need more caffeine." She checked the time on her phone and stood up. "It's gone eleven already, Paige, you'd better get ready. Do you have something to wear?"

"Yeah, I packed a few things." I licked the last bits of frosting off my fingers and drained my coffee. I could barely remember what I had packed, but I knew none of it would be right. I wondered what Madison would be wearing. Something gorgeous, no doubt.

"OK, good. Let me get you some cash before I go. I'll meet you outside of the town hall – sorry, City Hall – at two-thirty, is that OK? You'll know where it is."

"Can't miss it," Dad said, sliding off his stool and collecting the empty cups. "Let me know when you're leaving."

"Will do," I said, stretching and standing up as they both bustled away. I headed up the stairs – two flights was starting to feel like a workout now – and grabbed my carry-on case from the corner. I dumped the contents on the air bed and frowned. Why hadn't I made more of an effort with what I packed? All the good stuff was with the movers.

I threw my hair into a claw clip and wrinkled my nose. I looked tired and so pale that even my summer freckles seemed faded. I needed bronzer and mascara ASAP.

I looked around the bedroom – it wasn't quite *my* bedroom yet – and studied the selection of clothes on the bed. I needed to pick something cool, casual … like I'd just thrown it together.

Everything on the bed looked like I'd just thrown it together.

OK, let's start with the shoes. It was either the trainers I'd worn on the plane or my white Converse. Easy choice. I chucked the Converse over towards the bathroom door and picked up a yellow checked skirt. It was a little short, but it would be fine as long as I didn't drop anything. It joined the pile as I collected a long-sleeved black V-neck and my make-up bag.

I emerged from the bathroom a different person. I'd

29

scrunched serum into my hair so the curls that grazed my back were shiny and full of bounce. My skin was bronzed and highlighted and my lashes looked twice the length they had before, thanks to the miracle of mascara. I shrugged on an oversized denim jacket and grabbed a small crossbody bag. Lip balm, phone, purse – needed to get cash off Mum – and, on impulse, the letter. Oh, I hadn't forgotten about it, I just needed to decide when was the right time to bring it up. Or maybe I was in denial. Maybe I should show Mum this afternoon.

"Paige? I'm going, honey. Your dad has the cash," Mum called up the stairs. I double-checked my bag and ran down the steps to join her. "Oh, you look beautiful!" She fluffed my hair. "Not that you don't always."

"Yeah, yeah. Thanks, Mum." I followed her down the main staircase. "See you in a few hours."

"Bye, love. Be careful, OK?" I nodded. "Bye, Jake! Back soon!" she called into the kitchen and headed to the front door. "Oh, Paige, I'm going to get a key cut for you; we only have two. I'll give it to you later. Bye!"

"Bye, Mum." I watched her skip to the car and laughed as Dad appeared behind me.

"She will not be back soon." He laughed. "I'd be surprised if she even came home before she picks you up in town. Especially if she finds decent coffee."

"This is true." We waved as she pulled off and I saw Madison and Carter walk out on to their driveway and climb into a white car. "Looks like my ride is coming." I pointed. My stomach twisted in knots. God, I was nervous. At least Josh wasn't with them today: one less new person to deal with.

"Here." Dad handed me five ten-dollar bills. "Don't get used to that, we just didn't know what you'd need, how much things cost."

"Thanks, Dad. I'll bring back the change."

"No need, call it a moving gift." He looked at me the way he always did when he realized I wasn't five any more. "God, when did you get so grown-up?"

"Dad." I felt my cheeks go red.

"I'm not going to embarrass you, don't worry!" He laughed, opening the door wider as the white car pulled up at the end of the drive. "Well, maybe just a bit. Hi, guys! I'm Paige's dad. Look after her for me, OK?"

Madison stuck her head out of the window. "Sure thing, Mr Carmichael! Hey, Paige, you ready to hit the mean streets of Shorehaven?"

I took a deep breath and walked towards the car. "I guess so."

"You look so cute!" Madison said as we got out of the car a few minutes later. "I love your hair; I wish mine was curly. And that jacket, is it vintage? It looks vintage."

"Yeah, it was my mum's in the nineties." I smile, trying to tug my skirt down to a less offensive length.

"'Mum'. Oh my god, I love your accent." She linked an arm through mine as Carter walked ahead, leading us away from the car park. He'd been almost silent on the way over as Madison rambled away happily. "I bet you drink tea, don't you? I wonder if Grounded sells tea…"

"Oh, wow." I paused as we turned on to a cute little street.

"Really?" Madison stopped and tilted her head to one side, as though she was trying to see what I saw. Tall trees marched down each side of the street towards a large, official looking building, their leaves a million different shades of autumn. "I guess it's kind of pretty in the fall."

"Kind of?" I said. "It's gorgeous." Carter waited for us as I caught sight of a street sign among the fiery foliage. Main Street.

Of *course* it was called Main Street.

"You like it?" he asked. His voice was quieter today and he kept rubbing a patch beneath his sweater, up near his collarbone. "Is it like England?"

"No, not where I'm from anyway. We lived near kind of a big city."

"I wish we did," Carter mumbled. "It would make life much easier."

"Come on, Grumpus." Madison let go of my arm and slipped it through her brother's instead. "Let's go somewhere and sit down."

I followed them down the street, looking at as many

32

things as I could. It was lined with the quaintest shops I'd ever seen: antiques stores and cute little boutiques. I couldn't wait to explore properly. We stopped in front of a cluster of bistro tables and chairs on the pavement.

"In here." Madison pushed open a glass door that set off a little bell and a tall blonde guy raised his head from behind a rustic wooden counter. The word Grounded was swirled on to the wall behind him in white chalk, a list of drinks written below it. I scanned it quickly.

Cold brew. Hallelujah.

"Hey, Madison, Carter. How're you guys?"

"Justin, hey! What are you doing here? Back for homecoming?" Madison twirled a piece of hair around one finger and leaned on the counter. "Paige, what would you like?" She frowned as she studied the menu. "They only have Matcha tea, is that OK?"

"I'll get these," I said quickly, the fifty dollars Dad gave me weighing heavy in my pocket.

"It's fine, you can get the next one," she said, her voice a little higher pitched than normal. I looked from her to Justin and back to her again.

"Oh. *Oh*. Er, can I have a cold brew then, please?"

"Same!" She smiled, turning back to the counter and leaving me with Carter. A glance around showed the shop was almost empty.

"I guess we should sit?" I asked.

"Yeah, leave her to it. She's been lusting over Justin Astor forever." Astor. Why was that name familiar? Carter led the way over to a battered leather pair of sofas by the window. I sank down carefully, making sure I didn't accidentally flash him in the process. "So, how was your first night?"

"Fine," I mused, my fingers on the latch of my bag. I was desperate to show someone the letter, but was it too weird? They'd known me, like, five minutes. I left the clasp shut. Yes, it was definitely too weird. We hadn't even had coffee together yet.

"Just fine?" he asked. He had kind eyes, I decided, dark green, maybe hazel. And even though he appeared a little washed out, his skin was still more olive-toned than mine. Not as healthy and glowing as his sister's, but maybe he was under the weather. I wasn't sure about his ever-present beanie, though.

"Yeah, I'm sleeping on an air bed until our stuff arrives. Not the comfiest of things."

"True. But apart from that?"

"Well…"

"Here you go!" Madison appeared, flanked by Justin who wore a hessian-coloured apron that matched the coffee sacks that were scattered around the shop as décor. "A cold-brew for Paige, a pumpkin-spiced latte for Carter…"

"Do not judge me, I am a basic bitch and proud," he said in a mock stern voice as I held back a giggle. Madison placed the drinks on the table and turned to take the final one from Justin.

"And a cold brew for me. Thanks, Justin."

"No worries." He hovered for a moment as Madison sat down. I could feel his eyes on the side of my face. "Er, hi." I turned my head to face him. "Nice to meet you. I'm Justin."

"Astor!" I blurted, suddenly registering where I knew the name from. "Are you related to the guy running for mayor?" All three stared at me. I'd been speaking way too loudly. "Sorry" – I winced – "I saw the flyer last night and..."

"That's OK. Yep, that's my dad, good old Charlie Junior." He leaned forward and spoke with an exaggerated whisper. "Don't tell anyone, will you?"

"Oh! Sorry." He was holding his hand out so I shook it awkwardly. His palm was cool and clammy from holding Madison's drink. "I won't. Er, I'm Paige. From England."

Dear god.

"Hi, Paige from England." He smiled, ignoring the fact I was a bumbling mess. "You've found yourself some nice friends here. The twins will look after you."

"Thanks," I said as he wandered back to the counter. "Is that going to happen a lot? Not me making a fool of myself, that happens all the time." I sighed as the twins laughed. "The other thing. People randomly introducing themselves."

"Yeah, you're the first new blood around here in ages." My skin tingled at the phrase, but Madison looked

35

oblivious. She took a sip from the paper straw in her cup and sighed, watching Justin clean the huge coffee machine. "One day."

"You like him?" I asked, following her gaze.

"She likes everyone." Carter blew on his foamy coffee and Madison nudged him gently. "He's too old for you anyway, he's a college freshman."

"That's only a year. And I don't like *everyone*." She grinned wickedly. "Just the pretty boys."

I laughed and took a sip of my coffee. Stars exploded behind my eyes as the caffeine seemed to land directly in my veins. "Oh, that is good," I said. I drained half the cup and sat back in the squashy chair. "I needed that." The street outside was starting to get busy, and a battered pick-up truck parked outside of the large building at the end of the road. "What's going on down there?" I pointed.

"Where, City Hall?" Madison peered out of the window. "Oh, they're setting up the Halloween decorations."

"They decorate the City Hall?" I asked.

"They decorate the whole town." Madison laughed. "Don't they do that in England?"

"Halloween isn't a massive thing in England," I said. "My dad always missed all the trick or treating and stuff."

"Halloween is awesome." Madison put her cup down. "It's even better here because homecoming is on Halloween weekend. No one else really does it that late, but it's a whole

36

thing here in Shorehaven. Actually, Spirit Week starts on Monday. It's going to be epic."

"Sounds it," I agreed, even though I'd only understood half of the things she said. Spirit Week? Like, Halloween ghosts?

I had a lot of Googling to do.

I watched as a group of men congregated outside of the coffee shop and started to assemble scaffolding for a stage in the middle of the road, placing signs that read "Road Closed" at either end of Main Street. "What's that for? A concert or something?"

"Oh, it's the memorial tomorrow night." Carter pointed at a noticeboard near the door. A poster dotted with photographs of teenage girls and a large "28" was pinned in the middle.

"Memorial?" I asked.

"Yeah," Madison said. "When we remember all the girls who were murdered by the Shorehaven Ripper."

5

"That's, er, normal," I said, pretty proud of myself for not choking on my drink. I looked back at the poster – there were quite a few photos on there.

"It was a long time ago," Carter tried to reassure me. "Like, back in the nineties. When our parents were teenagers."

"Wait, so my dad knew about this?" I felt the blood drain from my face and chest. "Why didn't he say anything?"

"They were away at college when it all happened," Madison said cheerily. "Plus, he probably didn't want to creep you out."

"You think?" My mind was whirring. I loved true crime – no, since last year I had become unhealthily obsessed with true crime. Don't judge, we all have our coping mechanisms. So how did I not know that this had happened in Shorehaven? It certainly hadn't come up on my Google searches about the town, but I guess that the local tourist board probably had something to do with that. "Spill," I demanded, draining my drink and putting the cup down. "I need details."

Carter shrugged and pointed back at the poster. "This year is the twenty-eighth anniversary. Every year there's a memorial on the day the Ripper's first victim was killed, sort of in honour of them. There were five girls in total, but there should have been six."

"What happened? Did someone get away?"

"Hell yeah they did." Madison unlocked her phone and pulled up a photo. "Tiffany Brown. Well, she's Tiffany Vickers now but she doesn't use her married name much. You know Josh, who you met yesterday?"

"Yeah?"

"That's his mom. She escaped from the Ripper after he kidnapped her and her best friend on the way to their homecoming dance. Tiffany was Homecoming Queen and after she escaped, she ran to the school and arrived at the dance all bloodied and torn up." Madison slid her thumb across the screen and produced another picture. This one was a grainy newspaper print and showed a young woman in a long, light-coloured formal dress. She wore a tattered sash, no shoes and a tiara was twisted in her tangled up-do. "This picture is pretty iconic. Last year one of the seniors wore the costume to a Halloween party and Mr

Vickers lost his shit when he saw the posts. Banned this as a costume forever – I think it's actually in the town's bylaws now."

"Wait, Chase Vickers? Isn't he a local politician too?"

"Yeah, the current mayor and Josh's dad." Madison leaned in and lowered her voice. He's the one Justin's father will be running against. The Astors are old money and like to be in control of all things Shorehaven, but I think Mr Vickers will be voted in for a second term." She sat back, smiling over my head. "So, yeah. Tiffany Vickers is a for-real final girl."

"Oh my word." I leaned back into the seat and wrapped my jacket around me. "I can't believe I didn't know any of this."

"Well, there's no getting away from it in October." Justin appeared at our table to clear away the empties, and I hoped he hadn't heard the rest of our conversation. Madison had said he was from *old money*. So why was he working in a coffee shop? Didn't old money mean he was loaded? "That psycho and what he did haunts this town," he said angrily.

"This is not the afternoon I was expecting," I said, still incredulous. I watched Justin walk away. "It's only a small town, I bet everyone knew someone it affected?"

"Yeah," Madison said softly. "It had a pretty big impact. One of the girls would have been Justin's auntie, Phoebe Astor. And our moms probably wouldn't have come home

40

and got together if it didn't happen. It was *not* OK to be gay in nineties Shorehaven, but I guess people had a different outlook on things after so much tragedy." She glanced at me nervously. "And, you know, there were the Jacksons."

"What? The people who owned our house? What about them?"

Carter shook his head as Madison spoke in a small voice: "One of the girls who went missing was Nicole Jackson. She was with Tiffany the night of homecoming. She was the last one killed. And she used to live in your house."

"You're sure you don't need a ride home?" Madison jangled her car keys as we emerged into the daylight. I shrugged my jacket back on and nodded.

"I'm sure. I'm meeting Mum soon, so I'm going to explore on my own for a bit."

"I'm sorry to ditch, we'd stay but Carter gets tired and—"

"Carter is right here and he's fine," he interrupted, rolling his eyes at me. I smiled, but Madison was right, Carter did look tired. I hoped he wasn't getting ill.

"Yeah, yeah," she grumbled at him. "I guess we'll see you tomorrow? You're coming to the memorial, right?"

"Try and stop me," I said, eyeing the scaffolding that was still going up on the road. "My dad has got a lot of explaining to do."

"Go easy on him though, Paige." Carter fixed serious eyes on me and Madison nodded. "From what we know, it was pretty traumatic for everyone who went through it, even if they weren't actually in town. This place was like a real-life horror movie for a while. I'm pretty sure some people never recovered."

"Yeah." I dropped my eyes, shame flushing my cheeks. "You're right, thanks. I still want to come tomorrow, though. If this is going to be home, I want to know about stuff like this."

"Of course you do." Carter smiled but I could see it was strained. The circles under his eyes seemed to have darkened over the last hour. "See you tomorrow, then."

"Yeah, see you tomorrow. And … thanks, guys. It meant a lot for you to bring me out today."

"Of course!" Madison flipped her hair and smiled. "Anytime. I can introduce you to the rest of the gang tomorrow too."

"Great," I said, though my stomach wrapped itself in knots at the thought of meeting more people. I thought back to my so-called group of friends back home. In my limited experience people weren't all as nice as the twins.

I watched them turn the corner towards the car park and checked my watch. Time had flown once we'd got a second coffee and I felt the need to walk off my caffeine high. I decided to walk down to City Hall.

*

The hall was imposing compared to the rest of the street. A large stone building with columns along the front and a large dome that stretched up over a huge clock. As I glanced up, the large hand clicked into place and a bell chimed. Once. Twice... Two o'clock.

"What do you think of Shorehaven, then?" I turned to see Justin behind me. He was still wearing his Grounded apron but had shoved a black zip-up hoodie on over it. He smelled of warm coffee beans.

"So far so good." I smiled. "Apart from, you know." I nodded at the stage. It was almost finished now and some of the men in overalls had turned their attention to stringing orange and black bunting between the streetlights.

"Yeah. You can mostly forget about it for the rest of the year but October..." His voice trailed off. "Anyway, I was on my break and saw the twins leave. I just wanted to check you didn't need a ride or anything?"

"No, I'm good, thanks. I'm just exploring while I wait for my mum."

"Exploring?" He laughed, looking up and down Main Street. His teeth were super straight and white. "I bet we can do that from here in thirty seconds. Let me see." He pointed across the road. "Giuseppe's Pizzeria. Best – well, only – pizzas in Shorehaven."

"We had them last night," I admitted. "They were pretty good, though."

"Glad you approve." Justin pushed his dark blonde hair

off his forehead and pointed again. "Ackerman's Antiques. He only gets away with calling it that because of the alliteration, it's more like a junk store. He sells all sorts, actually. Hardware, haunted dolls, scratch offs—"

"SIM cards?" I interject.

"Yeah, I think he does. You need one?" I nod. "Well, come on, then, let's go in."

"You don't have to," I say quickly. "I don't want you to waste your break on me."

"Waste it?" He grinned over his shoulder as he started to cross the road. "You're the most exciting thing to happen to Shorehaven in years."

I was? God, this town must be dull.

"Er, OK." What was I supposed to say to that? I followed him across the tightly packed cobblestones. The front of Ackerman's Antiques was shabby compared to the rest of the shops, the window display full of dusty crockery and an old, wooden rocking horse with a porcelain doll perched on its back. Justin pointed at it.

"See?"

"That thing is definitely haunted," I agreed, staring at its mucky cheeks and fixed blue eyes. I shuddered.

"Definitely." Justin pushed the door, holding it open for me as another bell tinkled overhead. An old man in a shirt and tie was sitting behind a wooden counter. Long strips of random items from scratch cards to electrical fuses hung from the walls on either side of him. Justin gave a polite little cough and he finally looked up from behind gold rimmed glasses. "Mr Astor," he said, glancing back down at his newspaper. "What can I do you for?"

"Hey, Mr Ackerman. Just showing the new kid around." That got his attention. He looked up again, studying my face intently.

"The Carmichael girl," he said, looking back down at what I now saw to be a crossword. He didn't smile, in fact his face didn't move much at all. His bald head was creased, as though he was wearing a skin suit several sizes too big for him. "Heard he was back."

"OK, then," Justin whispered to me before raising his voice. "We're looking for a SIM card if you have one?"

"Probably do." Again, he didn't look up. I could see a few white wisps of hair dotted across his wrinkled head. "Go have a look around and I'll see if I can find you one."

"Sure thing." Justin replied, tipping his head towards the rest of the shop. I followed him slowly, making sure I didn't knock into any of the stands. Beyond the front desk the place was a maze, filled with mahogany end tables and old armoires. I stopped in front of a stack of ancient CDs and idly flipped through them.

"He seems … nice," I whispered, looking furtively at the front of the shop. Mr Ackerman still hadn't moved.

"Oh, yeah," Justin said, his voice low. "He's a peach."

"Wonder why he doesn't like my dad?"

"What do you mean?"

45

"Just the way he said, 'heard he was back'." I put down the CDs and joined Justin in front of a tall wood and glass cabinet at the back of the shop.

"Don't sweat it, he's like that with everyone. He's the town's grumpy old man."

"If you say so." I looked into the cabinet, my eyes landing on a silver necklace. "That's pretty cool," I said, pointing at the five-pointed hollow silver star. "Very nineties. In fact, I can almost guarantee my mum wore one of these. You think I should get it for her?" I looked up when he didn't respond and saw that his face was fixed in an angry scowl. "Justin?"

"That shouldn't be here," he said, his jaw set. He looked completely different from the friendly guy I'd met in the coffee shop. He turned his pale blue eyes on me. "He shouldn't have this in here," he repeated.

"Have what? What is it?" I looked back at the necklace.

"It's what he made them wear, when he killed them."

"Who?" I said.

But I already knew the answer.

6

"You still want this SIM card, missy?" Mr Ackerman's voice broke the tension and Justin's shoulders visibly relaxed.

"Um, yes, please." My voice was hoarse so I covered my mouth with one hand and cleared my throat as I took a step away from him. I headed back to the counter. "Yes, please," I repeated. Mr Ackerman looked over his glasses at me and handed me a brown paper bag.

"That's thirty dollars. It has data on there, but you'll have to top it up once that runs out."

"Thanks," I said, pulling three rough green bills from my bag. "It's just temporary. Until my parents sort out a new contract."

"Kids," he said, opening the ancient till with a ding and pushing the bills into the tray. He ripped off a paper receipt and handed it to me. "Can't live without their damn phones."

"Thanks, Mr Ackerman," Justin interrupted as he joined me. I shrank away a little – the look on his face before had creeped me out. Mr Ackerman grunted and settled back into his seat, uncapping his pen as he recommenced his crossword.

"Er, bye," I said quietly. I followed Justin to the door and breathed a sigh of relief once the fresh air hit my face.

"I'm sorry about that," Justin started, but I cut him off when I spotted a familiar rental car parked at the end of the road.

"What? About Mr Ackerman?" I ignored what he actually meant and waved to Mum so she wouldn't drive off. "Don't worry, we have grumpy old people in England too. Thanks for helping with this" – I waved the brown paper bag – "but I've got to run, my lift is here."

"Lift?" He looked past me to the blue pick-up pulled up near City Hall. "Oh, you mean your ride." He lifted a hand in a boy-wave to my mum and smiled at me. It was like nothing had ever happened. "No worries. I should get back to work. It was nice to meet you, Paige."

"And you," I said, watching as he crossed back over the street. What had that been about? I'd never seen someone's mood change so quickly. He'd seemed like a different person. I jogged up Main Street, going a little faster when Mum beckoned me through the open window.

"Get in," she called as I ran around to the passenger side. I pulled open the door and jumped in, letting it close behind me. "I don't think I'm meant to park here," she muttered, turning the steering wheel as she glanced over her shoulder. "Give me a second, let's find somewhere to park and—"

"Don't worry, I'm done for the day." I sank back into the leather and sighed. "People-ing is hard."

"Tell me about it. It took me years to get around the supermarket; I didn't know where anything was. I haven't made it home, so I have no idea how your dad is getting on with the movers and I'd forgotten how brain-melting it was to drive on the other side of the road and—" She sighed and glanced at me. "Sorry, honey. How was your afternoon? All OK?"

"Yeah, it was good actually," I said, pushing the weird moment with Justin from my mind. "Madison and Carter are really nice." I saw an opportunity and seized it. "In fact, they've invited me to this memorial thing in town tomorrow. Can I go?"

"Memorial thing?" Mum asked as she slowed for a stop sign. I could tell she was only half-listening.

"Yeah, you know, for the … murdered girls." The car jolted as Mum hit the brake a little too hard.

"Shit. Sorry. We should have got an automatic." She checked her mirrors. "What did you say?"

"There's a memorial on Main Street tomorrow. Apparently a load of girls were killed back in the nineties? You didn't know about it?"

49

"Well, yeah, I did. Kind of. Just stuff your dad told me when we were at uni, really."

"Like what?" I asked, trying to keep my voice casual.

"He knew some of the families, that kind of thing. He was living in DC then, remember? It was in 1995, a while before we met at Georgetown." Her voice was as light and casual as mine, but she reached up and scratched her nose. She only did that when she was nervous. She knew way more than she was letting on.

"Oh, right," I said, staring out of the window. "So, did you know we live in one of the dead girl's hou—"

"Oh, I got you something!" Mum butted in before I could finish my sentence. "There was a drive-through that had these amazing doughnuts, so I got a box for you to drop off at your friends' house, you know, to say thanks for today." She shook her head sadly. "Sounds like they've had it rough over the last year. Poor Carter."

My ears pricked up and I almost forgot she was trying to distract me. "What do you mean?"

"Didn't they tell you? Oh, maybe he didn't want you to know. Don't say anything then, just in case."

"Mum…"

"Carter has leukaemia, honey. He's having chemotherapy."

I felt the blood drain from my face. "He's … what?" Suddenly his pale skin and beanie made complete sense, as did Madison's protective sister act.

50

"For the last few months. It's almost over, I think, but he missed some school at the end of last year."

"Poor Carter," I said. Mum nodded as she signalled to turn into Ocean View. We were home. "Where are the doughnuts?"

"In the back seat. You want me to stop here?" She gestured at their house. Madison's car was already in the driveway.

"Yeah, it's a nice idea. Thanks, Mum."

Mum pulled up at the curb and I jumped out, my mouth instantly watering as she passed the box of glazed chocolate doughnuts through the window. "Don't worry!" She laughed. "I got us a box too. Don't be long?"

"Five minutes," I promised as she drove up to the house. I squared my shoulders and walked to the door, pressing the Ring doorbell. I didn't have to wait long.

"Paige! Hey." Madison flung the door open, her feet bare, nails polished neon pink. "I thought you were meeting your mom! You wanna come in?" She lowered her voice. "Carter's resting though, but we can go in the back room…"

"No, it's fine. I was tired too so we came straight home, but I wanted to say thanks for today. It meant a lot."

"Of course! Did you get a new cell number?"

"I did, but I haven't set it up yet."

"Well, here." Madison grabbed a pen and post-it from the extremely organized console next to the front door and scrawled two numbers down. "This is me and that's Carter." She handed me the note and I held out the box of doughnuts in exchange.

"I'll trade you. Thank you, again."

"Ugh, these are my all-time favourites." She took the box from me and inhaled deeply. "They're so good, thank you. I might wake Carter so I don't eat them all alone."

"I, erm…" I didn't know how to string the sentence together so I just blurted it out. "My mum told me about Carter. I'm so sorry, I would never have dragged you out today if I'd realized…"

"Oh, don't worry." Madison looked sad for a second before plastering a smile across her face. "He's dealing with treatment really well; he'll be fine. Totally fine."

"Great," I said. What else can you say? Just the word "cancer" was terrifying. "Well, enjoy. I have to go and take my whole life out of some boxes."

"Good luck." She was still smiling as I turned to walk down the drive. "Hey, do you want to come for dinner before the memorial tomorrow?" she called. "I know The Moms are dying to meet you." The Moms. I smiled. That was super cute.

"I'd love that," I called back, waving as I walked along the curving sidewalk. "See you tomorrow!"

Madison's front door clicked behind me as I walked the short distance back to 407. I could see the whole of our house from here, it dominated the top of the cul-de-sac. It really was gorgeous.

But now I couldn't stop thinking about the dead girl who'd lived there.

"Shake it off, Paige," I said aloud. I needed to lose myself in organizing my room, stick on a podcast or some music and—

That was it. I could listen to a podcast about the Shorehaven Ripper. My parents probably wouldn't tell me about it. I sped up a little and reached the end of our driveway.

The little flag on the mailbox was still down. I'd almost forgotten about the letter. It was definitely just some kind of mean prank, I decided.

Definitely.

I reached out carefully and opened the little door. Again, it was too dark to see inside the mailbox, so I reached my hand in and quickly whipped it out again when it touched something cold and smooth.

"Paige," I chided myself, "grow up."

I reached my hand in again, my fingers closing around the cool metal shape that sat atop a thick, cream coloured envelope. My stomach dropped as a five-pointed star winked up at me in the sunlight, one of its points threaded on to a thick black band.

It was the necklace from Ackerman's Antiques, and below it, another letter.

7

It couldn't be the same necklace.

My mind was whirring. There was no way Justin – or anyone for that matter – could have got the necklace here before us. Was there?

I slid it into my bag along with the new envelope and walked slowly up the drive. Mum wasn't familiar with the area, so it could have taken us longer than usual to get home, couldn't it? We might have taken a wrong turn or something. Could someone have beaten us to it? Plus, I'd stopped by the twins' house...

No. It was ridiculous. There was no way it was the same necklace; it had to be a different one. But was that better?

Or worse?

The bed of the pick-up was still open, so I grabbed the bags that Mum hadn't taken in yet and closed the lid with a bang. My thoughts were a tangled mess as I headed up the porch steps. Should I show them the notes now? It suddenly seemed like less of a prank.

No. I would go upstairs and open this one first, then I could decide what to do.

"Mum? Dad?"

"In here!" Mum yelled, her voice muffled. I placed the bags on the floor and entered the living room to see her standing at the fireplace, eyeing a large grey sofa covered in cellophane. She finished the doughnut she'd been eating and licked her thumb and forefinger. "It's too big."

"It's fine." Dad stuck his head around the door frame. "Hey, kiddo. How was your day?"

"Um, good, thanks."

"It is," Mum interrupted. "It's a monolith."

"It's a huge room," I said to her. "It can take it."

"See?" Dad grinned at me. "Exactly what I said."

"Fine." Mum threw up her hands, something she only did when she was about to lose her rag. "I need to get the rest of the shopping."

"I grabbed it, it's in the hall." I pointed. "Madison said thanks for the doughnuts, by the way."

"Oh, that's nice, honey." She rubbed my arm absentmindedly as she walked out of the room. "Right, the kitchen…"

"I think she's a little distracted." Dad sighed. "I think we all will be for a few weeks. It's hard getting somewhere the way you want it, and this place" – he gestured at the

55

faded wallpaper and scuffed floorboards – "well, this place needs more than a little work."

"Yeah, I guess." I followed him out into the entrance hall, marvelling to myself that our house had an entrance hall while I dodged the shopping bags. Should I mention that I was aware who the previous tenants were? He might talk to me about it while Mum was so distracted. "So, er, did everything arrive in one piece?"

"Yeah, I think so." Dad picked the bags up. "Your stuff should be in your room. I just let the movers put the boxes in the rooms as they were labelled and they unpacked, something to do with customs."

"Oh, thanks," I said, watching Dad head for the kitchen. Now or never, Paige. "Hey, we got this house pretty cheap, didn't we?"

"For what it is, yeah."

"And is that because—" I was cut off by a frustrated yell from the kitchen.

"Jake! Have you seen the state of this?"

Dad winced. "Coming!" He called back. "Sorry, P, I better go. You head up and have a look through your things. Your bookshelves and stuff should already be reassembled. I'll help Mom organize the kitchen the way she wants it and then I'm going to get the TV set up so we can watch something together after dinner. Sound good?"

"Sounds great."

"Good woman." He nodded to the kitchen. "Now go upstairs before you get a job too."

I didn't have to be told twice. We hadn't shipped any big furniture, we would get that here, but it was nice to see some familiar bits, including a pile of framed photographs. We'd shipped this stuff weeks ago and I was very glad to see a rack of my clothes hanging in the corner.

I ignored them for now and pulled the letters out of my bag, shrugging off my denim jacket as I flopped down on to the air bed. I placed them next to each other, studying each one. They were identical, down to the scrawl of my name across the paper. I opened the original one first, reading it again.

It seemed even more menacing now there was a second.

I pulled the necklace from my bag and placed that on the duvet too. It was a light, cheap piece of costume jewellery, something you'd get at Halloween or for dress-up. I couldn't say for sure, but the one at Ackerman's Antiques had appeared heavier. More like it was made from real metal. This one seemed to be a knock-off.

I stared at the sealed letter.

I had two choices. I could tear it up, put it in the recycling and get on with organizing my room. Or I could open it and then listen to a podcast about the serial killer who'd murdered a girl that used to live in my house.

Who was I kidding?

I ripped open the envelope.

Hello again, Paige.

You have been busy! Making new friends, learning about our town. Such fun!

407 Ocean View is teeming with new life – but there are still secrets. Oh, yes, many secrets.

Have you found what's in the walls yet?

Oh my god.

I swallowed down the bitter lump that had formed in my throat, but it was no good. My mouth started to fill with water and I raced to the bathroom, a combination of jetlag and a litre of cold-brew coffee making me retch. I leaned over the toilet and heaved, my stomach clenching and tears streaming from my eyes. My knees buckled and I kneeled over the toilet seat, emptying my stomach and trying not to think about the last time this bathroom was actually cleaned.

"Ugh." I rocked back on my heels, taking deep, shaky breaths. No one had come running up the steps so at least I didn't have to hide the letters. I sat down heavily, rubbing my face with the back of my hand. It came away streaked with black. I sat there for another minute, maybe two, the last line playing on repeat. *Have you found what's in the walls yet?*

It was time to talk to my parents; this had gone too far. I pushed myself up the wall to my feet, my brain looking for explanations. On one hand, it could be some creep who

58

wanted to mess with the new girl, though I don't know why they would go this far. On the other, there might actually be something in the walls.

I tried really hard not to be sick again.

My addled brain ran through the possibilities as I leaned against the wall in the dark bathroom. There could be rodents, boxes full of cursed objects...

Dead bodies.

"Stop it," I said aloud. I lurched to the sink, pulling the string light and squinting into the mirror. Mascara streaked my face and my cheeks were flushed, my hair a tangled cloud around a pale face. I sighed, grabbing a reusable make-up pad and rinsed it under the warm tap. I wiped away the damage, as the fan made its horrible rattling sound, then turned the light off and went back into my room.

The last thing I wanted to do now was organize, but there was nothing else to do. I dug through my carry-on case and pulled out my phone and a pair of AirPods. I took an earring from one ear and pushed it into the little SIM card drawer without even turning it on, making a mental note to sterilize said earring before I wore it again. I threw the old SIM into my case and inserted the new one before I powered up the phone. It took a few seconds to warm up and then a text came through: *Welcome to AT&T! You have $10 credit to use on data, calls and messages*. Excellent. I should be able to download a few podcasts before switching it on to airplane mode. I quickly opened WhatsApp and sent a quick message to my "Paige is leaving on a jet-plane" group to let them know I was here, I was alive and that I was without Wi-Fi until Monday. Not that they'd be bothered – no one had messaged the group since they dropped off that ridiculous card a week ago.

"Paige? Coming up!" I swept the letters and necklace to one side, throwing the duvet over them as Mum appeared at the top of the stairs, a cardboard box in her hands. She furrowed her brow. "You OK, sweetie?"

"I threw up," I said, sounding like a five-year-old.

"Oh, no! Are you still feeling bad?"

"No," I said, realizing I felt the opposite of sick as my stomach let out a loud groan. "In fact, I'm starving. I think not enough sleep and too much caffeine did it."

"Probably." She leaned down and placed her hand on my forehead. "You feel OK." She produced a huge sandwich from the box. "You want this, then?"

"You are the best mum ever!" I laughed. She set the box down and I bit into the sandwich. My all-time favourite – we call it the Irish sandwich after the ones my nana would make when we visited. White bread, ham, cheese, a bite of tomato and a squeeze of mayo. "It's perfect," I mumbled, even though the bread was a little sweeter than I was used to. My eyes welled up just thinking of my grandparents.

"Good. I'll leave you to it – just shout me if you feel ill again, OK?"

I nodded, my mouth full as I poked around in the box, pulling out a bag of crisps bigger than my head and a bottle of something called an Arnold Palmer.

She grinned. "You look fine to me. Just give it an hour up here though, OK? Don't overdo it. You have plenty of time to sort your room out."

"Thanks, Mum. Hey..." I pulled a small box out. "What's this?"

"Oh, I picked them up today. They're motion sensor lights for your stairs. Thought they'd be handy if you needed to come down for anything at night. They should just stick on the wall."

"Oh, cool, thanks." I dropped them back in the box and took another huge bite of the sandwich.

"See you later." I watched her blonde head disappear and picked up my phone again. I chewed as I typed "Shorehaven Ripper" into the podcast search bar.

Jesus. I had plenty to choose from.

I picked a couple and downloaded them, flicking the phone into airplane mode once they were done and I'd replied to my friends with some photos of my room. I wondered if any of them would follow through on their promises to visit and plugged my headphones into my ears, pointedly ignoring the place under the duvet where the letters were.

Time to organize.

I pressed play and grabbed a clear plastic bag full of

curly hair stuff I had panic bought and had shipped over. The soothing voice of an American woman filled my ears as I carried it to the bedroom.

"Back in 1995, the small town of Shorehaven was rocked by a series of so-called Satanic Panic murders."

Satanic Panic. That didn't sound good. I pulled the light switch. I could barely hear the clanking of the fan. Maybe headphones at all times was the way forward.

"In this episode we will explore the terror that gripped the community over the week of the Ripper's reign, from his first kill on October twenty-second to the evening of October twenty-eighth. Using first-hand accounts..."

Wait.

I double-tapped my ear bud, silencing the host. The fan was clanking as usual. But why exactly was it making that noise? Were the blades hitting something on their way around?

Have you found what's in the walls yet?

"No," I breathed as pieces began to click into place. I dropped the bag and put the toilet lid down before clambering up on top of it. I stretched precariously over the sink and peered through the dirty plastic slats of the vent. The fan itself was suspended in a compact metal box that had been built into a small cavity between the bathroom and outside walls – there should be nothing in there but dust and maybe a dead fly or two. I strained my eyes, but it was no good, it was pitch black. I jumped down and ran back to the bed, picking up my phone and turning on the torch. I balanced on the toilet again and angled the light so I could see in.

There, a dark shape, like a pile of … something that didn't belong there. I moved the light and something glinted back at me.

There was something in the wall.

8

"Do we have a screwdriver?" I gasped, sticking my head into the kitchen.

"Somewhere." Mum closed the door of the cupboard she'd been cleaning so I could see her properly. Her hair had dropped out of its bun and was sticking out every which way. She started to tie it up again. "Your dad must have it in the living room. What's so urgent?"

"Oh, nothing. Just … organizing my books and my bookcase needs tightening."

"We can do that tomorrow, honey." She opened the door again and started filling it with things she'd picked up from the store – dried pasta, jars of sauce.

"No, you're busy, I'll ask Dad."

"'K." She disappeared into the cupboard again. "Dinner and whatever we can find on TV at six."

"Sounds good." I passed through the hall into the living

room, where Dad was trying to lift a huge television on to a wall bracket.

"Oh, P, come and grab this with me." I rushed over and took the weight of one side. "Right, on three I want you to hook that lip over the plate on the wall, see it?" I nodded. Since when were TVs so heavy? "One, two, three!" We lifted it in unison and it clicked into place. "Great job."

"It's flipping massive."

"Yep." He smiled. "Isn't she a beaut?"

"You are getting more American by the second!" I laughed. He plugged it in and picked up the remote.

"Did I hear you ask for a screwdriver?"

"Yeah, can I borrow one? I won't be long," I promised.

"Have at it." He gestured to the tool bag on the floor and picked up a bottle of beer. "I'm going to unwrap the sofa and figure this beast out."

"Enjoy." I grabbed the tool bag and hesitated – was now a good time to ask about the memorial tomorrow? He seemed pretty chilled out compared to Mum, but I'd never discussed anything like this before.

"Hey, look, there's a whole channel of that true crime stuff you like." He shook his head. "I'll never understand the attraction. It's so … what's the word? Exploitative."

Not a good time to bring up all the murdered girls in his past, then.

I got back to my room and checked my phone. It was

just after four. Right, I'd quickly check the fan and then attempt to tidy a little.

I started to tug at the light switch before realizing that would set the fan off. I didn't want to explain how I ended up with one less finger, so I left it off, but it was dark in the room, the only light coming from my bedroom. I shivered.

Maybe I should leave it alone. Burn the letters.

Yeah, right.

I climbed on to the toilet, phone light in one hand and screwdriver in the other. I started in the top right corner, releasing each of the four screws that were holding the faceplate on to the wall. I put the screws in my pocket and lowered it into the sink, flecks of black grime flaking off the inside.

Moment of truth.

I took a deep breath and raised the torch. The interior lit up, thick with grey dust. I could see quite a bit of space behind the filthy blades of the fan and angled my light to get a better view.

There was something in there. I wondered if that was what had been making all the noise, if the fan had been brushing past it every time it was turned on.

"No way." Excitement and fear battled inside of me.

I couldn't believe there was actually something in the walls. Who would know that?

I stood on my tiptoes and reached my hand into the

cavity, batting away thoughts of teeth clamping down on me, or the fan starting up and slicing my hand to the bone. It wasn't too deep, luckily, and my fingers grazed something smooth. I patted around – it felt like a book of some kind and there was something lumpy and slick beneath it. I stood up as tall as I could and pushed my fingers underneath it, grabbing it firmly. I started to pull it out between the blades, my heart pounding, and peered in with my light. The lumpy thing was an ancient plastic bag, so I pulled that through too and climbed down off the toilet. I placed the bag on the floor and grabbed a wad of loo roll, wiping the cover of the book gently. It was made from red tooled leather in a swirling design.

And on the side, a lock.

"Shit."

I emptied the bag on to the floor, and an ancient Walkman and headphones fell out, followed by a sliver of silk and a chunky silver ring set with a black stone. There was no key, but I was still holding the screwdriver. I collected my treasure and walked into the light of the bedroom. The lock was a flimsy little thing. I didn't need the key.

I had it open in seconds.

"This is so weird," I whispered to the empty room. I lifted the cover with a faint creak, ignoring the little voice in the back of my head that was telling me to set it all on fire instead. I opened it to the first page.

There was writing.

The first line was printed, obviously one of many mass-marketed products. But the second was handwritten, little hearts dotting the "i"s.

This diary belongs to
Nicole Jackson

Holy shit.

It was the dead girl's diary.

Song of the Day: "Edge of Seventeen" (Stevie Nicks)

Dear Diary,

Well, that looks weird. Who am I even writing to? Myself, I guess? This is sure not something I want anyone else to read.

CJ gave me this gorgeous diary today, a gift for my birthday. He kept singing that song at me, even though it is ancient. I guess he was right, though.

Tomorrow. My seventeenth birthday. I'm literally at the edge of seventeen.

Tomorrow is also the last day of school. I wish I could be excited about summer break, but there is no way my parents are going to let me do any of the fun stuff Tiff will be doing. They would blow a fuse if they even suspected I was friends with someone like Tiff! I still have to sneak my actual outfit into school, so I leave the house wearing those suits Mom buys me, the ones that make me look like a pastor's wife. I guess that's their final goal for me, make sure I really am a Good Girl.

That reminds me: I need to find a good hiding place for this. My school bag will do for tonight, but if Pop finds out I am keeping a diary, I will be punished for sure. He would find some way to turn it into a sin. I need to think carefully, put it somewhere he would not even dream of looking. I'd hide it with my sanitary items, but Mom would find it there. No, I need somewhere better.

So what do people usually write about in diaries? Their day? That would be kind of boring most of the time, but today was a GOOD day. Mom and Pop were helping at the church clothing drive until six, so I knew I had some time before I needed to get home and make them dinner. Tiff and I went for a smoothie at the mall. (My parents would implode if they knew that. Mass capitalism = sin.) I am not a fan of mushed-up fruit, but someone told Tiff that CJ was home for the summer break, so we HAD to go. He looked super cute in his uniform - a teal polo shirt that totally brings out his eyes - plus he smelled like fresh oranges. Yummy. Anyway, when Tiff was busy, he pulled me to one side, all cute and shy. I haven't seen or spoken to him since spring break, so we were both a little nervous. To be honest, I thought he might meet someone and forget all about me.

But he hadn't.

He handed me this brown paper bag with his college logo on it. I was so confused at first, but when he showed me what it was, I wanted to kiss him. I could barely dare to believe he'd been thinking about me for all this time.

I wish I had kissed him.

So obviously you were in the bag, diary. All gorgeous and red, the color of sin - of Satan. That's not what CJ said, of course, but I know it's what Mom and Pop would think. I think you're beautiful.

But I really do need to find you a hiding place, ASAP.

So, in summary of a great day, I got to see CJ after all these months, and not only did he remember it was my birthday tomorrow, he gave me a gift too! I wish I had a way to see him more often. Maybe I should get creative. What would Tiffany do? (Or what wouldn't Tiffany do? Ha!) He is soooooooo cute and I'm sure he wants to see me this summer too. Maybe I could sneak him a letter or something?

He got that song stuck in my head. I keep thinking it's kind of my song of the day - you're only at the edge of seventeen once. Maybe I should have a song of the day every day. Yes, why not - I'm going to write one at the top of every entry. I almost caught myself singing it downstairs tonight, but singing is only allowed at church so I would have gotten a beating. Plus, Stevie Nicks definitely looks like she would dabble in a bit of Satanic worship. She has such a cool witchy vibe.

I'm going to bed before Pop gets out the belt to punish me for being up too late. He doesn't have to know I'll be lying there thinking about the cutest guy in the world. I can still smell the faint aroma of oranges from his shirt...

Night!

Kisses,

Nicole

9

I couldn't breathe. I closed the diary and stared at it, my eyes swimming a little, my contacts drying out. Nicole Jackson, the Shorehaven Ripper's final victim. I was holding the diary she wrote the year she died.

I flipped through the pages. It was only half-full, her sweet, almost childish handwriting filling each page. There were doodles in the margins, love hearts and squiggles, triangles and stars. Her personality seemed to jump from the book, even though I had barely scratched the surface of her entries, and the reality of the tragedy hit me properly. Five girls ripped from their families, some never found, all over the course of a week. This diary had been started in, what? I flipped back to the first page. June 1995.

Just over four months later she'd be dead.

"Do you know what's in the walls?" I whispered to

myself. Who would have known this was hidden here? And the bigger question – why did they want *me* to find it?

I checked the time on my phone, wondering if I'd have time to read some more before dinner. Five fifty-eight.

"Paige?" Right on cue.

"Coming," I called down to Mum, sweeping up the necklace and letters and shoving them all underneath a pillow with the diary. They'd be safe enough here for now. Mum and Dad weren't snoopers, unlike Nicole's parents.

I walked downstairs slowly, seeing the house in a different light. The home in that diary didn't sound like a happy one, but Nicole sounded like a free spirit. Rebellious, even. I wondered how many times she'd tiptoed down these steps.

I wondered who CJ was.

"There's our girl."

"Gramps!" I squealed, jumping the last few steps and rushing to squeeze the tall, white-haired man in the hallway. "Gran!" I threw an arm out and dragged her into the hug. She stiffened slightly but then gave in, laughing.

"Hello, darling." She kissed the top of my head. "Aren't you a sight for sore eyes!"

"Oh, I'm so happy to see you both!" I pulled away, drinking them in. "What are you doing here?"

"We wanted it to be a surprise." Dad joined us in the hall, two green bottles in his hand. "Cold one, Pop?"

"You know me too well. So, where are we eating?"

74

Dad led us all into the kitchen, where Mum was busy setting places on the island. "Sorry," she apologized, her face flustered, "we haven't got a dining table yet so we're up here this evening. Paige, will you grab those napkins for me?"

"Sure." I collected the packet of patterned paper serviettes from the counter and turned to watch as my grandparents settled themselves on to the high stools. Gran was as formal as ever, patiently waiting for her glass to be filled and making polite conversation, whereas Gramps was the total opposite, loud and exuberant, a white-haired version of my dad. He'd retired from the police force a few years ago, but he still told good stories, mostly when my mum and dad weren't listening.

Then it hit me. If they only moved away after Dad went off to university, there was a chance my granddad would have worked the Shorehaven Ripper case.

"Paige?" Mum held out a hand for the napkins. "Could you get the wine from the fridge and pour a glass for your grandmother?"

"Sure." I pulled open the door of the huge American fridge. Honestly, I could sit in this thing. I picked up the cool, green glass bottle carefully, glad to see that Mum had already opened and recorked it. I pulled the cork out and gave the wine a sniff, my nose wrinkling. Gross. "Here you go." I poured the pale golden liquid into the empty glass in front of Gran, who held her hand out for the bottle.

"It's a Viognier," Mum said as Gran studied the label. "I know how much you love European wine."

"Thank you, Sarah." Gran smiled, though it didn't quite reach her eyes. "That was very thoughtful of you."

I poured myself a Diet Coke and took a seat opposite my grandparents. Gramps was keeping Dad talking, but every now and then I caught Gran sneaking looks around the kitchen, something like disapproval in her eyes. I wondered if she'd known the Jacksons when she lived in Shorehaven. If she did, I'm sure she would have been less than impressed when we bought the house. I sometimes got the impression Gran wasn't a massive fan of my mum, like she thought she had stolen her son away or something.

"Dig in!" Mum placed a huge joint of beef in the centre of the island, thinly sliced and cooked to perfection. "Ted, I know you love my roast dinners, so I thought I'd cook one for our first meal together." She returned with a tray of Yorkshire puddings, golden brown and crisp on top. Dad hopped up to help, returning with a bowl of buttery mash and a tray of cauliflower cheese.

"Oh, my!" Gran laughed. "Look at all of these carbohydrates."

"Well, I think it looks mighty good, thank you, Sarah. I've been dreaming about those York-shire puddings since we were last in the UK."

I giggled, smiling at the way he pronounced York-shire as two separate words.

76

"Thanks, Ted." Mum sat down and filled her own wine glass as Dad placed a gravy boat next to the beef. My mouth watered but it came with a slight twist of longing for home.

Was I homesick already?

"Grace?" Gran held out a hand either side. We didn't usually bother with prayers before dinner, but I had forgotten how religious she was. I held her hand gently. It was wrinkled and cool from the wine glass and Mum grasped my other one. All five of us bowed our heads around the food. "Oh, Lord, for what we are about to receive, may we be grateful. Amen."

"Amen," we echoed. We dropped hands and Dad started to dish out food.

"Mom, I'll do yours." Dad put small portions of everything on to Gran's plate and placed it back in front of her. She'd never eaten much in front of me and had remained a tiny sparrow of a woman into her old age. I reckoned it was more of a control thing than a diet one, but what did I know? I piled my own plate high, pouring gravy over everything in sight. Who knew when Mum would cook a roast again?

"So, Paige, are you excited about school? You start Monday, right?" Gramps asked before he took a swig from his beer bottle.

"Kind of," I hesitated. "Yeah, I'm sure it'll be fine. I'm only there for a few months anyway; I have to start looking at colleges for next year."

"She's already made friends," Dad chimed in, "with the Garcia-Moore kids down the road. You remember Mia and Emma from my class at school?"

"The lesbians," Gran said, her mouth tightening. I felt my eyebrows raise of their own accord. Gran didn't approve of much, but I thought she was more open-minded than *that*. I thought of the little pride badge I'd worn on my jacket earlier today, and opened my mouth to say something when I was nipped on the leg. I turned my head to the right to see Mum make wide eyes at me, eyes that said, "There's no point."

Fine. I would change the subject if they were going to be bigots.

"Actually, Madison and Carter have invited me out again tomorrow. To that memorial thing." Mum nipped my leg again, but I moved away, ignoring her this time. "You know, the one for the victims of the Shorehaven Ripper."

"Excuse me?" Gran stopped pretending to eat and put her fork down.

"Yeah. It seems a bit weird to me, but I guess you guys are used to it?" I turned to Gramps. "Hey, you didn't work that case, did you? I mean you guys lived here then."

"I was at a couple of crime scenes—" An icy look from Gran silenced him. "Oh, but I don't really remember much. It was a long time ago. So they still hold a memorial, huh?"

"Seems like it." I placed my own fork down, my appetite gone.

The rest of the meal passed in silence. Dad took Gran into the living room as Mum and I cleared up and Gramps disappeared on to the back porch for an after-dinner cigar.

"Go on." Mum rinsed the gravy covered plates under the tap before loading them into the dishwasher. "Go and ask him while your grandmother is occupied."

"I don't know what you mean," I said innocently, slowly wiping the island with a damp cloth.

"Yeah, right. Go and quiz your granddad on that case while everyone else is busy. But I don't want to hear about it again. Deal?"

"Deal!" I threw the cloth in the sink and walked over to the utility room. The door to the porch was slightly ajar and I could smell the smoky sweet scent of my granddad.

"Hey there, trouble." His eyes crinkled as I pushed open the door and joined him outside. "Tell your dad this place needs a porch swing. It's nice out here in the evening."

"Good idea. You'll have to visit in the summer when the pool has been refurbished." I leaned on the wooden rail, careful in case the weight of my body broke through it and threw me on to the grass. The pool wasn't the only thing that needed refurbishing. "So."

"So," he repeated. He took a puff on his cigar and exhaled a blue cloud. "What do you want to know?"

I thought about feigning ignorance but Mum was right, I didn't have long.

"Did you really work on the Shorehaven Ripper case?" I blurted out. "When all those girls were killed?"

He looked at me like he was sizing me up and I knew that look, because I did it all the time. "What do you already know?" he asked.

Careful, Paige.

"I know the last victim lived here," I said. "The twins told me that today, but I haven't talked to Mum and Dad about it yet. And I know that tomorrow is the anniversary of when the first girl went missing and that it was all twenty-eight years ago."

"It's been twenty-eight years, huh? That's a mighty long time." He took another deep puff and exhaled slowly. He used to blow smoke rings to entertain me when I was little, but that was before I ripped up and flushed a whole packet of his cigars down the toilet when I found out smoking gave you cancer. "I was never officially on the case, but in such a small town you did a bit of everything when you had to." He leaned next to me, staring out towards the hedges that separated us from the house next door. "What you have to understand is that we had never dealt with a homicide before, never mind a serial killer. Mistakes were made in gathering evidence and such, I have no doubt about it. Most of the police business in Shorehaven before this happened involved chasing underage kids out of Devil's Den or arresting out-of-towners for a DUI."

"Devil's Den?"

"The state park off Route 6. It's a wooded area where … the girls were mostly found."

"Oh." My eyes widened. "Wait, mostly? As in, most of the girls were found there? Or … parts of them were?"

Gramps winced. "Both. Not every girl was found but there was … enough … to identify each of them." He pushed himself up to standing. "Sorry, Paige, that's all you're getting from me tonight. It was a dark, dark time for Shorehaven. Your grandmother didn't deal with it well, so we don't talk about it. She used to be friends with the Jacksons who owned this place; they went to the same church." That explained the disapproving glances from earlier. "We moved out to Seymour not long after that. Your dad was in college and I got a transfer, so it made sense. Thankfully I never saw anything like that again in my time on the force." He walked carefully down the steps and put out the end of his cigar on the gravel. "I wouldn't mention it around Gran again."

"OK."

He walked heavily up the steps and ruffled my hair, just like Dad did. "It's good to have you home, kiddo. We missed you."

I wrapped my arms around his waist and gave him

a quick squeeze, thinking of my other grandparents. "Missed you too."

I hung back as he went back inside. What he'd told me had only made me more curious. I was itching to get back upstairs and listen to that podcast.

And read Nicole's diary.

I went back inside and was just about to emerge from the utility room when I heard voices.

"… asking questions. You might need to talk to her about all this." Gramps's voice.

"I knew this would happen eventually, I just didn't think it would be on her first day in town. To be honest, I hadn't realized it was the anniversary, we've been so busy with the move." Dad. I froze next to the door and held my breath.

"It's that damn memorial. She's an inquisitive one, Jake. It might be best to come clean about everything."

"Not yet. Let her settle in a bit first. We can talk to her next week."

"Your choice." Footsteps now, walking away from the kitchen.

They stopped.

"Son? Just promise me one thing, will you?"

"Sure, Dad."

"For the love of God, don't let her see what's in the basement."

10

"Bye!" We waved my grandparents off from the end of the drive and walked back to the house in silence. Mum disappeared to the kitchen, probably to polish off that bottle of wine after a stilted conversation with Gran. I would have normally helped her with the small talk, but I hadn't been able to concentrate on a thing for the rest of the evening.

What the hell was in the basement?

"You guys want to try out the new TV?" Dad asked. "Watch a movie?"

"Sure." Mum appeared with a healthy pour in her glass. "Paige?"

"You go ahead." I forced a yawn which quickly turned real. "I'm still jetlagged. I'm gonna go to bed." I wished I could just come out and ask them – we were normally so open with each other – but a little cloud of doubt had settled over me. What if Dad never told Mum about the girl that lived here? Would I be starting a huge fight if I dragged up ancient history?

"OK, sweetie. I hope you had a nice time tonight. Oh, wait." She handed Dad her glass. "Take that, I just want to help Paige with the lights I bought." Mum followed me up the stairs to my room. "Where's that box I gave you?"

"Here." I handed her the automatic lights and watched as she unpacked them, willing her to hurry up. She took the palm-sized white lights out and examined them.

"Sorry we bombarded you with that today," she said, still not looking at me. "Your dad was desperate to see them, and we thought it would be fun for them to surprise you."

"It was fun. I'm just tired, that's all."

"Your grandmother isn't happy we bought this house," Mum continued, picking up a stack of metallic circles. She counted the discs and then the steps. "Here." She held out one to me. "There's enough for one above every second step. Peel the backing off this magnetic disc and stick it here."

"OK." I took it from her and slid a fingernail beneath the waxy backing sheet. "Gramps said Gran went to church with the family who lived here?" I placed the disc on the woodwork next to the top step. "Here?"

"Yeah, that'll do." Mum didn't answer my first question but instead peeled another disc and stuck it a couple of steps down. I left it; she clearly wasn't going to talk tonight. She carried on to the bottom, so I picked up the lights instead, studying the switch at the bottom before flicking them all to "auto" so they gave off a soft white glow. "Give me a couple of those?" she said. I padded down the stairs and watched as she stuck them on to the little magnetic circles. "These seem good," she said, watching as I stuck on the rest. The bottom two flicked off until she moved again. "And they work. Excellent."

"Thanks Mum," I blew her a kiss. "Enjoy the film."

"Night, sweetie." Mum blew a kiss back and disappeared through the door. "Shout if you need me. Love you."

"Love you too," I echoed. I sat on the top step for a second, watching each light go out until there was darkness on the stairs.

I got ready for bed quickly and jumped under the covers, pulling out the diary. Maybe I'd find some answers in here.

July 14, 1995

<u>Song of the Day</u>: "Dream Lover" (Mariah Carey)

Dear Diary,

I have just got back from the CUTEST date
with CJ. I've managed to see him at the mall a
couple of times with Tiff, and the last time he
said he wanted to take me on a date. We're going
to meet every Tuesday and Friday from now on, but
tonight was the first time and it was dreamy. We
didn't do much, just drove out of town and walked
around a different mall, but he held my hand the
whole time. IN PUBLIC. I might have even kissed
him in the car...

I'm so, so glad Tiff keeps me up to date on
what's happening outside of the Jackson family/
church bubble - it totally gives me something to
talk to him about, not that I struggle. He's so
kind and he really gets the whole parents-are-
religious-freaks thing.

Talking of Tiff, she told me today that the OJ Simpson case is hotting up, especially after they made him try on the killer's gloves last month. Crazy. Mom and Pop would beat me for sure if they knew I was even talking about something like this. We don't have TV in this house, let alone cable, so I rely on Tiff for my updates. I can't decide if he's guilty or not. No, scratch that. He definitely did it.

Anyway, as you can see, song of the day is a soppy but joyful one, and it's completely appropriate. I know I'm kidding myself with this whole CJ thing. He's going back to school at the end of next month and I'm stuck here for another year at least. He's not going to be some kind of dream lover and come to rescue me. I know that, but for now?

It's bliss.

Night,

Nicole

A muted beeping filled my ears and I pried my eyes open. My alarm. I slapped around the bed to find my phone and silence it before it woke the whole house and then lay in the quiet for a moment to gather myself. The diary was open next to me, along with my glasses. I'd fallen asleep while reading.

But at least I remembered to set the alarm before I did.

I squinted at my phone. Three a.m. What had I been thinking? Nothing good ever happened at three a.m. My room was dark, even with the streetlights outside the window, but I ignored that and threw back the duvet, shrugging on the hoodie I'd left next to the air bed. I was already dressed in leggings and thick, fluffy socks, so I picked up my phone and propped it against the glass on the window sill. I stayed low, making sure I could see the mailbox, but no one would see me if they glanced up. The little flag was still down but that just meant we hadn't put mail in to be taken away. The whole system was very confusing to me. I rubbed my eyes and looked longingly back at the bed. This could be a ridiculous idea, today's letter might have been the last one, but I had a feeling that if someone was sneaking around, the dark hours before the dawn would be the best time to catch them.

I set the phone to record a time-lapse and dug out my headphones. I skipped to the next episode of the podcast and listened to the recap, wondering if I should leave the phone recording until the morning and just go back to bed.

"Episode 2: Satanic Panic in Devil's Den."

Devil's Den? That's the place Gramps said the bodies were found. Parts of them, anyway.

Wait.

I tapped my headphone again and sat in the silence, my brain still foggy with sleep as the evening came back to me. Gramps had told Dad not to let me see what was in the basement.

Why?

I crept back to the window. There was no movement and a scroll through the very short video confirmed that nothing but a cat had passed by. I weighed my options. I could leave this on record and go and check out the basement while everyone was in bed. Mum and Dad would be long asleep by now, and there wouldn't be a better time for a while. But what if there was something *nasty* down there? Should I take my phone for safety? Maybe film it…

Was I ridiculous for even thinking about it?

I chewed on my bottom lip. It wasn't that bad surely, and it wasn't like I was leaving the house. I trusted Mum and Dad that there was nothing dangerous down there. Maybe there was just stuff the old owners had left behind.

Oh my god.

Maybe it was *her* stuff.

"Ten minutes, that's all," I whispered to myself. Catching the letter writer would have to wait. There was no guarantee they would turn up tonight anyway. I crept over to the stairs, phone in hand, when a light flashed on. The skin jumped off my bones and my heart hammered until I realized I hadn't been caught in the act after all, it was just the motion-sensor lights switching on. I took a shallow, shaking breath and crept down the stairs, cursing each lamp as it illuminated. When I snuck into the hall and closed my bedroom door, I was glad to see only a sliver of light escape from the crack at the bottom. I stood still, glad my parents' room was at the other side of the house, and waited for them to switch off. After what felt like forever the darkness resumed and I continued down the second staircase. The basement was directly below, so when I turned at the bottom I was faced with a plain white door.

A single key hung from a hook on the door frame. Dad clearly hadn't thought to move it yet; it was like he trusted me or something. I sighed, hating myself a little bit as I slipped it off the hook. I pushed it into the door.

It wouldn't turn.

Damn it.

I paused, thinking of the front door of our old house in Manchester. You had to almost lift it up with the key before it would unlock. Maybe this was temperamental too. I tried a dozen different ways that didn't work, then I pulled the doorknob towards me with one hand while I turned the key with the other.

A dull click echoed through the hallway and the door began to swing open.

"Here we go," I muttered, flicking on the torch on my phone and regretting my life choices. The air at the top of the basement stairs was cool, and I wrinkled my nose as a damp smell drifted up. The darkness swallowed my torchlight, so I could only see two steps in front of me.

I stepped further in and then hesitated. What if the door shut? What if there was no phone signal in the basement?

What if there were monsters down there?

I gave myself a shake. *Stop, Paige. Think clearly.* I eyed the door and pulled off a fluffy sock, wedging it underneath so the door didn't close all the way. I still had the key so I shoved it into the front of my hoodie, just in case the door did shut, and took a deep breath.

I tried not to think of every scary movie I'd ever seen.

The basement stairs were made of unfinished wood, and I could feel tiny splinters working their way into the sole of my bare foot as I crept down. The air grew even colder as I reached the bottom, but the darkness stayed thick and close, my light barely piercing it. I turned slowly, tracking my phone along the wall in case there was a light switch at the bottom of the steps.

There, on the far wall.

I held my breath as I flipped the ancient switch. A bare bulb started to glow in the centre of the room, dim but better than my torch. I switched the phone to camera mode and started to film. You know.

Just in case.

The basement was huge, almost the size of the ground

floor of the house. My bare foot dragged through a thick layer of dust as I walked across the freezing concrete floor to the other side, beneath the kitchen. There were a few windows high up on the wall at the back of the house, though they were either whitewashed or so thick with dust that you couldn't see out of them. Under these were a couple of old, broken chairs and a large cardboard box that was splitting along one side. I moved closer, aiming the camera at the contents that poked out.

Nothing but newspapers. Dozens of them, yellowing and brittle, ready to spill out across the floor if I so much as breathed at them wrong. I backed away – I wasn't in the mood for a clean-up job or a mould-related illness.

I glanced around the empty room. This was it? The way Gramps had warned Dad not to let me down here, I thought I was going to walk into John Wayne Gacy's basement.

My gaze dropped to the floor as I walked back to the stairs. There were definitely no hand-dug graves that I could see. I used my socked foot as a duster just in case, sweeping a large patch of the floor clean.

My torch flashed on something white.

"What was that?" My voice echoed in the empty room, and I regretted speaking out loud – I had thought it would be comforting but the dank air swallowed my voice and cooled the blood that was pumping through my veins. I looked around the basement for a sweeping brush, or maybe a mop, anything that I could clean the floor with. There was nothing. I crouched down and hesitantly ran one finger across the white patch. It was rough, like the concrete felt on my bare toes. Was it paint?

I removed my other sock and put it over my hand, wiping away wide strips of dust and trying not to sneeze. The white patch revealed itself to be a thick line, like a paintbrush had been dragged in a straight line across the floor.

Why would you paint the floor? Or more accurately, why would you only paint a part of it?

I kept going, wiping away dust until that line intersected a second one, then a third. There was some kind of pattern forming now and I lost myself in the task, my upper arm burning as I continued to literally sweep the floor by hand. The first line continued straight until it almost reached the wall and then started to come back on itself at an angle, forming a triangle with the original line.

Wait.

I'd seen this pattern before.

I was starting to get warm now, my lower back and chest slick with sweat. I swept every inch of the floor that I could reach, trying to film the whole thing at the same time. Dust tickled my nose and dried out my eyes even more than usual. When I reached the other side of the room it became painfully clear that I was now just moving dust from one place to another. My sock was thick with black grime, and I peeled it off my hand as I ran around to the steps, climbing halfway up for a better view through the open treads.

I knew it.

Five thick white lines crisscrossed over one another in a star shape that took up the entire open part of the basement floor. The pentagram was surrounded by a circle that stretched to the breezeblock walls, the symbol identical to the one on the necklace in my bedroom.

The necklace sent to me by a stranger.

The necklace the dead girls had worn.

11

I made sure the whole thing was visible on screen and then stopped the video, snapping several photographs. There was one difference between this symbol and the necklace, this one had extra symbols around the star, five of them in total. I didn't know what they were, but they sent a shiver down my spine all the same. We'd eaten dinner above this ... whatever it was. And my parents knew about it? I felt sick. I tiptoed back down and flicked off the light before running up the stairs as fast as I could, yanking my spare sock from under the door and pushing it closed behind me, past caring if I was caught or not.

I leaned back against the basement door. *What the fuck was that?*

I took a shaking breath. The air up here was so much fresher, but it rapidly cooled my sweaty body and I started to shiver, my teeth chattering. Eventually, I caught my breath and I pushed myself upright. I had so many questions. What was that symbol? Why was it in our basement? And why didn't Gramps want me to see it? I made sure the door was locked and hung the key back on the hook. I was filthy, sweaty and full of dust from who knew when. I tiptoed up the stairs, no other sound in the house, and welcomed the motion lights when I opened the door to the top floor. I crept up to my room, each light switching on in turn, and made my way to the bathroom. I washed my face and hands in the dark, relishing the warm water and the clean smell of the soap. It was almost four a.m., but the sun wouldn't be up for hours and now that I was properly awake, I doubted my screwed-up body clock would rest. I changed my filthy pyjamas and was heading for bed when a movement outside caught my eye.

There was a dark figure standing out on the road.

I dropped to my knees and scrabbled for my phone. It was them, the letter-writer. It *had* to be – who else would be skulking around at this time? I didn't even think – I ran back downstairs as quietly as I could, phone in hand, towards the front door. There were tall, frosted windows on either side so no one could see in, but it meant that they were useless because I couldn't see out, either. Should I open the door? I pushed that idea away – this person could be dangerous. I couldn't let them see me.

Then it came to me – the utility room. I could go out of that side door and watch the mailbox from the porch. I walked quickly, concentrating on the unfamiliar layout of the house so I didn't bump into anything. I didn't look up until I got to the door, about to turn the key in the lock when something made me look up at the small window.

A face stared back at me.

The privacy glass blurred it into oblivion, but it was definitely a face – I could make out the dark blur of features. I clapped a hand over my mouth to muffle the scream that had started deep in my chest. My eyes had shut involuntarily so I forced them open, standing stock still as I did.

There was nothing there.

My body almost melted with relief and I checked the door was locked. Screw this. I ran back into the entrance hall, heading for the stairs. Mum and Dad hadn't stirred – my scream must have been more of a squeak. I crept up the second flight of stairs and ran to my window, looking out into the night.

The road was empty. Still.

Had I imagined it?

I took some deep breaths to calm the pounding in my chest and crawled back into bed, propping my pillows up against the wall. I stared at the sky and wondered why the hell my parents had bought this house.

I wasn't going to sleep now, so I grabbed my phone and flicked through the photographs of the basement, finding the clearest one and putting it into Google image search. I flicked through what felt like fifty different images of chalk art until I reached something that looked similar.

The motion sensor light at the bottom of my stairs flicked on.

Shit, Mum *had* heard me. I dropped my head down and locked my phone, feigning sleep, but there was no sound, no footsteps on the stairs.

In fact, I hadn't even heard my door open.

My eyes popped open just as the light turned off. A faulty light, that was all. We would have to exchange it for a new one. I took a shaky breath and stayed burrowed down, the duvet pulled up to my chin as I unlocked my phone.

The light turned on again.

My rational brain was telling me to go and sort it out, flick the switch over to off and leave it until the morning, but my body wouldn't respond. I lay frozen as the next two lights along flashed on.

Then another.

And one more.

I squeezed my eyes shut and burrowed my head under the covers, holding back a sob. Every primal thread of my being was screaming the same thing.

There was someone in my room, and they weren't friendly.

I held back tears and curled myself into a ball, making myself as small as possible. Even as I did it, I was horrified at myself – I should be fighting, standing my ground or running as fast as I could. Instead, I was frozen, a sitting duck just waiting to be hunted. I clasped a hand over my mouth as a groan threatened to escape. I couldn't see the lights any more but I heard the faint clicks as each one turned off. One. Two. Three. Four.

Five.

They didn't switch back on.

My brain whirled. If there was someone up here, the top light would turn on if they moved, just like it did when I walked around the room. I stayed still for what felt like hours but there was nothing. No click, no shuffling movement. Not even any breathing, apart from my own, though that seemed so loud it could hide the sounds of ten people stood out there. I steeled myself, wrapped a hand around my phone and flung the duvet off, ready to charge at them and run.

There was no one there.

I stood up from the bed and flashed my torch around, setting off the top motion light, proving that it was working as it should. There was nothing. I checked the bathroom to make sure no one was hiding in the shower, though I could see through the open door that it was empty.

Was I totally losing it?

I sat down heavily, rubbing my sore eyes. I was exhausted. We had moved halfway across the world less than two days ago and already I was getting embroiled in my own true crime show, one that I wanted no part in. That was it, tomorrow I was coming clean with Mum and Dad. I'd show them the letters, we could call the police and they could catch the sicko that was trying to scare the new girl. I pushed aside the thought that it could be something else, something dark and unnatural. Something that had followed me up from the basement. After all, it was just a coincidence that my lights had started playing up once I'd seen the exact same symbol on Google image search.

I opened my phone and clicked on the tab again. It said the same thing.

The symbol in our basement was a devil trap.

12

"Paige? Are you up?"

"Hmmmmm?" The world came slowly into focus, starting with the sensation of sandpaper in my mouth. I cracked one eye open, the other smushed into my pillow. "What time is it?"

"One p.m."

"WHAT?" I sat bolt upright as Mum appeared at the top of the stairs, a steaming cup in her hands. The motion sensor light flicked on and the whole of last night came rushing back to me. I clocked the filthy pile of clothes next to the bed and flung my duvet over them. "Why did you let me sleep so long?"

"You were shattered, honey." She knelt next to the bed and handed me the cup, pushing the flyaway hair out of my eyes. "Listen, I have some news."

I studied her face. We'd been here before. "Why do I have a feeling it's not good news?"

"It's not." Mum sighed. "Your grandmother was taken to hospital in the early hours of this morning. She's fine" – Mum stopped my fluster in its tracks – "but she was having chest pains. It could be a small heart attack. Dad just found out, poor Ted only just got around to calling him. We're going to drive up to see her now."

"I'll come too." I set the mug down and started to get out of bed.

"There's no need; we want you to carry on with your day as normal, especially with school tomorrow." Mum shook her head. "Plus, visiting rules are strict: it's one in one out at the moment. I'm only going so your dad doesn't have to drive alone."

"But what if I don't see her before…?" I said, my voice small. I couldn't do this again, it was all too soon.

"I promise you will. She's awake and … fairly coherent. She's just being monitored. We'll only be a few hours and will definitely be home by the time you get back this evening. Dad's already spoken to the Garcia-Moores and they're expecting you for dinner before you go out later. OK?"

"I guess." Mum put the cup back in my hands and stood up. "Drink your tea then come and give Dad a hug before we go."

"OK." The light on the top of the stairs didn't click on

this time. "Hey, Mum? I think the lights might be faulty or something. They went off on their own last night and now that one has stopped working."

"They did?" She pulled it from the wall and studied the bottom. "They might need charging. There's a lead in the box." She pointed at my cup. "Don't be long, we're leaving in ten."

I drained my tea in three gulps and shoved a clean jumper on. The house was quiet and when I got to the hallway Dad was already there, pacing up and down. "Dad?"

"Oh, hey, Paige." He held one arm out for a hug.

"You OK?" I gave him a cuddle and tried to avoid looking at the basement door. A cold shiver trickled down my back.

"Yeah. Gran's fine, it was just a scare, but I wanna see her. You'll be OK? Emma and Mia are going to cook you dinner."

"I'll be fine," I lied. I didn't know how I was going to spend time alone in this house after last night. "Give Gran a big hug for me."

"I will, of course I will."

"Ready?" Mum appeared in the kitchen doorway, car keys in one hand.

"Yeah." Dad gave me another squeeze and took the keys from Mum. "But I'm driving."

"Thank god." She sighed, kissing my cheek. "Right,

Paige, I'll text when we're leaving. Visiting ends at six so we should be home for seven. There's money on the island."

"Thanks." I stood in the doorway and waved as they pulled away. I hoped Gran was going to be all right. I felt kind of guilty that I had brought up a serial killer at dinner, I didn't want that to be my last conversation with her. I hoped her visit here hadn't caused a heart attack. I was glad I hadn't mentioned the basement, this morning would definitely not have been the right time.

I jogged back up the stairs to my room. I needed a shower; I could smell the basement grime in my hair. Then I needed to get out of here for a bit. Maybe I could go for a walk or something, explore the neighbourhood. Walking past the window, I remembered I hadn't checked the mailbox this morning. I peered out on to the street. If I really had seen a figure skulking around last night there could be one in there, but the last thing I wanted to do was go and look. I wished I'd shown Mum and Dad, but how could I now? I didn't want to stress them out even more. I looked down the street and saw that Madison's car was in the drive. I wondered if she'd come for a walk with me.

I wondered how weird she'd think I was when I told her about the notes.

I sent her a quick text message, plugged my phone in to charge and then scrubbed myself clean. Grey water pooled around my feet as I washed my hair, the last of the basement dirt draining away. What had happened in this house?

Oh my god.

The diary.

"Paige," I chided myself as I rummaged around for a half-decent outfit. It had to be tiredness – how didn't I think of this earlier?

There would be answers in the diary.

My phone pinged from its charging station on the floor. A message from Madison.

Madison 13:30
No one walks around here. Plus Sunday is literally my only day of rest. Come over and hang out instead? We can get ready together!

I grinned, typing back. I wouldn't have to spend the day here alone after all.

Paige 13:31
Perfect, my parents had to go out. Give me twenty minutes and I'll be there :)

I looked at the clothes I'd picked out and hesitated. What did you wear to a memorial service of people you didn't know, who had been killed almost thirty years ago? I rummaged around the rack and the unpacked cases in my room and decided to wear leggings and a hoodie to Madison's, then threw a bunch of stuff in my backpack that might work later. I added my make-up bag and started to towel dry my hair with one hand while I dug under my pillow with the other. Should I take everything? The letters, the diary, the necklace? I looked down at the strange little pile. Oh, why not? I placed them all in the bag. I'd show Madison everything.

I had to prove I wasn't going insane.

I combed out my curls, shoved my feet into trainers and slung the backpack over my shoulder, pausing only to grab my phone and then switch every motion sensor light to "off" on my way downstairs. I texted Mum to tell her I was spending the afternoon with Madison, grabbed my house keys and practically ran down the driveway. I glanced back at the house, almost expecting to see a shadow in my window.

There was nothing. The house looked rundown but innocuous. Innocent.

But if that was true, why were there occult symbols in the basement?

I shuddered, regretting my wet hair as a cold breeze blew past. I started the walk to Madison's but couldn't avoid the mailbox. It stood there, squat and menacing, its little open mouth leering at me.

I froze. Why was it open? I had closed it, I was sure of it. Or had I?

I really wished I was the kind of person who could walk past, just ignore it and deal with it all later – or better yet, let my parents deal with it. But I wasn't. Even as I was thinking I should just leave it alone, my hand was already in the open mailbox, feeling around. It landed on something glossy, slick, and I held my breath as I removed it from the darkness.

It was a just a flyer.

"Oh, god." I laughed, my knees wobbly with relief. Chase Vickers stared back at me, his eyes crinkled in a friendly, white-toothed smile. "YOU CAN TRUST IN ME" was emblazoned across the top along with two little American flags. It was another election leaflet. I shoved it back in, but beneath the glossy flyer there was something thicker. Rougher.

I pulled out a thick cream envelope.

I couldn't even look at it. I shoved it into my pocket, forcing back the tears that were threatening, closed the door and speed-walked past the four houses that separated my house and the twins'. At home it would have taken seconds – living on a terraced street meant the houses were wedged together in a row, with no space between them, but here everything was detached, and they all had a lawn and a driveway. I tried to focus on the Halloween decorations that dotted the yards – gravestones with bony fingers reaching from the earth, ghostly figures dangling from giant trees. The house next to Madison's had a giant inflatable pumpkin in the front yard, its generator whirring loudly as I got close. Down the street I spotted what seemed to be a fifteen-foot skeleton lounging over someone's garage. I couldn't help thinking about the dead girls – ghosts and gravestones all seemed in slightly poor taste now.

I turned on to the Garcia-Moores' driveway and tried to pull myself together before I knocked on the door. I wondered how Carter was feeling today. Then, as if I had summoned him, he appeared.

"Hey."

"Hey," I replied, twisting my toe into the driveway like a nervous five-year-old. I hadn't seen him since Mum told me about the cancer thing and it was enough to temporarily overshadow the letters. "You OK?"

"I am now." He held the door open and my heart skipped a beat. "I mean, I'm glad you're here. Mads is being even more annoying than usual and you are about to save the day. Madison!" he shouted up the stairs. "Paige is here!"

"Bring her up!"

Carter opened the door wide and pointed to the stairs. The house was set out differently from ours, so I kicked my shoes off by the door and walked straight into the sunken living room. There was a staircase on the right and beyond it I could see the kitchen, up a couple of steps towards the back of the house. I followed Carter upstairs, looking at super-cute photos of them as tiny tots that ran all the way up the wall. He reached the top and walked along a long hallway before ducking through an open door near the end.

"Paige!" Madison jumped up from a large double bed and gave me a hug. I responded awkwardly, my arms seemingly glued to my sides. "Just the person. I need you to tell Carter that *all* of my ideas are *good* ideas. Here, sit." She pulled me on to the bed and I dropped my bag down on the floor at the side, happy to be distracted. Madison produced two small white boxes and handed one to me.

"What is this?"

"Madison's *great* idea." Carter sighed. He sat back into a huge egg chair that dominated a corner of the room. It was full of fuzzy blankets and he folded his feet in underneath him.

"It's a DNA test," Madison said. "You know, like one of those Twenty-Three and Me things. They help you trace your, like, third cousins and whatever."

"Oh, cool." I turned the box over in my hands and looked at Carter. "So why is it a bad idea?"

"Because I'm pretty sure our Moms will disown us if they find out."

"What? Why?"

"Because we're IVF donor babies." Madison rolled her eyes. "The Moms used Mama's eggs and Mom carried us to term—"

"Oh my god," I interrupted, "I didn't even know you could do that! That is the loveliest thing!"

"Yeah, yeah, it's a beautiful love story." Madison waved her hand, clearly used to the reaction. "Thing is, you need more than an egg to make a baby."

"I'm sure Paige doesn't need to have 'the talk', Mads," Carter said. His face had gone bright red.

"Stop being so prudish, brother. As I was saying, you also need a sperm donor. The Moms chose someone, but it was an anonymous donation."

"You want to know who it was?" I asked. Carter shook his head.

"Not really. But we watched that documentary about the doctor who had used his own, er, you know, with his patients. The kids are all grown up now and started doing these tests" – he nodded at the box in my hands – "and they found out they had tonnes of siblings all over the place. Some of them had even *met* each other."

"I watched that!" I said. "They were worried that their kids might meet and have relationships without knowing and... Oh." I looked at Madison who winced. "You want to make sure you're not going to shag your own brother?"

"Shag?!" Madison howled with laughter and Carter cracked a nervous smile. "Oh my god, I love it. *Shag*." She put on a faux-English accent. "That is the best word. But, basically, yeah. I don't want to hook up with some

110

hottie at college and find out they're my half-brother, do I?"

"I mean, that sounds fair." I threw the box towards Carter. "Very sensible, in my opinion."

"Thank you," Madison said pointedly. "Come on, Carter," she whined. "For meeeeee."

"There's just no point," he said, throwing his hands up. "We're twins! Same eggs, same sperm donor, same DNA results. Plus after all the chemo I've had, that swab will probably melt on contact with my saliva."

"You can't use the cancer card to get out of this one," Madison argued half-heartedly and I felt my eyes widen at what she'd said.

"Of course I can." He grinned at me and his eyes lit up with mischief. "It's got to be good for something, right?" I laughed, glad he wasn't upset. "I've had an idea, anyway. Let Paige do the other one."

"Oh, fine." Madison picked up the spare box and held it out to me. "You want to? It's already paid for, and you just need to swab the inside of your mouth. My friend Iris's mom works at the lab near Boston so we'll get the results back super-quick; I think she's telling her it's for a science project or something."

"Sure." I shrugged, opening the package. "It'll be a waste, though, my parents are both only children of only children."

"Your dad is from Shorehaven though, right?" Carter

asked. "You might have some second cousins or something hanging around."

"And shagging second cousins is almost as bad as shagging half-brothers," Madison said wisely, opening her box and grimacing as her terrible English accent sent Carter and I into peals of laughter. "Please don't tell anyone how bad that impression was."

"I will." Carter grinned and I found it hard not to grin back. He was cute when he smiled. Very cute.

I copied Madison, taking out the little plastic swab and wiping it around the inside of my cheek – it was nothing but a stick with some cotton wool on the end, and when I was done I dropped it into the plastic vial it came with and sealed the whole thing up. Madison had already filled in Carter's details so I just left them as they were and repacked the box.

"I'll give them to Iris later," she said, just as the door slammed downstairs.

"Hi, kids!"

"Oh, shoot." Madison jumped up and shoved both boxes under the bed. "Hey," she called. "Paige is here, we'll be down in a sec!"

"They didn't buy you the tests?" I asked.

"Hell, no. Abandonment, remember?" She batted her big brown eyes at me. "I am totally innocent."

"Come on, Al Capone." Carter pushed himself off the chair with a clear effort. He was out of breath by the time he got to the door. "Let's go and be Paige's back-up while she faces the inquisition."

"I'm sure they're not that bad." I laughed, getting off the bed. Carter and Madison shared a glance. "Oh."

"Prepare to share your life story."

"So lovely to meet you properly, Paige, and I'm sorry about your grandmother. Sounds like she'll pull through, though." The Moms – Emma was Mom and Mia was Mama, which had made me laugh as the whole family started to sing Abba songs – had been utterly lovely and stuffed us with fresh cookies. Madison and Carter looked slightly disappointed that they hadn't given me the third degree.

"Yeah, thank you. Actually, I should see if my dad has sent me an update, if that's OK?"

"Of course!" Emma cleared our plates from the large glass dining table and Mia stood up to help her. "Dinner will be ready at five so we can get to Main Street by six – be ready to go, guys."

"Sure thing." I stood up and pushed my chair in, thanking them again. The three of us climbed the stairs and I picked my phone off the bed to see a message from Mum.

Mum 15:24
All fine, Gran staying in tonight. Home tomorrow if she continues to improve. Dad happy. Xx

"Everything good?" Madison furrowed her brow and Carter took his seat in the egg chair again.

"Yeah, seems to be." I breathed a sigh of relief that turned into a sob. "Oh, god, I'm sorry," I hiccupped, mortified. "It's been a really weird few days."

"I bet. Here." Madison patted the edge of the bed and I sat next to her. "I can't imagine moving across the world. You must miss your friends and now this happens. I'd be a nervous wreck!"

"It's not just that. Can I show you both something?" I sank on to the floor and opened my backpack before I could change my mind. The letters and necklace sat on top of the diary, so I pulled the whole lot out and took my seat on the bed again. Carter pushed himself up and joined us, so the three of us were sitting in a circle on the white duvet. I placed everything in the middle, including my phone. "Please don't think I'm weird," I muttered, "but I have no one else to tell."

"To tell what?" Carter asked gently.

I started at the beginning, from opening the mailbox on Friday to the weird scene with Justin in Mr Ackerman's shop. I passed the letters around and told them that not only had I got home to a second letter after our coffee date yesterday but also a necklace that was identical to the one Justin had flipped out over.

"Oh, Paige, I'm so sorry," Madison said, dangling the necklace in one hand. "This is horrible. It's probably just

114

some asshole from school who heard you were moving into the Jackson house, you know? It's spooky season and you're the new kid; it's a great story for homeroom on Monday morning, that's all."

"Maybe," I said carefully, running a hand over the diary. "But then I found this." I explained about the fan in my bathroom and handed the red notebook to her. "It's hers. Nicole Jackson's diary. It was exactly where the second letter told me to look – in the walls. Who would know something like that?"

"Wait, really?" Madison flicked open the pages and gasped. "Oh, shit. This is intense." She passed it to Carter. "You know her body was never found, right? Well, not all of it."

"Jesus, Mads," Carter breathed, giving his sister a sidelong glance. "How do we even know this is real? The house has been empty forever, it could all be some wild prank."

"I guess," I said. I wasn't convinced.

"Have you read it yet?" Madison asked.

"Just the first few entries," I admitted. "I tried last night but fell asleep. There was a bunch of other stuff with it: a dress, one of those old Walkmans. I haven't looked at it all properly yet. Her parents sounded kind of strict, though. She was sneaking different clothes into school, lying about who she was friends with, that kind of stuff. It makes sense she'd have a hiding place."

"Yeah, I think they were pretty heavily involved in the church." Madison lowered her voice. "You know there was a whole Satanic Panic thing here in the early nineties? Not long before the murders happened."

"Well, that" – I pulled up the picture of the basement on my phone – "might explain this."

"What is that?"

"My basement. I went down last night and—"

"What? *Why?*" Madison gawped at me as Carter left the room in silence. Great, I'd upset him too. "I don't even go in our basement during the day."

"That's because you're lazy and that's where the laundry is." Carter reappeared, a slim silver laptop in his hands. "Let's see that symbol again?"

I handed him the phone and explained what my gramps had said about not letting me see what was down there. "So obviously I had to."

"Because you got told not to?"

"Well, yeah."

Madison thought for a second and nodded. "Seems legit."

"The Jacksons must have been deep into the whole Satanic Panic thing," Carter said, spinning his computer around. The symbol from my basement filled the screen, only this one was black on white. "It's called a Devil's Trap. It's used in certain types of exorcisms."

"Holy shit," Madison breathed.

"Exactly," I said.

None of us smiled.

"There's something else." I told them about the dark figure and the face in the window, the lights going off even though there didn't seem to be anyone there. I slid the new letter from my pocket and placed it in the middle. "Then today I found this."

"Another letter?" Madison breathed. We all stared at it as though it might bite.

"Yeah. I haven't opened it yet." I picked it up. My name was slashed on the front, as usual. It felt quietly menacing.

"You want me to?" Carter asked. I nodded, handing him the envelope. He carefully peeled back the flap and slid out the thick paper, unfolding it and laying it on the bed. This was different immediately – a small hand-drawn pentagram decorated the top right corner.

I held my breath and read.

Hello again, Paige,

I'm quite disappointed that you haven't started to put the pieces together.

I hope you haven't already forgotten what I told you.

Did you discover what was in the walls?

What about ... the basement?

407 Ocean View holds secrets and, dear Paige, I'm afraid it's down to you to expose them.

Otherwise, history will repeat itself.

117

"What does it mean, history will repeat itself? The murders?" I said it aloud, even though I hadn't meant to. The twins didn't answer. I traced my finger over the five-pointed star on the page as Madison picked up the necklace again.

"Is it weird that a symbol found on a bunch of dead girls – and now on one of your creepy letters – looks the same as a demon trap?"

"Very," I said. "You think there's a connection? Between the necklaces and the Jacksons?"

"Maybe." She dropped the necklace. Carter had picked up the letter and was studying it, as though he might find the sender's name hidden somewhere in the text. "I don't know that much about the whole thing. The Moms don't talk about it and the memorial is kind of the same every year. The mayor welcomes the town, then Tiffany Vickers speaks. We take a moment to remember the victims and then everyone drives out to Devil's Den."

"Wait, what? You go out to where the bodies were found?"

Madison squirmed uncomfortably. "It sounds kind of gross now, but, yeah, it's a high-school tradition." She looked at her brother. He put down the letter and shut his laptop. "We were going to go tonight, but I feel a bit weird about it now."

118

"No, let's go," I said. I'll get to witness the memorial and now I'll get to see Devil's Den too. "I think it's time we found out everything that happened in 1995."

13

"It's so busy," I said as we pulled into the same parking lot from yesterday, though this time Madison struggled to find a space. We ended up squeezing into a corner that was surrounded by a patch of manicured grass and a tiny fence.

"It always is for Memorial Day," Carter said from the back seat. "I never realized how morbid it all is, though."

"Same." Madison checked her reflection. Her hair was in a high ponytail and she twirled the two loose pieces of hair at the front, sighing. "Let's change the subject. Do you think I should get bangs again?"

"Nooooo." Carter climbed out of the car. I followed suit and discreetly tried to adjust the waistband of my leggings. "Last time you got bangs you cried for two weeks straight."

"Bangs?" I asked as I followed them towards Main Street. "Am I missing something here?"

Madison stopped and stared at me. "You don't know what bangs are?"

"Er, no? Should I?" I felt heat creeping into my cheeks, embarrassment rising.

"When you cut the front of your hair short, like this." She flipped her ponytail forward and draped it across her forehead. I burst out laughing.

"Oh, a *fringe*! Aw, do it! I think you'd look cute with a fringe."

"Fringe?" Madison rolled the word around on her tongue and repeated it, trying her best to mimic my accent. "Fringe, fringe, fringe. Oh, I love that, what a fun word!" She laughed and threaded an arm through mine. I relaxed slightly. "Yes, I might get a *fringe*."

"Good one, Paige." Carter rolled his eyes, but he was smiling. "That's two weeks of hell for me."

"Quiet, you." She nudged him. "Oh, look. Everyone's here already!" Madison dropped my arm and walked ahead to a group close to the stage. Everyone was holding those white candles with the plastic shields around them. I'd only ever seen them on TV, usually for victims of mass shootings or something like that. That thought triggered my paranoia.

"Hey, can people have guns here? Like, is it allowed?" I asked Carter. I studied the crowd, suddenly wondering if everyone was hiding a firearm. It wasn't something I'd ever worried about at home.

121

"What, here? Like, at the memorial? I guess so." My shoulders retained their hunched position up by my ears. "You have to have a permit, though."

"Oh." I think that was meant to make me feel better. It hadn't worked. "People don't really have guns in England unless they're, like, criminals. Or really posh people in the countryside. Or farmers, maybe?" I was babbling so I took a deep breath to reset myself. "It's a bit scary to think that anyone here could have one, that's all. I've never even seen one in real-life."

"Really? Huh. I guess it's just a normal thing here, kind of wild that it's not like that everywhere."

"Yeah, wild," I echoed.

We fell into step and walked over to Madison. There were probably ten or twelve people clustered together – a few guys who slapped Carter on the back and girls who came over to give him a hug and ask how he was. He introduced me and I smiled and nodded, repeating my name over and over while knowing I would never remember all of theirs. But everyone was … nice. I'd been expecting a caricature of American high school – jocks and nerds, cheerleaders. But there was a real mix of people, and – unless one of them had sent me the letter – everyone seemed delightfully normal.

Until I turned around and stood face to face with the most beautiful person I'd ever seen in real life.

"Hey." The girl smiled at me, a perfect American smile

that even my dad would be jealous of. "You're Paige, right? I'm Shay, I'm on the cheer squad with Madison. We had practice yesterday and she didn't stop talking about the cool British girl who just moved on to her block, so I had to say hi!"

"Um, hi." I tried what I hoped was a smile. Me, cool? To these guys? "It's so nice to meet you."

"Oh, I love your accent!" Honestly, I couldn't stop staring at her face. She had glowing golden skin and big wide eyes that were surrounded with the thickest lashes I'd ever seen. I wondered if they were real. "So, I went to the UK when I was, like, twelve," Shay carried on, oblivious to me staring. "We went to the Tower of London, did you live near there?"

"No." I laughed. "Miles away. I'm from the north of England, a place called Manchester? It rains a lot but it's a pretty cool place."

"As in Manchester United?" A tall, muscular guy appeared behind Shay, draping one arm over her shoulder. Ah, here were my stereotypes: this guy had to be on the American football team because Shay was clearly his hot cheerleader girlfriend. She kissed his hand, confirming my suspicions.

"Yeah, like Man U. I used to go to the matches with my granddad."

"Awesome! Soccer is cool; I play real football, though. I'm Hunter, by the way."

"Hey, Hunter, I'm Paige."

"Nice to meet you, Paige. You need a candle?"

"Um, sure, I guess?"

"I got you one!" Madison appeared next to me, bouncing on the balls of her feet. "It's not a real one, you just flick a switch on the bottom."

"Thanks." I turned the candle upside down and turned it on while watching Hunter from the corner of my eye. He disentangled himself from Shay and melted into the crowd, leaving the three of us standing there. Madison looked everywhere apart from at Shay, and I got the distinct vibe that something was a bit off between them. Shay seemed oblivious though, her eyes on the stage as a very smartly dressed man climbed the steps and approached the microphone.

The crowd fell silent instantly.

"Good evening, Shorehaven, and thank you for joining us on this special evening." The man was tall, with broad shoulders and dark hair that was greying at the temples. I recognized him from the leaflet I'd crumpled up earlier. Chase Vickers: current mayor of Shorehaven, Josh's dad and husband of Tiffany Vickers, sole survivor of the Shorehaven Ripper. "I say 'special' because it's a testament to our town that we continue to honour the memories of the five amazing women whose lives were so cruelly taken away. In a moment, I'm going to introduce my fearless wife, Tiffany, to remind you exactly why we are here."

"If she can climb the steps," Madison said behind her hand. "We just saw her down a glass of wine behind the stage."

"I think I would have too," I muttered back, looking at the crowd. There must be five hundred people here; the whole of Main Street was packed with bodies and more were joining every second.

"Please welcome my wife, Tiffany Vickers." Chase stretched out an arm in the direction of the steps that descended from the right of the stage. A petite black woman in a tailored trouser suit walked across the stage and the couple exchanged a practised kiss on the cheek. Chase retreated to the back of the stage as Tiffany stood in front of the microphone, pulling a wad of notecards from her pocket.

"Good evening, everyone." Her voice was steady – either it hadn't been wine she was drinking or she was used to downing a glass like water. "First, I would like to thank you all for joining us here tonight. Today marks the twenty-eighth year since our lives changed irreparably. October 1995 saw events like no other in Shorehaven's history and, despite the time that has passed, I am secure in the knowledge that law enforcement continue to look for ways to identify the killer and bring them to justice."

"Wait," I whispered. "They never caught the killer?"

"No," Madison whispered back.

Shay shook her head. "Scary, right?"

"Yeah," I said, thinking of the letters. They had just been a prank, hadn't they? "Very."

Tiffany continued her speech and I studied her carefully. Her hair was worn in natural curls but obviously professionally styled, her nails bright and manicured. Her make-up was perfectly tasteful for a woman in her mid-forties and the hot-pink suit that she wore complimented her skin tone beautifully. She looked expensive, an aging beauty queen who had done well in life. "Please join me for a moment of silence as we remember the young women who were taken too soon. Brittany Hendrik, Misty Bonucci, Phoebe Astor, Erin Ackerman and my best friend, Nicole Jackson."

The crowd bowed their heads and I copied them, looking down at my Converse as Main Street observed the silence. I recognized some of the surnames – this really had affected the whole town. I wondered what it had been like for Tiffany, being the target of a killer, her best friend the final victim. I wondered if she was still like the Tiff Nicole had mentioned in her diary. She had sounded fun and a little reckless but had clearly been a good friend.

I wondered if she felt guilty for surviving.

"Thank you," she breathed into the microphone and the crowd erupted into applause. Chase took over, thanking the spectators for coming, and as quickly as it had started, the whole thing was over. The crowd dispersed before my eyes, disappearing towards the parking lot or into the restaurants and coffee shops that had stayed open late.

"What now?" I asked Madison, but Shay was the one who answered.

"Now we party!" she squealed, drawing looks from an elderly couple walking towards Grounded. "Oops." She giggled. "Sorry. I'm just excited."

"Let's get going, then." Madison stood on tiptoes to scour the crowd. "Carter! You ready?"

"Coming," he called, saying goodbye to the guys he was talking to. Josh was there now that his mom had finished her speech and he caught my eye, nodding in my direction. No wonder he'd looked so weird at my house. I waved back at him and wondered what he had heard over the years. Carter and Josh weaved through the crowd to join us and Carter's cheeks grew red as he saw who we were with. "Oh, hi, Shay."

"Hey, how're you doing?" Her eyes filled with sympathy and I suddenly felt massively protective over Carter, which was ridiculous since I'd known him for two days. But in that moment, I saw that she was looking at his illness, not him, and that sucked.

"Yeah, good, thanks." He said, though he looked deflated at the question. Josh cleared his throat and changed the subject for him.

"Are you guys coming out to— "

"Josh! There you are." Chase Vickers appeared behind his son and Josh pressed his lips together as a large hand landed on his shoulder. "We wanted to see you before we set off."

"Oh, hey, Dad. You know Shay and the twins, right? And this is Paige Carmichael. She's just moved from—"

"England," Chase finished, removing his hand from Josh's shoulder so he could crush my hand in a short handshake. He was much more imposing up close, taller than Josh and he still had the build of a football player. "You're Jake Carmichael's daughter."

"I am." I discreetly wiggled my sore fingers. "We just got here yesterday. Nice to meet you."

"Likewise." He turned his attention back to Josh. "Come say bye to your mom before I take her home."

"Sure." Josh turned to us. "See you later." He followed his dad back to the stage area and I watched as he begrudgingly allowed his mum to fuss with his hair and the collar of his green polo shirt. Did she know he was going up to Devil's Den tonight? I couldn't imagine she would ever want her son anywhere near the place she was almost murdered.

"Are you ready to go, Paige?" Madison said, digging car keys out of her bag.

"Oh, yeah. Sorry," I turned my attention back to Shay and the twins. "So, that was the mayor of Shorehaven."

"Sure was. Carter, you ready?"

"Yeah." He was still making doe-eyes at Shay. "Do you, um, do you need a ride? We have space," Carter asked her. Madison looked like she might pop a blood vessel.

"No, I came in Hunter's car." She gave him a twinkling smile and scanned the crowd. "Thanks, though. See you guys there!"

"Bye, Shay," I said as she went to find her boyfriend. Carter looked crestfallen and something stirred in the pit of my stomach.

Was I *jealous*?

"Snap out of it, Carter." Madison rolled her eyes. "It's never gonna happen."

"I know," he said quietly, studying the pavement as we passed Grounded. I glanced in the window, trying to distance myself from sibling talk and saw Justin was staring out at us. He waved, a milk jug in one hand, and I waved back, a little uncomfortable.

"Will Justin be coming tonight?" I asked.

Madison raised her eyebrows. "Why?"

"Oh, no reason." She gave me a look that made it clear she thought I was interested in him. "OK, to be honest he made me a little uncomfortable yesterday. And then I found the necklace in my mailbox…"

"You don't think he did it?"

"No." I opened the back door, climbing in quickly so Carter could sit up front. "I don't know. Maybe he did? It's a pretty weird coincidence."

"It's all pretty weird," Madison said. "Come on, let's get there and show our faces so we can leave. I'm suddenly not in the mood for Devil's Den."

We drove in silence until Carter connected his phone to the speakers and started playing music. I watched houses turn to country roads as we drove. "How long is the drive?"

"About twenty minutes." Carter twisted his head to talk to me. "Just long enough for me to play you half a Sam Hunt album."

"Never heard of him," I admitted. I kind of liked it, though.

"This album is *Montevallo*. Listen to the lyrics. Some of them are really clever. He's a great songwriter." Carter turned it up and a deep bass beat filled the car.

"Plus, he's hot," Madison shouted over the music. "Very, very hot."

I grinned as the twins started to sing together in the front seat, seemingly back to normal. It had always amazed me how siblings could go from bickering to besties in a matter of seconds. I was a tiny bit jealous as I watched them alternate the high and low parts and try to outdo one another when the singer started to rap. The music slowed to a more relaxed rhythm, and the singer's raspy voice filled the car with lyrics about stars and treetops, driving out to the woods. If I was to have a song of the day, like Nicole did, it could be this one.

But without all the kissing he mentioned.

Sam Hunt, Montevallo. I made a mental note to download the album when I got home tonight. It would give me something else to talk to Carter about.

"Here we go," Madison said, turning down the music and slowing the car. The headlights flashed on a tall sign emblazoned with the words: "You are now entering Devil's Den. Please drive carefully." We took a right turn and straight away trees closed in on either side. We curved slowly upwards. "We have to park up here and then walk in a little bit."

"OK." I checked my phone. Seven p.m. "How long do you think we'll be? I just want to give my parents an ETA. They should be home soon." I hadn't actually heard from them since Mum's earlier text, so I hoped everything was OK with Gran.

"An hour?" Madison said and Carter nodded in agreement. "We'll be home before nine, anyway. It's your first day of school tomorrow, you'll need your wits about you."

"Ugh, don't remind me." I'd managed not to think about school too much, what with everything else going on. Now it loomed large in front of me. To be honest, I'd kind of *forced* myself not to think about it because when I did, little black vines of anxiety started to creep into the corners of my vision. Pretending it was just another normal week was the only thing that kept me from overthinking every single aspect of a new school.

"You'll be great. It's a super fun week, what with

homecoming this weekend." Madison pulled into a parking area, the woodchip covered ground crunching beneath the tyres. She caught my eye in the rear-view mirror. "You *are* coming to homecoming?"

"I don't even really know what homecoming is." I laughed as her face went slack with shock. "You can tell me all about it on the way back."

"Oh, don't you worry," Carter said as he unbuckled his seat belt. "She will."

A couple more cars pulled up as we started the walk into the woods. It was so dark out here, but the sky was amazing, a scattering of silver stars across dark blue velvet. I'd never seen anything like it.

"Pretty special, huh?" Carter asked, pulling a thick black puffa coat around him. It wasn't freezing but I wondered if chemo could make you feel the cold a little more than normal.

"Yeah, it really is. Are you feeling OK?"

"Yeah, just tired. Don't worry about me, I'm not the one about to be thrown to the wolves."

"What?" My blood ran cold then, goosebumps exploding down my arms.

"Oh, no, I just mean you're the new blood. Everyone is going to want a piece of you tonight." He stopped. "Eww, I just heard how that sounded. Sorry."

"Come on, you two!" Madison called from the trees up ahead.

"Coming!" Carter looked at me. "Sorry, I didn't mean to be weird. I just meant that everyone would want to meet the English girl, that's all. You're big news around here." We crunched through the trees and into a clearing. The stars were even brighter here, and I could see that the edge of the path fell away behind a thin metal barrier.

"I hope that is all," I tried to joke. There were about thirty kids here already and in seconds Madison was dragging me around, introducing me to everyone. Even though it was still early, a lot of them were already dancing to music that was blasting out of a portable speaker. Massive coolers spilled out a variety of drinks on to the ground and when a can of beer was thrust into my hand, already popped open, I decided not to drink out of it under any circumstances.

The evening was flying by in a blur, like so much of my life had over the last few days. I wondered if I'd ever get used to the change. I learned and forgot a bunch of new names and saw Shay and Hunter dancing together a couple of times, but Carter and Madison had both disappeared, so I went on to autopilot, nodding and smiling, answering questions about England and if I really drank cups of tea and if I had met Prince Harry or not. I finally excused myself and checked the time, looking for somewhere to ditch my still-full drink – my parents would be home soon. I wondered how Gran was.

"Hey." A familiar voice broke through my maudlin

thoughts. Justin stood in front of me, holding a can of his own.

The hairs on the back of my neck prickled and I hugged my coat a little tighter.

"Oh, hey," I said, looking for the twins as discreetly as I could, but Madison was on the other side of the clearing and I couldn't see Carter anywhere. "I didn't expect to see you here."

"Why, am I too old?" he said, laughing humourlessly before taking a swig of his drink.

"No," I rushed to say, even though, yeah, he kind of *was* too old. Justin was a college freshman. Was it skeezy that he was at a high school party? "I thought you'd be working late or something."

"Nope, all locked up." His eyes were a little glassy and I wondered how many of those cans he'd downed already. I really hoped he wasn't driving. "Listen, I wanted to say sorry about the other day. About the necklace."

"What?" Panic crushed my chest and I scanned the crowd for someone I knew. "What necklace?" I squeaked.

"The one at Mr Ackerman's. I know I upset you, it just ... triggered me. I haven't had a chance to say sorry about that."

"Oh, I didn't even notice," I said, trying to sound casual, but hoping he didn't hear the squeak in my voice. Why would he bring that up out here of all places? "Don't worry about it," I said, almost jumping in joy when I saw

Madison. I waved furiously, not caring what Justin Astor thought about it. "There's my ride. Nice talking to you!" I left without waiting for him to respond and practically ran over to my friend.

"Hey," she said, raising her eyebrows. "You OK?"

"Yeah." I glanced over my shoulder. Justin had joined another group but was still looking our way. "That guy gives me the creeps. Does he usually go to high school parties?"

"What, Justin? Oh, he's harmless." Madison lowered her voice slightly. "I just found out he got thrown out of college. Not sure why, but the rumour is Grandaddy Astor has cut him off. That's why he's working at Grounded."

"And probably why he's drunk," I said. "Anyway, forget him. Sorry, but I need to get home. Are you ready to go?"

"Yeah, I just need to find Carter."

"I'll come with." I followed her through the clearing, echoing her goodbyes to the group. Someone had started a fire in one of the barbeque pits and I breathed in the deep, smoky smell. It reminded me of my grandparents' open fire back at home and my eyes filled up a little. "I haven't seen him for a while, have you?"

"No. I have a feeling, though…" She trailed off and I followed her back the way we had come, towards the car park. "I knew it."

"Hey, Madison! Paige!" Shay called from her cross-legged position in the roots of a huge tree, a can of

135

White Claw cradled in her hands. Carter sat on a tree stump across from her – they had obviously been deep in conversation. "Are you guys leaving already?"

Madison's jaw was set in a tight line, so I rushed to give an excuse. "Jetlag. I'm still getting used to the time difference."

"Oh, yeah!" Shay said. She climbed to her feet, a little unsteady. "Ow, dead leg, dead leg!"

"I've got you." Carter rushed over and she put an arm around his shoulders, squealing with laughter. My stomach flip-flopped.

"Aahhhh, it's like jelly!" She laughed.

Madison let out an audible huff. "Are you coming, Carter?"

"No, I'm not ready yet." He narrowed his eyes at his sister, daring her to argue. "I'll get a ride off someone else; you go."

"You know how much shit I'll get if I don't bring you home," Madison warned. Shay let go of him and moved her foot around experimentally.

"No one's going to leave the kid with cancer out in the woods, are they?" He snarled the words and Madison flinched. "I'll deal with the Moms when I get home."

"Carter—"

"We'll bring him home," Shay interrupted. I could feel the fury coming off Madison in waves, but Shay seemed oblivious. "Hunter is the designated driver and we have space."

"See?" Carter glared at his sister. "*Hunter* will bring me home."

"Fine." Madison spun around in the soft ground and marched towards the car. I hesitated.

"Bye, Paige!" Shay said merrily, her foot back to normal. Carter stalked off towards the party. "See you tomorrow!"

"Um, bye." I waved, watching her leave before I hurried after Madison. She was already in the car, so I climbed into the front seat beside her.

Her face was wet.

"What's going on?" I asked carefully. She pulled a sleeve over her hand and wiped her face, the light material coming away streaked with make-up. "Are you worried about Carter? We can wait for him."

"No." She started to reverse the car and drove down towards the entrance. "He can do what he wants. He's right, no one will leave him there."

"So what is it?"

"Shay." She turned on to the country road and started to pick up speed. She didn't put any music on and didn't offer any more information either. We drove in silence until the road started showing signs of life. "She's bad for him."

"Were they … together?" I asked, realizing I wasn't sure I wanted to hear the answer.

"No. I think they got close once but then Carter got

sick and she kind of … distanced herself from him. Like she couldn't handle it all. Then she started dating Hunter." She spat his name.

"Why do you say it like that?"

"Because darling Hunter was seeing someone in secret at the same time." It took a second for me to register that *someone* was Madison. "We hadn't made anything public yet, but I was all in. I thought he was the one, you know? Then he just ghosted me over the summer." Houses started to appear in the distance, Shorehaven creeping ever closer. "When we got back to school a few weeks ago, they were this official couple and Hunter and I were ancient history. Or worse, really, because no one ever knew about us."

"Oh, Madison, I'm sorry. And now Carter is into Shay. That sucks."

"He's not just into her," Madison said, concern in her eyes. She shook her head sadly. "I'm worried he's obsessed with her."

14

"Welcome to Spirit Week!" a peppy white girl with long black hair boomed as we approached the school building. I ducked my head and smiled shyly — I recognized her from the memorial crowd last night but couldn't remember her name. Carter stalked past Madison and I sighed. The atmosphere on the drive over had been icy at best, the twins were clearly not talking after their fight last night. At least Carter had made it home in one piece.

"I'm so excited!" Madison ignored her brother and ran to hug the girl. "Paige, you remember Kacey, right?"

"Yeah, hi." I glanced up at the enormous banner that hung over the entrance, obscuring most of the school sign. A huge, snarling bear had been painted on a long stretch of cloth along with the words: *GO, BEARS*. Must be the school mascot. "This is pretty intense!" I laughed.

"It is?" Kacey tipped her head, puzzled. "What do you do for homecoming in the UK?"

"They don't have homecoming," Madison whispered conspiratorially. "Can you believe it? This is Paige's first time."

"A homecoming virgin!" Kacey crowed, delighted, as I waited for a hole in the ground to open up and swallow me. "Oh. This is going to be so much fun!" she insisted. "Spirit Week is the best!"

"I can't wait." I hoped that didn't sound sarcastic; I was genuinely looking forward to seeing the chaos unfold this week.

"Kacey, we'll see you at lunch. Paige, come on, you need to get your class list from the office." Madison skipped through the crowd.

"Bye," I said weakly, catching up with Madison before she disappeared. The school building was full of students but was light and airy, the reception area surrounded with glass. Madison's loose curls bounced as she pushed open the door, the red velvet ribbon that held them back from her face striking against her dark hair. I realized how lucky I was that the twins had adopted me so readily. This whole place – Spirit Week, homecoming, all of it – was so foreign to me. I'm not sure I'd be able to survive it on my own.

"Yes, girls?" The woman behind the desk addressed us curtly, as though she was too busy to deal with students. Her greying hair was pulled tightly back at the temples and she wasn't wearing make-up. Her shirt was buttoned up to the collar and a pair of unflattering glasses perched halfway down her nose.

"Hey, Mrs Richardson. This is Paige Carmichael?" Madison said it like a question. "She's new here?"

"Ah, Paige, yes." Mrs Richardson put her head down and riffled through a pile of folders on her desk. "Here you go." She started to push it across the desk when the phone next to her rang. "Wait there, girls, one second."

"I wonder if they've assigned your homeroom yet," Madison whispered as I watched Mrs Richardson's face grow pale. I widened my eyes at Madison and tipped my head. She stopped talking, watching the receptionist too.

"Let me call you back, there are students here. Yes, of course. Two minutes." She replaced the receiver, her hand shaking slightly. "Sorry about that."

"That's OK." I smiled. I wondered what the phone call was about – Mrs Richardson had appeared unflappable just a minute ago. She pushed the folder towards me again and switched to autopilot. "This is all for you. Take it home, there are some consent forms for your parents to sign for school photography, things like that. The instructions for the parent portal are in there too, so they can set up an account. Your class schedule should be fairly self-explanatory and there's a map of the school so you can find your way around." She glanced at the clock on the wall. "If you come back at recess we can have someone take your picture and sort out your student ID and library card." She flattened her lips into what I assumed was a smile. "I think that's all. Any questions?"

"No, thank you."

"Then school starts in five minutes. You've been assigned a homeroom, but if you'd rather join Ms Garcia-Moore that's fine, I can amend your timetable later. Have a good day, girls."

"Thank you." Madison pushed me out into the corridor as Mrs Richardson disappeared into a small office and picked up a phone. She started talking and closed the door gently.

"What do you think that call was about?" I asked as Madison took the folder from my hands.

"Oh, could be anything. Last Spirit Week someone chained all the teachers' cars together!" She chuckled. "They never found out who did it. Things can get a little ... raucous."

"Sounds fun," I said, though I couldn't shake the feeling that it had been a more serious phone call rather than news of a prank. "So, where am I going?"

"One sec." Madison pulled out the timetable. "Yes! You're with me and Carter for homeroom, so you don't have to switch. I was hoping you'd be in with us."

"Oh, good." I took the folder from her. "I was worried I'd have to sit on my own."

"Come on, it's this way." I followed her past a row of

lockers. The hallway was rammed, students everywhere. Everyone wore their own clothes too, not the scratchy grey-and-green polyester uniforms we had to wear back home.

I felt like I was in a movie.

"In here." I followed Madison into a classroom. It was standard enough, but the chairs were different from home – there you would have tables that sat two people, and plastic chairs, but here each chair had its own little table attached to it. I slid into one next to Madison, and she introduced me to what felt like a million more people until the bell rang. Carter sat alone at the other side of the room, and I was surprised to see Josh run in at the last minute.

"Hey, guys," he whispered, sliding into a seat behind us. "Have you—"

"All right, simmer down." A young blonde teacher walked into the room and placed a travel mug on the desk. "I know it's Spirit Week but let's start it right."

She started to take the register – though she called it roll call – when Josh leaned forward again.

"Hey," he hissed at Madison. "You see the news?"

"What do you mean?" She tilted her head back.

"They found a body at Devil's Den."

"What?" The word was loud and the teacher glared in our direction. "Sorry, Ms Bailey." She waited until names started to be called again. "Are you serious?" she hissed.

"Yeah, look." Josh clicked the screen on his phone and Madison dug hers out too. He'd sent her a link. She arranged the books on her desk so they'd hide the cell and then opened it.

"Shay Kalani? No?" Ms Bailey said, glancing around the room.

"Shay's not here?" Madison asked. "But we have practice later. She better not miss that; the game is on Friday." I glanced down at her phone. There was a news article that had been updated less than twenty minutes ago. *Body found in local beauty spot.* "Wait. You don't think…"

"No, of course not," I breathed, my eyes catching snippets as she scrolled. *Identity still confidential. Unconfirmed homicide. Suspicious circumstances. Police presence. Road closed.* "Maybe she's sick, or at the dentist."

"Yeah." Madison's usually tanned skin had a grey tint to it. "I'm sure you're—"

"This is an important announcement," the voice of someone who was clearly not a staff member came over the Tannoy system, making almost everyone jump out of their seat. Ms Bailey rolled her eyes in exasperation and took a swig from her cup. This had obviously happened before. "Go to TikTok and follow *@RealLifeCrimeGuy*. He's live at Devil's Den."

"Wait – what?" Ms Bailey put her cup down. "Do not get your phones out."

"Oh, god, it's true." A girl at the front held up her phone. "He's live-streaming a police crime scene."

"What?" Ms Bailey ran over to her, looking down at

the phone. "No, put it away!" Everyone started digging in bags and pockets for their phones and soon the room was full of screens that displayed a cordoned off area in the trees. "Put your phones away!"

No one listened.

Even Ms Bailey fell quiet as we watched the scene unfold. The camera feed was handheld and shaking as the person filming ran towards the cordon, narrating in a breathless whisper. *"I'm here at Devil's Den, where the police have confirmed a body was found by joggers early this morning."* He paused as he climbed over the tape, his breath coming in gasps. *"The cops are down at the parking lot interviewing the witnesses and, man, those joggers are pretty distressed. I heard one of them use the word mutilated to describe the body. OK, I'm in. I dodged the officer stationed at the cordon. I'm going to see if I can gather any clues the cops might have missed."*

"Oh my god," someone in the room said. "He's trying to find the body."

"Turn it off." Ms Bailey started to go around and remove the phones from people's hands, but she wasn't quick enough. I couldn't believe what I was seeing. The first rule of true crime was you didn't mess with evidence. Well, that and ask for a lawyer. This guy had no idea what he was doing.

"The crime scene is through here," the voice said, his mouth close to the mic, leaves and branches brushing against the camera. *"Oh, no."* A gasp caught in his throat. *"Oh, god."*

We were glued to Madison's screen.

"*There is a body here. A young woman. It's… I need to go.*"

"*Hey!*" A deep voice sounded off-screen and the cameraman started to run, the screen wobbling before it fell and hit the ground. "*What the hell are you doing?*"

"*I'm sorry.*" The guy was sobbing now and the screen stayed dark, like it was face down on the floor. "*I need to get out of here.*"

"*Come with me.*" The camera moved, showing a close-up of the mulch that covered the ground. A retching noise filled the speakers and the phone fell again, only this time it got stuck at an angle.

A young woman's body filled the screen.

She didn't look the same as she had last night. Her hair was full of twigs and dried blood trickled from her open mouth. Her eyes were white and cloudy yet bloodshot at the same time. She stared into the distance, but it was clear she couldn't see anything.

"Shay?" Madison sobbed. "Is that really Shay? Is she…"

"I think so," I said, taking hold of her hand. The classroom was silent as the camera moved again, giving a full shot of the body. It wore the same jeans and strappy top that Shay had on last night, though the straps had been cut and the white fabric was a dark reddish-brown now, soaked in blood. A silver pentagram necklace sparkled at her throat. That had not been there yesterday.

"Wait, is that … writing?" Josh said behind us.

146

"Writing?" I squinted to look, but the camera wobbled again, and the live feed was cut off, leaving the screen blank.

But I'd seen it.

Everyone had.

Someone had carved the word "SINNER" into Shay's sternum.

15

"The letter was right. It's happening again," I muttered as the classroom erupted into chaos. People, including Ms Bailey, were making calls, some sobbing into their phones. It seemed as though normal rules had been abandoned. Was this my fault? The letter had told me that history would repeat itself. Could I have stopped this from happening?

Was the letter writer also the killer?

"Madison?" Carter came over and dropped into a crouch next to his sister. Madison's face was ghostlike, tears streaming down her face.

"I… She…" She let out a sob that hurt my heart. "She's dead." Carter leaned forward and wrapped her into a hug, her body heaving as she cried.

"Paige?" he asked. He looked broken.

"I'm OK." The words came out in a whisper. I didn't

know why I'd said that. I was far from OK. A girl I had met yesterday was dead. Murdered. Was I meant to have stopped it? "I mean…"

"I know." He nodded, stroking his sister's hair. "That was… I don't even know."

"Seniors, I need you to listen." Ms Bailey stood at the front of the class, her voice raised above the sobs. "I've spoken to the office. You need to make your way to the auditorium. The principal is waiting for you there." Questions erupted from every corner of the room, and she held her hands up. "That's all I know, I'm sorry. We've obviously just witnessed something extremely traumatic and it's our job as a school to make sure you are all safe from this point forward. So, please, make your way to the auditorium and let's see what the next steps are."

"Come on, Mads." Carter lifted her to her feet and nodded at me to help him. I grabbed my bag and her books and we walked to the door in silence.

"I'm so sorry you had to see that," Ms Bailey said as we walked past. Madison didn't reply, just stared straight ahead, as if trapped in a nightmare. Carter thanked her and dragged his sister along the corridor.

The auditorium was at the back of the building. The corridors were busy again; students were spilling out of rooms every twenty feet, most of them either crying or looking like they had just stopped. I felt numb – what we'd seen was horrific, but it didn't seem real. It was like something out of a horror movie, or a true crime documentary.

"You know that … what was on Shay's…" I gestured to my chest, struggling to find the right words. "You know what that was, right?"

"Some kind of writing?" Carter said, looking down at Madison. She didn't react.

"Yeah, but did you read it? It said… It said sinner. It's what the Shorehaven Ripper did to his victims."

"I didn't see it properly before the video ended. I didn't want to look. I mean that was… That was Shay." Now Carter's eyes filled with tears. "She was our friend."

"I'm so sorry." *Shut your big mouth, Paige.* Now wasn't the time to go in with true crime theories. "Let's find a seat."

We entered the auditorium. Hundreds of feet squeaked across a shiny floor that was striped with white lines. A basketball court. Hoops hung at either side and a digital scoreboard dominated the wall over the furthest one. The seating was the kind that pulled out from the wall, a series of benches that stepped up to the ceiling. Bleachers, maybe? They were mostly full but before we could even start to choose a seat, a blur of faces surrounded us.

"Madison." Kacey threw her arms around the twins in a quick hug and placed a gentle hand on my forearm. The rest of the cheerleaders rallied around as Kacey addressed us. "Did she see it?"

"We all did," Carter replied.

I nodded and she squeezed my arm gently before letting go and hugging Madison again.

"Oh, honey, we did too. I just… We can't believe it. Poor Shay." Her voice cracked. "She must have been so scared."

"Seats, please," a deep male voice echoed out through the speakers and the last few stragglers found a space. We sat at the front, Madison enveloped by her squad mates as I perched next to Carter on the edge of a bench.

"Who is that?" I asked. A tall, balding man in a grey suit and thick-rimmed glasses stood behind a microphone in the centre of the court.

"Principal Goldberg," Carter said. "He's a decent guy. He'll tell us what's going on."

I nodded. I didn't think I wanted to know what was going on.

"Thank you, all." His voice quieted the last few whispers. "I know many of you have just witnessed an unfortunate incident, but I would like to stress that we do not have all of the information yet." He paused to adjust his glasses. "While I would like to say more, at this time we as a school feel it is important that you receive the correct level of support. School will remain open and classes will continue as normal, though if you feel that you need to speak to the counsellor we can arrange that."

I'd half-expected a few groans but the hall remained quiet. The shock in the air was tangible.

"I am going to invite Officer Tatum to speak to you on behalf of the Shorehaven Police Force." Mr Goldberg beckoned to the doorway. A young officer in full uniform walked to the microphone, his nerves visible as whispers started in the bleachers.

"That's Rory Tatum's older brother," Carter muttered. "He only left here a couple of years ago. He's not going to tell us anything useful."

"Erm, good morning." The young man's voice was higher pitched than the principal's and hesitant. "My name is Officer Tatum and I'm here to address a very serious incident." He cleared his throat and removed a piece of paper from his breast pocket, unfolding it carefully. He cleared his throat again. "At four fifty-eight a.m., two joggers in Devil's Den came across the body of a young woman. Her family are currently being informed, so at this moment we cannot confirm her identity." Whispers continued to travel around the auditorium and Officer Tatum raised his voice above them. "We have reason to believe some of you may be able to help with our enquiries. Please, if you were out at Devil's Den last night, make yourselves known to a teacher so we can ask you some questions over the course of the day." He looked back at the paper and stopped – he had clearly come to the end of his prepared statement. "Er, thank you."

The hall erupted. Kids up at the top of the bleachers

shouted questions and Carter tensed as Madison started to sob once more. "Told you that would be useless," he said through gritted teeth.

"Thank you, Officer Tatum." Principal Goldberg took the mic once more and raised his hands for quiet. "This is an unprecedented event, and we will deal with it as best we can. As I said earlier, school will run as normal, so when I dismiss you, please report to your next class. If we need to speak to you throughout the day, you will be collected. We will keep you informed of any new developments." He paused as another teacher ran up and whispered something, her face turned away from us. Principal Goldberg nodded. "You are all dismissed."

We stayed sitting down as the cheerleaders whispered. I didn't need to hear them to know what they were saying. We had all been there last night, at Devil's Den. We had all spoken to Shay on the last night of her life.

Was it possible the killer had been at the party too?

"I'm taking Mads to the nurse's office." Carter nodded his head at her. She was practically comatose, her large, bloodshot eyes staring at the wall opposite. I followed her gaze.

"What are they?" I pointed at the five framed pictures that hung in a row against the opposite wall and regretted it immediately, realizing what I was looking at as soon as the words were out of my mouth.

"It's them," Madison croaked as we looked at the

photographs of the Shorehaven Ripper's victims. "The original dead girls."

"Right, let's get out of here." Carter led his sister out into the corridor and I followed, unsure what else I could do. It was so busy, students standing, talking, walking everywhere. I kept my head down until a loud, metallic bang cut through the whispers.

"Hunter, calm down!" Josh's voice. Madison broke away from us and raced towards the noise. We followed, reaching her just in time to see Hunter slam his huge fist into a locker. Judging by the blood pouring down his fingers, it wasn't the first time.

"Hunter, stop!" Madison grabbed hold of him and he turned to her, his face a mask of fury. I baulked at the sight of him – there was nothing but rage behind his eyes. "Hunter, it's OK. It's me, it's me." His shoulders sagged as Madison spoke to him in a comforting tone. She wrapped her arms around him in a hug and he returned it, pushing his face into her hair.

I had the feeling there was a lot to be resolved between these two.

"Let's get out of here, Madison." Carter's voice was cold. His sister flashed him a look of irritation.

"I'm going to take Hunter to the nurse's office," she said, lifting her chin defiantly. I could feel the fury rolling off Carter as they stared each other down.

"Fine," he spat, stalking away. Madison held Hunter's

uninjured hand and directed him down the corridor, making soothing noises as she did.

All I could do was stand there, alone, as my only two friends went in different directions.

16

I was so relieved when the day was finally over. The police officers had pulled us into the principal's office in small groups, which, in my opinion wasn't the right way to question anyone, but I guess they had a lot of people to get through. There were a lot of seniors at Devil's Den last night; the place must have been a CSI's nightmare.

"Here's the welcome party," Carter muttered as he pulled the car into the driveway where The Moms were waiting. Madison hadn't been fit to drive; she had been crying all day. She sat quietly in the front seat, a hollow shell of the girl who had driven us that morning. Carter hadn't been much better, but he'd held it together so far. Losing Shay must have been tearing him apart.

I still wasn't sure how that made me feel, but it really wasn't the time to start examining romantic feelings.

Carter had barely opened his door when Mia wrapped

him in a hug, Emma running around to get Madison. I got out of the back seat awkwardly. What should I do? Wait? Say goodbye? Or just walk home? I chose the latter.

"Paige, *carina*." Mia reached out to me, and I let her wrap me in a hug that sent me to the verge of tears. "Your first day of school. I'm so sorry. You must want to see your family." I nodded, words sticking in my throat. I really did want to see them.

"I'll walk you home," Carter said. I started to argue but Emma beat me to it.

"No, Carter, you need to rest." She walked Madison over to the front door. "Besides, we want you both at home, where it's safe."

"And I want Paige to be safe," Carter countered as his mom's lips tightened. "I'll make sure she gets home and then we can bundle in for the night."

"I'll stay here and watch," Mia reassured her wife. "I won't let him out of my sight."

"Fine." Emma sighed. She looked at me with guilt in her eyes. "I'm sorry, Paige. Carter's right, you need to be safe too." She looked past me. "Are your parents home yet? The car isn't there." I followed Emma's gaze. She was right, I hadn't even noticed.

"Mum texted to say she'd be back for five. Dad should be home though, he was only out for the morning."

"If they're not home you come back here, OK? You shouldn't be alone."

"Emma," Mia hissed, "stop scaring the girl."

"Come on, Paige." Carter walked ahead. I mumbled my thanks, waved to Madison and then followed him, jogging to catch up.

"How are you feeling?" I ventured. We hadn't spoken much today as he'd been busy making sure Madison survived. "About … everything."

"Kind of … numb, I guess? Like it's not real. She can't be…" His voice trailed off and I knew he couldn't bring himself to say the word. Dead. He scratched his head beneath the rim of his hat. "When I was diagnosed, I went a bit wild. I figured if I was going to die young I might as well have fun, you know? Do whatever I wanted." He gave me a sidelong glance and I carried on walking, looking straight ahead. "When we started senior year, I asked Shay out. She was already dating Hunter but I thought, screw it! I might die! No harm in telling her how I felt."

"What did she say?"

"No, of course. Who wants to date a guy with no hair who has to go into hospital every few weeks for the next couple of years? A guy who might die before his twenty-first birthday?" The corner of his mouth quirked in a half-smile and I wondered how he could joke about it so easily. I guess what doesn't kill you really does give you questionable coping mechanisms. "My diagnosis did save me from an ass-whupping by Hunter, though. He could hardly beat on the kid with leukaemia, could he?"

"Now that's a silver lining," I agreed, hesitating before asking the next question. "So your prognosis … is it bad?"

To my surprise, Carter laughed out loud.

"Who taught you that dirty word?" He shook his head. "It took me for ever to explain to my friends what a prognosis was."

"My granddad had cancer, back in the UK. My nana had dementia, so we were the ones who looked after him." I paused, remembering. "His prognosis was not good."

"I'm sorry," Carter said. "My default is to make a joke about it, but cancer really does suck for everyone involved." He took a deep breath. "My prognosis is good. The docs think my treatment is working and hopefully in a few months it'll be like nothing ever happened. Well, apart from sticking me with lifelong trauma and questionable coping mechanisms, but you know what I mean." I smirked at his use of the same phrase I'd been thinking. We really were alike.

"That's good news." I smiled at him, noticing a line of freckles that traced along his jawline. "I'm glad you'll be OK."

"Thank you." We paused at the bottom of my driveway. "You want me to walk you up?"

Yes. "No, I'll be fine," I lied. Dad would probably be inside, and I didn't want to get Carter into more trouble with his moms after everything that had happened over the last two days. I could do with some time to process too. I took a deep breath and tugged down the little door on the mailbox. Empty. "Doesn't look like there are any new letters at least."

"That's good." Carter stuffed his hands in his pockets. "I'll wait here until you're in, just in case." A shiver took hold of me. Just in case what? Just in case there was a murderer in my house?

I shivered again when I realized that was exactly why he was going to wait.

"See you in the morning?"

"Yeah. I'll drive if Mads isn't up to it. She's so cut up. I know her – she's feeling guilty. Her and Shay had history, you know? It wasn't all good but most of it was. We've all known each other a long time."

"I get it." I smiled weakly and gave him a little wave as I headed to the house. "I'll see you guys in the morning."

"See ya." He waved back with a little salute, and I jogged up the steps, pushing my key into the front door. I paused as I pushed it open.

"Mum? Dad?"

Silence.

I turned to see Carter stood firm at the end of the drive. He looked exhausted.

"Dad's home," I called to him, hoping it was true. "See you tomorrow."

"Bye, Paige." I watched him start the walk home and stepped inside, closing the door behind me. The house was so quiet I could hear the hum of the fridge from the kitchen. I looked at the stairs. I didn't know if I wanted to be alone up there.

I hauled my bag into the kitchen and dumped it on the island. What a day. The image of Shay's body was imprinted on to my brain – I don't think I'd gone more than a few seconds without thinking about it. There was one thing in particular though, one thing that no one had really wanted to mention today.

This had all happened before.

I dug out my headphones, plugging them into my ears as I opened the podcast app on my phone. I restarted the last episode, wrapped my curls up into a messy bun and retrieved a glass from the cupboard.

"Shorehaven had traditionally been a strict white-Christian town," the woman drawled as I rummaged in the fridge for something to drink, *"but in the years preceding 1995, it had evolved into a much more diverse community. Though this was welcomed by most residents, there was still a small faction who thought that their community should remain as it had been a hundred years ago."* A classy way to say Shorehaven had an active bunch of racists in 1995. Noted. I bet the Jacksons were part of the "small faction". I poured a glass of something called Sierra Mist and took a sip of the clear, fizzy liquid. *"Though the murders were not ever linked to this group, it has always been thought that the town's own Satanic Panic was, in part, responsible for the deaths of these young women."*

I found the cupboard with the snacks in, even though I wasn't hungry. I just needed to keep my hands busy. I began studying the contents – Doritos, Lays, Cheetos. I was praying to find something salt-and-vinegar flavoured when I felt hands rest on my upper arms.

"No!" I twisted out of the grip and spun around, pushing out with as much force as I could. Adrenaline rushed through my body, and it was the opposite of the other night in my bedroom.

This time I was ready to run.

"Whoa, Paige! P, it's me!" My dad stood in front of me, gasping and rubbing his chest. I'd given him a hard shove in the solar plexus. "What's going on? Are you OK?"

"Dad? Oh, god, I'm sorry." I pulled my headphones out. "Why did you sneak up on me?"

"Sneak up on you? I called you like three times." He tapped his ear. "You had that turned up loud, huh?"

"I guess." I was panting and everything was blurry.

"Are you crying?" Dad came closer. "Oh, P, I'm sorry, I was just messing around. I thought you were ignoring me."

"PAIGE?" The front door slammed, and Mum's voice echoed down the hallway. "Paige? Are you home?" She appeared at the doorway, taking in my tears and Dad's confused face before racing over and wrapping me in a hug. I buried my face in her hair and sobbed.

"What's going on?" I heard Dad say as Mum sank down to the cold kitchen floor with me. I let myself cry and listened to her tell him she'd had an alert from the school when she finished work, a message that confirmed that a body found out at Devil's Den was a Westpoint High student.

"Paige?" Mum tucked a finger beneath my chin and lifted my face to hers. I wriggled away.

"Can I have a tissue?"

"Here." Dad thrust a full kitchen roll at me. I ripped a piece off and blew my nose.

"Paige?" Mum repeated. "Did you see it? The video?"

"The what?" Dad looked confused but Mum silenced him with a look. I took a deep shaking breath and nodded.

"Oh, baby." She hugged me again, rocking me gently like I was little. "That must have been awful for you. I'm so sorry."

"I met her. Last night, I met her at the memorial." My voice cracked. "She was called Shay. She was so nice to me and now…"

"Shhhh, I know, sweetie." Dad joined us on the ground and wrapped his arms around us both. "I'm so sorry." We sat there for a couple of minutes until Dad stood and pulled us both to our feet. "Family night," he declared, pushing us towards the living room. "No excuses or arguments. I want my girls where I can see them."

"I want to get changed first." I gestured at my jeans. "Put some pyjamas on."

"Fine, but if you're not back in five minutes I'm coming

163

up. Me and your mom need to catch up for a minute anyway." I started to climb the stairs. "Oh, Paige? The internet is all set up, I left the password on your stairs." I watched my parents disappear back into the kitchen. Dad clearly wanted to know what the hell was going on.

I got to my stairs and collected the little card with the Wi-Fi details on. Finally. I jogged past the muted motion sensor lights and dug my laptop and charger out of my carry-on case. I really needed to sort this room out but today was not the day. I plugged it in and connected it to the Wi-Fi, ignoring the flurry of WhatsApp messages that came through. I'd respond to my friends back home later. What was I supposed to say? "Great first day, apart from the brutal murder"? I closed them down without reading and opened a web browser instead.

I typed "Shorehaven Ripper" into the search bar.

I knew it. News reports from as recent as eight minutes ago flooded my screen, accompanied with pictures of Shay and the area of Devil's Den where her body had been found. The press were already linking the killings in 1995 to Shay's death, even if my new friends weren't. The TikTok video had been taken down, but I had no doubt there would be screenshots of it if I cared to look further.

I did not.

Instead I focused on the date. Something about it had been bothering me since I started listening to that podcast. Last night had been the memorial and that was held on the day the first victim had been killed. Between that and the letter saying history was repeating, I followed a hunch, pulling up a calendar for October 1995.

I knew it.

The 22nd of October 1995 had been a Sunday. Yesterday was a Sunday. I pulled up the calendar from the corner of my screen and compared it to the old one. The dates and days all matched. There was no way this was a coincidence.

I went back to the search bar and pulled up the Wikipedia entry for the original murders. The victims were listed, along with the dates they had died. The first one had been killed on yesterday's date, just like Shay.

The date next to the second victim was today's.

17

"Madison?"

"Hey, no, it's Carter." I heard him shuffling around on the other end of the phone and could almost see him peering out of the front window. "What's up, are you OK? Is someone home?"

"Oh, yeah, everything is fine. I was just checking in."

"You scared me for a minute." There was a muffled thud. "She's resting. Mom gave her a sleeping pill so she's pretty out of it." The phone rustled. "Say hi, Mads."

"Hi, Mads." Her voice was thick with sleep and she followed the words with a giggle.

"Wow," I said. I couldn't quite face a laugh. "I'll go, I just wanted to make sure she was safe."

"What do you mean?" Carter was on the move again and I heard a door close softly behind him. "Paige?"

I took a deep breath. "This is going to sound … well, this is going to sound weird."

"Today can't get much weirder."

"True, but… Oh, sod it. I've been reading about the Shorehaven Ripper."

"I figured you would, what with the diary and stuff. Have you read any more yet?"

"No." My school bag – with everything in it – was downstairs. "Shit, I need to go and get it."

"Then spill quickly. Why were you checking on Madison?"

"When you google Shorehaven Ripper now, news articles about Shay come up."

"What? Wait a second." I heard the tapping of keys before Carter sucked in a breath. "Oh, Jesus. You're right. They think her death is connected to the old murders."

"It was my first thought too," I admitted. He was typing again. "Because of the necklace and the letter."

"Yeah." His voice was faint. "So you think he's targeting cheerleaders or something? Is that why you called?"

"No, I'm not sure what's going on yet," I admitted, "but something else occurred to me."

"Go on…"

"The dates. Yesterday was the memorial and it's on that date because it was when the first victim was killed in 1995, right?"

"Yeah, it's on a different day every year."

"Exactly. So I looked up the date each victim died and guess what? The days and dates in October 1995 match up perfectly with the ones this year."

"They do? You mean the twenty-second was yesterday, on a Sunday, and it was also on a Sunday in 1995?"

"Exactly."

"OK, but what does that mean?" Carter was starting to sound frustrated, and I was fairly sure he would be rubbing his forehead beneath the band of his hat.

"It might not mean anything," I said, "but it seems like a pretty big coincidence. The days lining up like that makes it seem ... I dunno ... purposeful somehow?" Was that even a word?

"I don't know..." He sighed.

"Well, when I looked at the dates the other girls died, they all happened within this week. One of them was killed on Monday the twenty-third."

"Today. That's why you called Madison. You think someone is going to get hurt tonight."

"Yeah."

"Oh, Paige. She's here and she's fine, I promise."

"Good. I don't... I'm not friends with anyone else. Do you think you could send a message out to her friends? Ask them to stay home, be safe?"

"Sure, if you think it will help."

"It might," I said. "At least we tried if anything does happen."

"Yeah." There was silence on the line for a few moments. "It'll be fine, Paige. This isn't what you think it is. It can't be."

"I hope not, but thanks for hearing me out."

"Of course." A slight smile crept into his voice. "That's what friends are for, right?"

"Well, in that case, thanks for being my friend."

"You're pretty cool, Carmichael, for a newbie."

"Thanks, I think?" I did laugh this time.

"Don't mention it." His voice turned serious. "You keep safe and don't leave the house until I'm beeping at the end of your driveway at seven a.m., you hear me?"

"Loud and clear. Thanks, Carter."

"Don't mention it. G'night, Paige."

"Night."

I sat on the air bed for a second, analysing the feeling in my stomach. I … liked him.

This was the last thing I needed. In my experience, people let you down and I didn't have the energy for another emotional roller coaster.

"Paige, you OK?" Mum called. I jumped up and stuck my head over the railing.

"Just checking on Madison," I said as she stared up at me from the bottom of the stairs. "I'll be down in a minute."

"Of course." She blew me a kiss and then lowered her voice. "Just don't be too long, OK? Dad's taken it upon himself to cook."

"Oh, *god*."

"It's only nachos. Everything is in a packet so he should be fine, but we thought that last time."

"I'll be quick as a flash," I promised. Last time Dad made nachos he'd managed to burn the tortilla chips but not melt the cheese. I mean, how is that even possible? I grabbed some clean pyjamas and headed for the bathroom, resigning myself to a cosy night and, very probably, a takeaway.

"Bye," I called into the kitchen, a triangle of toast dangling from my mouth. I started to close the door and was horrified when Mum caught it behind me and started to follow me down the driveway to the twins' car. "What are you doing?"

"Nothing," she said innocently. "Just going to work." I narrowed my eyes. "Fine, but remember I'm your mother. Morning!" She raised her voice on the last word and waved at Carter and Madison. Carter rolled down his window as I opened a door and shuffled into the back seat. I tried to ignore the fact that he looked as if he'd spent the night crying.

"Hey, Mrs Carmichael," Carter said. Madison smiled beside him but she didn't look good either. There were dark circles under her eyes and her skin and lips were ashy. I didn't think she was wearing make-up at all.

"Hi, Carter, Madison. How are you both?" They both shrugged and Madison's eyes welled up.

"Mum," I warned.

"Sorry, sorry. I wanted to make sure you'd bring Paige home, that's all, what with everything going on. If you have other commitments let me know and I can collect her."

"I'll be coming straight home." Carter smiled reassuringly. "She'll be with me, don't you worry."

"Thank you." Mum's face was still knotted in a frown as she directed her gaze at me. I slotted my seat belt into place. "You call me if anything happens, Paige. Promise?"

"Promise," I mumbled. "We need to go now."

"Have a good day, kids." She backed away from the car. I lifted my hand in a wave as Carter pulled away from our house and I slid down in my seat.

"Sorry, guys." I closed my eyes. "She means well."

"Don't worry, it's nothing compared to the fuss our moms made this morning." Madison turned to look at me. "You OK?"

"I think so." I nodded. "You?"

"No. But I will be."

Madison turned back to stare through the windscreen, and we spent the rest of the journey in silence. It wasn't awkward though, just the opposite. We all needed a quiet five minutes before school.

"What's going on?" Madison's voice pulled me out of my daze. "Is the parking lot closed?"

"I don't know." Carter slowed to a crawl. A police cruiser blocked the entrance to the car park and Officer Tatum was waving cars away. When we got closer to him, Carter put his window down again. "What's happening, Officer?"

"School has been suspended for the day. You kids need to go back home."

"What? Why?"

"Look." I leaned forward and pointed to the football stadium. The rear entrance was at the far end of the car park, and you could only see one end of the bleachers from here, but it was enough.

"Don't you kids go over there," Officer Tatum warned, but Carter ignored him and pulled the car away. The road was rammed so we barely crawled along. I kept my eyes on something that looked like a white tent being erected over by the bleachers. My breath caught in my throat. I'd seen white tents like that hundreds of times.

On true crime shows.

"Pull over," Madison said. Her head was bent over her phone screen, strands of hair falling loose from her French braid. She was typing furiously.

"I can't, I'll get a ticket or something; the cops are right there."

"Fine." She opened the door and jumped out on to the road, stumbling a little but catching herself.

"Jesus." Carter looked around in desperation. "There really is nowhere to pull over."

"I'll go." I unclipped my seat belt and he slowed the car to a stop.

"Thanks. I'll circle around the block, just keep an eye on her. I'll try to park up."

"Will do." I grabbed my bag and got out, weaving between cars as I looked for Madison's white jacket. I spotted her halfway to the stadium entrance and jogged to catch up. "Hey," I puffed when I reached her. She was still typing so fast I expected to see smoke coming from her fingers.

"It's happened again," she sobbed, glancing at me but not stopping. I matched her pace, my blood turning to ice in my veins.

"What has?"

She said nothing but held the phone out so I could see it. It was a cheerleader group chat. I squinted until one message jumped out.

They've found another body.

"No," I whispered. I looked around for the car, but it was nowhere to be seen.

The white tent.

School being cancelled.

It all added up.

"Hey, do you guys know what's happening?" Madison had got away from me and approached a group of kids I didn't recognize.

"Yeah," the tallest one said. He was wearing a checked

173

shirt and a backwards baseball cap. "Apparently it's Kacey Molloy."

The blood immediately drained from Madison's face. "Kacey? What about her?"

"That's her in there." He pointed to the white tent beyond the gates. "They found her body this morning when the janitor was opening up."

"What? No." Madison crumpled to the ground and started sobbing.

"Are you sure?" I asked. Baseball cap nodded.

"We got here just after he found her. He was hysterical, kept saying something about a necklace and a sinner?"

Madison stared up at me. "Like Shay," she whispered. I nodded.

Just like Shay.

18

"Car. Now." I shoved my hands under Madison's arms and hauled her up. She followed blindly as I desperately searched for their car in between the traffic, which had doubled in seconds. Huge vans spewed out people with cameras and microphones – the press had already found out what was going on. The whole place had become a media circus in less than five minutes. News anchors fixed their hair and scoured the crowd for someone to interview. A woman in a bright suit fixed her gaze on Madison and I tugged on her arm once more.

Not on my watch.

"This way." I manoeuvred her in front of me and fumbled for my phone.

"Hey." Carter picked up on the first ring. "I can't get back in. What's going on?"

"There's been another one," I mumbled, trying to keep my voice low enough so Madison wouldn't hear.

"Shit. Where are you?"

"Looking for you. The press have turned up and the whole parking lot is turning into a newsroom."

"I'll pull up at the 7-Eleven around the corner. Mads knows where it is."

"OK." I ended the call. "Madison? Hey, you with me?"

"Yeah," she croaked. Her face was completely slack, like all the energy had been sucked out of her. "Was that Carter?"

"Yeah. He's at the 7-Eleven. Can you show me where that is?"

Her eyes cleared a little and she nodded. "Of course." She held out a hand and I grabbed it gratefully. We walked against the tide of people arriving at the scene – obviously school hadn't got the message out about closing in time to stop people coming in – either that or they had completely ignored it. Cars were being abandoned outside the parking lot as curious students made their way over to the stadium and I could see Officer Tatum starting to lose his patience.

Eventually the crowd thinned, and we turned a corner on to the main road. The 7-Eleven was a couple of blocks down and my shoulders relaxed as I spotted the twins' car.

"He's over there," I said, pointing. Madison nodded but didn't let go of my hand. I squeezed it tight as we picked up the pace.

"Hey," Carter said as we climbed into the car – Madison next to him and me in the back. I let my body relax against my seat and sighed.

"Hey," I echoed. Madison pressed a button and the doors locked with a click. Seconds ticked past in silence.

"Mama called," Carter said, turning to look at Madison. Her face was soaked with tears, but she didn't make a sound and her eyes were vacant, glassy. She must be in shock or something. "She's stuck in Boston, she has a damaged tyre, said she must have driven over a nail or something. And Mom is at work, she's in a meeting until eleven so she won't know what's happened, but Mama has left a message for her to come home. It probably won't be until lunchtime, though."

"Come to my house," I blurted, suddenly realizing I had no desire to be alone, but Madison shook her head.

"I just want to go to bed," she whispered, closing her eyes. "This is a nightmare."

"Paige, you can come to our house." Carter started to reverse out of the parking space. "You better call your mom too. She was pretty clear this morning."

"Yeah." I dug my phone out to see I already had two missed calls and a bunch of messages. I dialled her number and stared out of the window as the phone rang.

"Here." Carter handed me a steaming mug and I took it gratefully, the heat melting through to my palms.

177

"Thanks." I placed it on the side table, careful not to disturb Madison. She'd flaked on the sofa pretty much immediately and her head now rested on a cushion that was wedged up next to me. Carter draped a blanket over her and sat on the other sofa, turning the TV on but leaving it muted. I picked up my drink and blew on it, the chocolatey smell soothing my nerves slightly as I watched a series of images flash across the huge screen. Drone shots of Devil's Den, Shay's class photo, the scenes outside the school earlier. "Wait." I sat up straight as archive footage appeared on screen. "Sorry," I whispered, wincing as Madison stirred next to me, "but will you turn that up?"

"Sure." Carter picked up the remote and sound filled the room. I held my breath as Madison stirred once more but then settled.

"That's Josh's mom?" I asked.

"Yeah." A young Tiffany Brown was flanked by officers as she entered a police station. Judging by the way she was dodging the press, it couldn't have been long after her escape from the killer. She wasn't wearing the famous prom dress, but I bet it was only days later.

"Similarities have been drawn between this week's incidents and the horrific murders that shook Shorehaven in October 1995. Westpoint High School has been closed for the rest of day, though they hope to be open in time for the homecoming football game on Friday evening."

"They're still going ahead with that stuff?" I hissed. "That's ridiculous. Two girls have been found dead." I hated that I'd been right about the next murder, but I felt so lost. Was I supposed to stop it from happening? How?

"I kind of get it." Carter shrugged, sipping his hot chocolate as I raised my eyebrows. "Horrible things happen and people just … carry on." He rubbed the skin beneath his hat. "It's awful but it's life, and some people are gonna find it easier to just carry on as normal."

"God, I'm sorry."

"It's fine." He sighed. "Life has been a shitshow recently. Homecoming was meant to be one normal thing for us all to do together." I stared at my cup, slightly mortified. Who did I think I was? I'd been here five minutes. Those girls were his *friends*.

"Carter, I didn't think. I really am sorry."

"Thanks." We sat without talking, Madison breathing softly next to me as the same images paraded across the screen on a loop. "Do you think they're really linked to the Shorehaven Ripper case?" he asked.

"I don't know," I admitted, taking a sip. "They seem to be, don't they? The same MO."

"MO? What does that actually mean? I hear it on cop shows all the time, but I've never thought about it."

"It stands for *modus operandi*. It basically means a certain way of doing something. So the Shorehaven Ripper's MO was … well, all that horrible stuff he did to them, then the

179

necklace and the word 'sinner'. It's a pretty unique MO."

"So either the original killer is back or someone is imitating them?" Carter set down his cup and yawned.

"I guess. He was never caught, was he?" I felt a yawn forming in my throat too and stifled it as best as I could. "Do you think it could be the same person?"

"Wouldn't they be ancient now, though?" A small voice came from somewhere around my right elbow and I looked down at Madison. Her eyes were still closed but she'd clearly been listening.

"Not necessarily," I said, shifting in my seat as she pushed herself up to sitting. Threads of ideas I'd had over the last few days started to weave into something more coherent as I spoke. "We don't know how old he was. If he was our age when he committed the murders, he'd only be, what, mid-forties? Even if he was thirty at the time, he'd only be around sixty now."

"Like I said, ancient." Madison pulled the bobble from the end of her fraying braid and played with it. "So either some old guy is going around killing all my friends or someone new is doing it?"

"It could be a copycat, yeah," I agreed. Both the twins stared at me. "That's what they're called, people who copy an earlier killer. Someone could have read about the Shorehaven Ripper, noticed that the dates this year matched up to the ones in 1995 and decided they were going to make history repeat itself. Or it could be the original person – I mean, why did they stop? There's no real theory, is there? There are loads of cases where a serial killer stopped because they had a family or something, like the Golden State Killer, or BTK. But they just couldn't help themselves and eventually went back to killing, sometimes even taunting the police. Serial killers always like to think they're smarter than everybody else and sometimes it leads to their downfall. Do you guys think I should be taking the letters to the police? The necklace?"

"Maybe…" Madison picked at the glitter polish on her nails. "Would they take us seriously, though? Maybe you could ask your granddad?"

"No." I softened my voice – that had come out much more abruptly than I'd intended it to. "It's too much for him. Last time I brought the old murders up it gave my gran a heart attack."

"That wasn't your fault," Carter said softly.

"I know, I know. I just … no. I can't bother him yet."

"That's fair, I think." Madison visibly deflated and leaned back on the arm of the sofa, tucking her feet up so she was facing me. "I'm worried it's someone we know. It could be, couldn't it?"

"I guess so," I whispered.

"What do you think, Mads?" Carter's voice was suddenly cold, and he levelled his sister with a stare. "You think anyone has been acting weird recently? Hunter, maybe?"

"Well, sure, yesterday was brutal, but he was dating Shay. Of course he'd be acting weird."

My phone started to vibrate on the side table, interrupting whatever fight the twins had been about to have. "It's my dad." I scanned the message. "He's back and apparently in possession of a lot of flatpack furniture."

"You want me to walk you home?" Carter started to stand, but I waved him back into his seat.

"No need, he's walking down to meet me." I stood up, blew Madison a kiss and then stopped. "Just, watch me out of the window maybe? Until I get to him."

"Sure thing."

I gathered my phone and bag and walked to the front door, slipping back into my shoes. I froze as the door started to open.

"Carter? Madison?" Emma's voice entered the room before she did, and I let out a huge sigh of relief.

"Here, Mom," Carter said behind me as the door opened wider. "You're back early…" His voice trailed off as we saw that Emma wasn't alone.

"Carter Garcia-Moore?" the taller of the two police officers asked.

"Yes?"

"What's going on? Mom?" Madison joined us at the door, looking between Emma, who wore a similar look of shock to her daughter, and the two police officers. "Wait, has something else happened?" They ignored her and two more officers appeared behind them, flashing a piece of paper before forcing their way into the house.

"We have a search warrant and will be taking your cell phone and any other device that connects to the internet," the officer said.

Emma regained her senses and started to argue. "Are you *arresting* him? There must be some mistake," she said. "Carter is a good kid. What's this all about?"

"He's not under arrest. Yet." The officer turned back to Carter. "We're taking you in to the station for questioning. As you are under eighteen you may be accompanied by a parent or guardian." The officer began to lead him towards a squad car.

"Wait, I need my shoes." Carter froze on the driveway as we followed him out, Emma holding his boots in one hand. "Why are you doing this?" The officer stopped, took Carter's shoes and exhaled. Madison threw her arms around her mum as I saw my dad start to walk down from our house.

"Carter Garcia–Moore, you are a suspect in the murder of Shay Kalani. Now get in the car."

19

"Paige?"

I stood frozen to the spot. I could hear Dad shouting, his feet pounding on the pavement as he ran to join us, but it was like I was underwater or watching from really far away. All I could do was watch as Carter's head got pushed down into the back seat of the police car.

"You be careful with him." Emma had finally snapped out of her shock and her tone was sharp. "He's in the middle of chemotherapy."

"Yes, ma'am," the short officer said, closing Carter's door and opening the driver's one. "You can follow us down to the station. Like I said, if he's under eighteen he's a juvenile, so he can have a guardian present."

"You're damn right he can," Emma growled. She unlocked her car. "Madison, Mama is going to be here any second, OK?"

"What?" Madison snapped out of her stupor too. "No way; I'm coming with you!" She grabbed a pair of sneakers from inside the door and closed it, following her mum to the car. "This is ridiculous; he couldn't have done it. He was with me the whole time!"

I rubbed the back of my neck. That wasn't true, was it? We'd left Carter with Shay at Devil's Den and Madison had even told me he was obsessed with her.

How obsessed?

"Paige?" Dad put a hand on my shoulder, out of breath. "What's happening?"

"It's Carter... They think he did it."

"What?" Dad paled as he watched the police car pull out, closely followed by Emma and Madison, wheels squealing as they raced behind. "They think he killed those girls?"

"I guess so." Tears threatened to overspill, so I took a deep sniff to mask them.

"Home. Now." Dad wrapped an arm around my shoulders as he marched me back to our house and I snuggled in gratefully, suddenly feeling like a child again. Nothing could happen to me with Dad around, could it?

"What about the IKEA stuff?" I gestured at the pick-up, a mountain of brown cardboard packages strapped into the rear of it.

"They can wait. Mom will be back soon and we're

all home for the night – Detective Coffey has imposed a darkness falls curfew. Come on."

"Darkness falls?" I asked. Sounded ominous.

"Yeah, no one out after dark without good reason." He dropped his arm from my shoulders and pressed the key fob to make sure the car was locked. I took advantage of the distraction and glanced towards the mailbox.

I couldn't deal with more letters.

"Come on, pud." Dad climbed the steps and unlocked the front door. That got a wry smile from me – I don't think he'd called me pud since I was a little kid. "Let's get some lunch."

I followed him into the house, dropped my bag and kicked off my shoes on autopilot. I could hear him rummaging in the cupboards as I stuck my head into the kitchen. "I'm not hungry, Dad. Sorry."

"That's OK." He stopped and looked at me. "You wanna talk about it?"

I hesitated. I couldn't tell him about the letters now, could I? They could make Carter even more of a suspect. I didn't want that on my conscience.

"It's fine," he rushed to say, "whatever makes you feel comfortable. You can talk to me, or your mom."

"I know." I dropped my gaze to the floor.

"Honey, I'm sorry. For your friends, for bringing you here, this whole … mess. None of it was planned this way, I promise."

"I know," I repeated. As if he knew this would happen. "I'm going to try and take a nap. Is that OK?"

"Sure it is. You want a drink of something? Here." He quickly filled a glass with water. "Take this up, at least."

"Thanks, Dad." I took the glass from him and started to drag my feet out of the kitchen.

"Oh, Paige, wait! There's a letter for you. It's on the console at the bottom of the stairs."

"A what?" My mouth was suddenly bone dry. I took a big swig of water.

"It looks like an invitation, maybe? Did you get invited to a party already?"

"Oh … er, yeah. A party."

Dad shook his head sadly before commencing his search for lunch. "Shame, I bet it won't happen now. Oh, well, there'll be others."

"Yeah." I felt numb as I walked back out into the entrance hall and made a beeline for the little half-circle table. How did I miss this? It glared up accusingly, the scratchy letters that spelled out my name mocking me. Thank god Dad had found it; Mum would *not* have let it go so easily. She would have had five hundred questions about a party.

I snatched it up and doubled back for my bag before racing up the stairs two at a time. My bag buzzed with a text message, probably Mum, but I ignored it for now. I threw myself on the air bed and ripped the envelope open,

187

slicing the skin on my knuckle in my haste. "Ouch!" I dropped the letter, the cut from the thick parchment paper welling with blood. I stuck it in my mouth and flipped the letter open with my other hand.

There was no doubt it was from the same person.

Hello, Paige,
    What a shame about the two pretty little dead girls.
    I'm afraid that's just the start.
    You think you know what happened to the last girl who lived at 407 Ocean View. But do you?
    The killer was never caught.
    Read the diary, Paige.

"Holy shit," I said, removing my finger from my mouth. The air stung it. I turned the page and the envelope over, but as usual, there was no indication of where it had come from. This read more like a threat than any of the other letters, but that wasn't what I was focused on. The writer knew I had the diary.

Someone was watching me.

My phone buzzed again.

I tipped my bag upside down on to the bed, sending books and papers flying. My half-empty water bottle thudded on to the bed and my phone bounced out on top of it. The screen was full of text messages from Madison.

Madison 11:57
WTF just happened?

Madison 12:03
Pulling up at the precinct now.

Madison 12:08
I'm not allowed to see him. Mom has gone in.
I'm sitting in the waiting area on my own.

Madison 12:10
Paige? Please don't ghost me. He didn't do it. I
know he didn't! It's Carter FFS!

Poor Madison. I started to type but just took a photo of
the letter and sent that instead.

Paige 12:12
Not ignoring you, sorry. Got another letter.

Madison 12:13
The diary? What the hell? How do they know?

Paige 12:13
I dunno.

Unless it *was* Carter. Only he and Madison knew about this whole thing. What if he was writing the letters?

What if he *was* killing the girls?

No. It couldn't be Carter. He was … nice. But then again, BTK was the president of his church council, wasn't he?

No. I refused to believe I was that wrong about him.

Paige 12:14
I guess they've been watching me.

Madison 12:16
Jesus. Your dad is home, right?!

Paige 12:16
Yeah.

Madison 12:16
So what do you think? What do they want you to do?

Paige 12:17
Read the diary, obviously? There must be a reason it was hidden. Maybe there's a clue in there.

> **Madison** 12:18
> Maybe something in there can help Carter? Find the real killer?

I hesitated. The police wouldn't take Carter in for nothing, would they? Had they learned about his obsession with Shay, too?

What had I got myself into?

> **Paige** 12:18
> Maybe.

> **Madison** 12:18
> You have to read it.

> **Madison** 12:18
> Please.

> **Madison** 12:19
> It could help my brother.

Read the diary. Easier said than done. I pulled it from the tangle of books on my bed and turned it over in my hands. Even though I'd flipped through it, carried it around all week, I still felt wrong having it. It was a *diary*. Something private, full of hopes and dreams. Secrets.

A dead girl's secrets.

I switched my phone on to silent and pushed everything but that and the diary back into my bag. I dragged the duvet over my shoulders like a cape and sat cross-legged, staring at the book.

I wasn't really doing anything wrong, was I? If it could help prove that Carter was innocent, I should read it. And if it didn't ... well, I could cross that bridge when I came to it. *If* I came to it.

"OK, Nicole," I whispered, cracking it open. "Let's see what you're saying."

I scanned the pages quickly, her large handwriting making it easy to skim through several entries. They were all kind of the same – about her conservative parents, sneaking out to meet Tiff or CJ, details about outfits and accessories that she bought and hid in the air vent. She seemed cool, and it was sad to think these were some of the last things she ever did. Wait – the other things she'd hidden. I jumped up and rummaged in the case I'd hidden them in, taking the plastic bag back to my bed.

I studied the items more carefully now, picking up the silky gold slip dress first. It was creased with age but still had a tag on – she'd obviously never got the chance to wear it. The thought filled me with a sense of loss I could barely describe. I folded it carefully and picked up the Walkman

192

next, turning it over in my hands. I only knew what it was
from watching old TV shows.

How did this thing work?

It was a small rectangular piece of blue-and-grey plastic.
The front was clear and I could see there was a cassette tape
in there, so I pressed the buttons, even though I knew that
twenty-eight-year-old batteries wouldn't work any more.
The eject button did, though, and the little door popped
open. I carefully removed the cassette and saw there was
writing on the label.

Nicole's Mixtape, Summer '95

Wow. I stared at the tape. Could I listen to this? I popped
open the battery compartment and saw it was empty. The
springs looked healthy, and I was sure I could salvage some
batteries from somewhere, so I harvested a couple from
my digital alarm clock and clicked them into place. The
Walkman had an ancient pair of headphones plugged into
it. I slipped them over my ears, closed the little door and
pushed down the play button.

Music filled my ears.

"Oh my god," I whispered. I recognized the song, one
that I'd heard played acoustically in Irish pubs with my
grandparents since I was a toddler. It was The Cranberries.
Dolores O'Riordan's lilting voice filled my head and tears
pricked at my eyes. I picked up the cassette case and saw

a list of songs scrawled on the insert card – "Dreams", The Cranberries was listed at number four. At the bottom of the list was written: "For Nicole, love CJ".

Nicole had never seemed more real to me than she did in that moment.

I left the music on and picked up the diary again, skimming through it when a word jumped out at me.

"Sex".

I glanced around my room, as if someone might catch me reading, then refocused my eyes and found the beginning of the entry.

<u>Song of the Day: "Always" (Bon Jovi)</u>

Dear Diary,

I can't believe I'm about to write this - in fact, I'm pretty sure my parents will send me off to a convent (or worse) if they ever find out - but tonight CJ and I did it. We went all the way.

We had sex!!!

Let me go back to the beginning. Tonight was my last date with CJ before he goes back to college tomorrow and, even though we said we'd try the long-distance thing, I don't see how it can work. It's not like I can tell my parents about him, never mind go and visit. So tonight was the perfect way to say goodbye.

I've grown up being taught that sex is wrong - well, no, that's not even true. I've been taught nothing about it at all. But between church sermons, being removed from sex ed and my parents' distaste for anything that even shows my ankles, I've been conditioned to think that sex is a sin unless it's between two married adults. And then you can only do it in order to procreate. "Only sinners fornicate, Nicole." But how can something so beautiful be a sin? I've never felt more loved or cherished than I did tonight, and I know CJ felt the same. When he was dropping me off he gave me a mixtape of all my songs of the day - how thoughtful is that? He remembered so many of them. I keep listening to the last one on repeat - it wasn't a song of the day until today. It was CJ's addition and couldn't be more perfect.

I really wish we could be together.

Maybe next year, when I go to college.

When I escape this town.

Arggghhhh, I wish I could tell someone about this! But with everything going on in the church at the moment it's not safe, for me or for CJ. I can't even tell Tiffany about it.

Especially not Tiffany.

Kisses,

Nicole

Go, Nicole! I smiled, happy for her until it hit me that this had probably been the last time she ever saw CJ.

I wondered who he was. And why couldn't she tell Tiffany, her best friend?

My phone buzzed.

Madison 13:27
Anything?

"Paige? You want to help me move that stuff now?" I whipped the headphones off as Dad called from the bottom of the stairs. Dammit. Just as things were getting interesting. "We can build your bed; the mattress is being delivered this afternoon."

"OK, two minutes!" I listened to him close the door and fired off a response to Madison.

Paige 13:29
Not yet, I'm up to August, though. Need to go help my dad but I'll carry on later.

Paige 13:30
Is Carter out yet?

I packed the diary and other bits into my bag and stood up. I needed to hide it all if Dad was coming up. My phone buzzed from the bed, so I picked it up with one hand and opened the bathroom door with the other.

Madison 13:31
Nope. Mama is here now, they won't let her in at the same time as Mom so she's making angry phone calls to her lawyer friends.

Paige 13:32
Good. Keep me updated? I'll do the same once I've started reading again.

I really didn't know if I wanted to carry on reading. My head was a mess, constantly flip-flopping between finding Carter innocent and guilty. I didn't know what to think. I glanced at the extractor fan and briefly thought of hiding everything in there before shaking my head. My parents weren't snoops. I could trust them, unlike poor Nicole.

Madison 13:32
You promise?

I hung my school bag on the back of my door and vowed to come back to it later.

Paige 13:33
I promise.

20

Something tickled at my face, and I woke with a start, my heart racing. Flashes of last night's dreams replayed themselves as my groggy brain tried to make sense of where I was.

Looking in a mirror, letters carved into my chest. They were backwards but I knew what they said. Nicole writing in the diary and hiding it, turning to me with dead eyes and a finger to her lips, the universal signal that we shared a secret. I'd dreamed of running through forests and getting trapped in the basement, a dark figure standing over my bed.

The last one had jolted me to full consciousness.

I pushed the diary away from my face, looking at the last entry I'd read. There had been pages and pages about school and church, nothing as interesting as when I'd started it. No wonder I'd fallen asleep reading. I forced myself to sit up and look around. The room was as we had left it once we'd built the new bed – which meant it was still a mess. There were piles of my belongings everywhere, and the air bed was now a sad pile in the corner. There was no way I could tell if anyone had been in the room or not.

No, I must have dreamed the figure, along with the rest of the stuff my subconscious decided to dredge up last night.

I relished the comfort of my new mattress as I reached for my phone, which was charging on my new bedside table. It was just past six a.m. and I groaned. I missed lie-ins already.

I propped my pillows on the headboard and my eyes widened at the view. We'd set the bed up so it was facing the window, like the air bed had been, but I couldn't see much last night. Today, all of Shorehaven stretched out before me and I could see the ocean sparkling blue in the distance. My eyes drifted closer to home, and I noticed Emma's car was parked in the drive at Madison and Carter's house.

Did that mean he was home?

I looked back down at my phone and turned off the Do Not Disturb setting. Notifications flooded my screen, most of them text messages from Madison.

Madison 01:52
Anything?

> **Madison** 01:58
> Sorry, you must be asleep. We're still here. I'm tired and cold and ready to go home.

> **Madison** 02:05
> You're definitely asleep. I've just found some quarters at the bottom of Mama's purse so I'm about to raid the vending machine.

> **Madison** 02:19
> Slightly regretting that Snickers bar. Think it expired before my fifth birthday.

> **Madison** 04:42
> We're home. Call me when you wake up?

So they *were* home. I was desperate to know what had happened but first things first. I checked the Westpoint High website, a banner appearing on the screen immediately. "School will remain closed on Wednesday October 25. We will communicate any further updates via the parents' portal." I relaxed into the bed. Thank god for that. I couldn't face trying to be sociable with strangers today, especially when one of them could have murdered two of my classmates. I shook my head. How was that even a real thought? I missed my boring life in Manchester. Even hanging out with the people

201

who'd half-forgotten me already was more appealing than all this.

I flicked to another tab and refreshed the news story from the night before. It had been updated just before I'd woken up, mainly regurgitating the two original stories. I scrolled through quotes from family and friends and a statement from the Shorehaven Police Department. Nothing I hadn't read yesterday, which I hoped was a good thing. New bodies would have meant new articles.

I shivered and burrowed myself down into the new duvet. This one didn't smell of home, but it was soft as a cloud, comforting. I decided to text Madison rather than calling her this early, but my thumb hovered over the screen. What was I supposed to say? I didn't actually know them that well – in fact, I'd known them for the grand total of five days. Sometimes people knew each other for a whole lifetime and still never found out their deepest, darkest secrets. But they'd both been so kind to me, so welcoming. And it wasn't like I had any other friends, was it? I typed.

Paige 06:12
Hey, sorry. I fell asleep reading the diary. Nothing yet but I'll keep reading today. School is shut. Hope everyone is OK?

No response. I hadn't expected one. If I was Madison I'd be fast asleep. I rolled over and closed my eyes, trying to force sleep, but it was no good. I was wide awake now and the faint aroma of coffee had started to drift up the stairs. Coffee meant breakfast and I realized I was starving. My stomach growled in agreement and I sighed, pushing the duvet off and grabbing my dressing gown from the floor. I cocooned myself in it and padded down the stairs, avoiding eye contact with the basement door. If I ignored it, it wasn't there.

Right?

"Morning," I said through a yawn as I entered the kitchen.

"You're up early!" Mum was dressed for work, filling a thermos with coffee from a shiny new pot. "There's no school for you today."

"I know, but I couldn't sleep." I opened the cupboard doors in turn, searching for bowls and cereal. I still couldn't remember where everything was.

"How are you feeling?" She screwed the lid on tightly and opened the cupboard over her head, pointing at the boxes of cereal. Frosted flakes for me, wheat things for Dad and some weird whole food stuff for her. I shuffled over and she kissed my forehead.

"Thanks. I dunno, to be honest." I grabbed a bowl and filled it to the brim. For once I didn't get told not to waste it.

"I bet." She collected her bag from the island and slung it over one shoulder. "I wish I was off with you, but I have to be in the office all week for induction. I won't be able to work from home until next week." She looked me in the eye. "I'll call in if you want me to stay home, though."

"No, it's fine, it's your first week; I don't want you to miss anything." I opened the fridge and pulled out a huge carton of milk. "Dad will be here, though, right?"

"Of course." She took a deep breath. "Listen, I know they're your friends, but just stay away from the twins' house today, OK? Stay home with your dad."

"Why?" Like I didn't know why. Whose mum would want their child hanging out with a murder suspect?

"They've all had a shock." Mum chose her words carefully. "And Carter is a poorly boy. He needs a break."

"OK." I didn't want to push it. And she never said anything about FaceTime. I grabbed a spoon from the drawer, and she tapped her foot on the floor impatiently.

"Is Dad out on a run?"

"Yes. He said he'd be back by now."

"Just go. I'll be fine. I have my phone and I can lock the door behind you."

"Not a chan—" She was interrupted by the click of the front door opening.

"Hey, Sarah, I'm back!" Dad appeared in the doorway, panting slightly. His face was bright red, the same colour mine went any time I attempted exercise, and his forehead was beaded with sweat. I wrinkled my nose as he planted a kiss on Mum's cheek.

"About bloody time," Mum grumbled, rolled her eyes and blew me a kiss. "I'll be back as soon as I can, I promise. Look after our daughter." She aimed the last sentence at Dad.

"You know it." He walked past and ruffled my hair. I rolled my eyes back at Mum and she smiled.

"Bye, you guys." She bustled out and I heard the jangle of keys before the door slammed shut.

"Good run?" I asked. Dad was making some kind of protein shake that smelled like death and I wondered what it was like to be able to go for a run alone, in the dark, when there was a killer in town. I made a mental note to remind him of his white male privilege later. I don't think I'd done that this week.

"Not bad. Bit eerie out." He looked at me and I raised an eyebrow as if to say, "No shit". He pulled a face at his protein shake. "Screw this. You want a bacon butty?"

I looked down at my untouched cereal.

"Oh god, yes." I pushed the mush away and listened to him bang around in the cupboards. "Hey." I pointed at the rolled-up bundle he had dropped on the other end of the counter. "Is that today's newspaper?"

"Oh, yeah. The kid started delivering them this morning." He paused, tilting his head out of the fridge. "I don't know if it's a good idea for you to read it, Paige."

"Like it'll tell me anything I haven't already seen on the internet?"

He stared at me. "Fine, I guess you're right."

I leaned over and grabbed the paper, unfolding it so I could lay it out flat on the worktop. Predictably, the front cover was splashed with photographs of Shay and Kacey, smiling selfies in their cheerleader uniforms and holiday snaps lifted from their social media. I scanned the text as the smell of frying bacon started to fill the room. Nothing I didn't already know there. I flipped through the rest, the newsprint tacky beneath my fingers. The last time I'd read a paper was out loud to my granddad when he was in hospital. The first few pages were all about the murders, but the stories quickly dwindled and the pages filled with ads for local businesses and stores that would make you a corsage or rent you a tuxedo for homecoming.

"Do you think they'll still have the homecoming stuff this week?" I mused aloud. Dad dropped slices of sourdough bread into the toaster and headed back to the pan so he could flip the bacon. My mouth watered as the fat sizzled and spat. It wasn't like the rashers we got at home, this was streaky bacon, but hey. Bacon was bacon. It was one of the only things that kept me from being a proper vegetarian.

"I don't know, to be honest. I guess if school reopens tomorrow or Friday it will ... why? I didn't think you'd be into all that stuff."

"I'm not really." I shrugged, folding the newspaper back up. "But I was interested to see it all in real life. It's so different from home, you know? The football game, the big dance. It would have been cool to see."

"Yeah, it's a pretty big deal around here. I bet they've never cancelled one before." The toaster popped and Dad pinched the slices out with the tips of his fingers and dropped them on a plate. "Hot!" He waved his hand around. "Let's see what happens, that's all we can do."

"Yeah."

Dad busily buttered toast and layered bacon between two slices.

As I put the newspaper to one side, two glossy flyers slipped out. "These guys again? How many leaflets do they need?" I said, looking down at the grinning faces of Chase Vickers and Justin's dad, Charles Astor Junior. "They're obviously not campaigning for the environment."

"Local elections are a big deal around here," Dad said, bringing over my sandwich. He'd barely put the plate in front of me when I grabbed it and took my first bite. I sighed in satisfaction as the bread crunched on the outside but melted on the inside. My eyes welled up a little. It tasted like home.

"Good?" Dad grinned through a mouthful of bread.

"So good," I agreed. "Like Grandma used to make them."

"She trained this American boy well," he replied,

chuckling, "I remember she damn near had a fit when I first met her. I asked if she was putting maple syrup on the bacon." I grinned. I could just imagine her face at the suggestion. Sacrilege. We ate in contented silence until there were only crumbs left, and I collected those with the tip of my finger. "It's OK, you know. To miss them. To miss the UK. It's your home." He wiped his hands on a paper towel. "Even if things were rough in the last couple of years."

"I know." I pushed my plate away.

"I know I'm your dad and I'm the last person you want to talk to about boys, or friends, or *feelings*" – he exaggerated the word – "but you can, you know?"

I nodded. The last thing I wanted to do was discuss all the things we had left behind.

"OK, then." Dad sighed. "What are you doing today? I guess you haven't got much schoolwork yet?"

"I need to check online actually. I don't want to miss anything and I have some catching up to do in general. There's a lot of required reading I need to get hold of. Have you heard of a book called *Catcher in the Rye*?"

Dad's eyes widened.

"Have I heard of … go on, get outta here. Sounds like you're in need of a *real* education. I'll clean up. Maybe you can sort your room out a bit if you don't have too much to do." He collected the plates in one hand and squeezed my shoulder with the other. "I'm here whenever you need me."

"I know. Thanks, Dad." I pushed out from the island and my feet touched the cool tile floor. I was going to spend the day on my laptop.

I just wouldn't be doing schoolwork.

21

Five missed video calls.

"Madison?" I asked as the phone connected. I waited a second for the movement on the screen to stop and tried again. "Are you there?"

"Yeah, one second," she whispered, obviously sneaking around the house. Everyone must be asleep. "OK, I'm here." She came into focus in a room I wasn't familiar with, and it took a second to register the figure behind her.

They must be in Carter's room.

"How are you both?" I asked. Madison shuffled up the bed while holding the phone, until she was sitting with her brother. I could see both of them on screen now, and Carter did not look good. He had a black hood pulled up over his head, which accentuated his thinning eyebrows and made the shadows under his eyes look like bruises.

"Tired," Madison said. Carter pulled the duvet up to cover his face. "Oh, no, you don't," Madison snapped at him. "You promised you'd tell her."

"Tell me what?"

Madison's jaw was set tightly and I briefly thought about ending the call and blaming it on technical problems. I didn't want to end up in the middle of a sibling fight.

"Why they had the search warrant for my devices," Carter croaked. He sounded as though he'd been crying. "You were here, so you deserve to know."

"OK…" I left the word hanging, nerves knotting my stomach. Was this it? Some kind of confession? I darted a glance at my stairs, as if Dad would be able to overhear from two floors down. I reached for my headphones, just in case.

"I'd been messaging Shay," he said. "But not as myself."

"He was *catfishing* her," Madison blurted.

Carter's face crumpled. "You make it sound so sleazy," he complained. "Do you know how hard it is to be me at the moment? To have everyone around you constantly say 'Oh, don't you look *well*' or 'You're so *brave*'. And I have to smile and nod and say 'thank you', all because they're not telling me I look like shit, when I know I do, because I feel like shit. I spend half the day worrying about dying and the other half consoling everyone else. It's exhausting. I was just pretending to be someone else for a while."

"I get that," I said.

"Do you? Because Madison doesn't seem to."

"Of course I do. I just don't know how you let it go so far, or why you didn't tell me!" she hissed. Their parents were clearly not meant to hear this discussion and I got the distinct impression that Madison was more upset her brother hadn't confided in her than anything else. "You were having conversations with Shay like you were a whole other person."

"Because it was easier than being me."

We sat in silence for a minute.

"Um, thanks for telling me," I tried. He was in such a shitty situation; I could empathize with wanting to hide away from your real life for a bit, I just wasn't sure this had been the right way to handle it. Carter shrugged but didn't say anything. "I am sorry about Shay, you know. I know how much you liked her."

"I don't even think it was her that I liked," he admitted. "I think it was the way she treated me when I was acting like somebody else. Like someone who wasn't living under a potential death sentence."

Madison started to cry.

"Oh, come here." Carter put an arm around his sister as she sobbed into his shoulder. "Let's talk about something else. Mads said you were reading the diary?"

"Yeah." I relaxed slightly, thankful for the change of subject. "Nothing that might connect the new mur— What has happened this week with the Ripper, but I'll keep reading." I lowered my voice so Dad really wouldn't hear. "She did reveal some juicy details, though."

Madison stopped crying and sniffed loudly. "She did?"

That was all it took. Carter and I started to laugh and before I knew it, I was spilling the details about Nicole's secret tryst. "I feel so sorry for her," I said, pulling the diary from under my pillow and running one hand over its cover. "Her parents sound like something out of the eighteen hundreds and she couldn't tell anyone how wonderful this guy made her feel. Plus, he was going back to college, so she was on her own again. She wouldn't even tell her best friend about it."

"That is sad." Madison took the phone back from her brother. "I wonder who CJ was." Her eyes lit up. "I bet he's in one of The Moms' yearbooks."

"Do you have them? I saw my dad's yearbooks once, but I think they're still at my grandparents' house. They're not really a thing in England," I said, rolling over on my side and propping the phone on the pillow next to me.

"They're not?" Madison said. She popped something in her mouth and chewed. "Weird."

I shrugged. I was glad I didn't have a bound hardback to remind me of school, but maybe that was just me.

"I wonder if he was ever a suspect?" Carter asked. "I mean, if last night showed me anything, it's that the cops always suspect a potential love interest, right?"

"And if he was shagging her, he was more than a potential love interest," Madison said.

I snorted with laughter. "Shagging?" I repeated.

"Yes," she said defiantly as Carter's shoulders quaked beside her. "I'm adopting it."

"Anyway," Carter said, shaking his head. "How old was this CJ guy again? Does it say? It might help us to track him down. He might remember something she said, something that points towards the Ripper."

"That's assuming it's the same killer. Here, let me check…" I flipped through the start of the diary and scanned the pages. "It says here that he was home from college for the summer. And it says later he was going back. I don't know what year he was in, though."

"Well, college is four years. So he had completed at least one year and had at least one left, so that makes him a sophomore, junior or even a senior, right?" Madison said.

"A what now?" I asked, confused but impressed with her quick maths. "I hear those words all the time, but I have no idea what they mean."

"It's the same as high school," Carter explained, taking back the phone. "First year you're a freshman. Second you're a sophomore, third is junior and fourth is senior. Make sense?"

"I think so." I thought carefully. "So that would make him anywhere between nineteen and twenty-one at the time?"

214

"Yep." Madison counted on her fingers. "If Nicole was a senior at Westpoint High, and he was going back to college, he must have already done a year at college at least, right? So he would have been two years older than her, three at the most. The Moms were a couple of years older than her, so if we look in their old yearbooks, we might be able to figure it out."

"How do you know he went to Westpoint High?"

Madison rolled her eyes. "Have you seen the size of this town? Everyone goes to Westpoint High."

"Fair. She never mentions him by name, just calls him CJ, so you could start there, I guess?"

"Already on it." Madison disappeared off screen and I could hear the door close behind her. It was just me and Carter.

"Thanks for not freaking out," he mumbled, looking off to the side of the screen. "You're a good person."

"You're having a shitty time. And we all make mistakes. One day I'll tell you about allllll of mine."

"Promise?" He gave me a half-smile, meeting my eyes again.

"Promise."

"OK."

We let the silence linger for a moment.

"I'm going to go," I said. "There's some stuff I want to look up. Let me know if you find anything?"

"Will do. And, honestly, thank you. Not just for

trusting me, but for not doing any of that shit I talked about earlier."

"Well, now you mention it, did I tell you how well you look—"

"Hanging up now!" Carter laughed. "Speak later."

"See ya." I smiled as he hung up the phone. He looked like a different person when he laughed and I had to admit, I was pretty relieved he'd been released. Maybe I could stop doubting him now. I pushed the thought of Carter's smile away and sat up.

I had stuff to do.

I pulled out my laptop and refreshed the browser.

Nothing new.

This was good, surely. Maybe the media circus around the first two killings had scared the killer off. Maybe it was all over? Still, it was time for a deep dive.

I typed in the URL for my favourite time-wasting website. I'd read about more unsolved true crime and creepypasta on there than I'd care to admit, but it usually wielded some kind of result, even if it was just a conspiracy theory. The little skull logo appeared at the top of the page, and I quickly typed what I was looking for into the search bar.

The screen filled with results.

"I knew it," I whispered. Good old Deddit.

I scrolled through the chats. Some were years old, musing on why the Ripper had never been caught, discussing the victims as if it was their own fault someone had preyed on them. Just the same old misogynistic shit you got in these cases, when some people liked to chime in to victim blame. As if anyone deserves to be murdered. One thread about Tiffany Brown being the sole survivor caught my eye. When I scrolled down, someone had pasted in the now famous photo of Tiffany in her prom dress. I took a closer look at it.

It was grainy, a scanned in photo that had been taken on a throwaway camera. You could just about make out the outside of Westpoint High because it looked exactly the same, though the entrance was filled with students dressed for homecoming, blurry figures in suits and dresses, all peering out of the glass doors at the scene in front of them. Tiffany was being held up by an older man and you could see the make-up smeared down her slack-jawed face. Bloody patches decorated her pale silk dress, and the bottom of it was shredded, ripped into tatters that had caught the wind. Her hair was still in its formal up-do, the lengths twisted and knotted in an elaborate pattern, but twigs and branches were tangled in it, and bits had come loose, her tiara knotted in it all. Her lip was split and there was a long scratch down her right arm. She was a mess. My eyes travelled to the caption beneath the picture.

What does she know?

I sat up straight and typed her name into Google, opening the Wikipedia hit that came up. I scanned the article, realizing I only knew three things about her – she was Josh's mum, she had almost been murdered by a serial killer and she was married to the mayor. I scrolled down the page and skipped straight over the "Early life" section, instead focusing on the part that was headed: "Sole survivor of the Shorehaven Ripper".

> *Vickers (née Brown) was the only known survivor of a terrifying series of murders that rocked the east coast town of Shorehaven in 1995. In interviews, Vickers has only ever given brief details of her time with the killer, choosing to focus more on the memory of her friend, Nicole Jackson, who was abducted with her, and the other victims. Few details are publicly known, other than the killer's MO and the names of those who were identified. Vickers worked closely with the police, though most details have remained confidential due to the case still being classified as open. Vickers speaks at a local memorial in Shorehaven each year and is in talks to write a memoir focusing on the week of the murders, for a rumoured seven-figure sum.*
>
> *See __Shorehaven Ripper__ for more details on the case.*

I leaned back, thinking of the caption below the photo. What *did* Tiffany Vickers know?

I picked up the diary. Maybe Nicole could help me out here.

September 6, 1995

<u>Song of the Day</u>: "Dreams" (The Cranberries)

Dear Diary,
    Sorry I haven't written for a few days, but guess what?

I'M A SENIOR!

    I can't believe this year is finally here. I had the best summer <u>ever</u> with CJ and Tiff. (I haven't even written about the movie she took me to yet! It was called Clueless and I have been thinking about Cher Horowitz's outfits ever since. How I wish I could really wear what I wanted!) Anyway, I feel like spending time with them has really shown me what I want from the rest of my life. I want to go to college, and not some religious college that my parents decide is good enough. Somewhere fun, somewhere where I'll have friends. I visited the guidance counselor today and she gave me a bunch of brochures, but I left them in my locker so I can read them during study hall. I need a plan.

I have dreams, goals. One of them is to convince Mom and Pop to let me go to homecoming this year. They might, if I let Mom be a chaperone and don't talk to anyone but the church kids.

Either way, I can always sneak out to the afterparty.

Gotta go – homework is no joke this year, and I need to keep my grades up if I want to get into college!

Write soon,
Nicole

22

"Sorry we couldn't talk yesterday," Madison said. It was Thursday morning and school was closed again. The place must still be a crime scene. I shook out my damp hair, squeezing it with my designated curly girl T-shirt as she chattered on the phone. "Do you want to switch to FaceTime?"

"No, I'm doing my hair," I explained, scrunching serum into my curls as I avoided my earphones. "Tell me what you've got."

"Not much. A list of CJ names but there weren't even many Cs. Carter has been trying to quiz The Moms but they're not in a good place; they're both really upset with him. I might try again later."

"So we're no closer to finding out who CJ was." I sighed. "It probably doesn't matter, anyway, he probably told the police what he knew back in '95."

"What about you?" Madison asked.

"Not a lot. The diary isn't giving up much apart from how Nicole was looking forward to leaving this town. Her parents sucked but Josh's mum did seem like a really good friend to her. Oh, and I looked Tiffany up too. You know she's never spoken publicly about what happened?"

"Huh. No, I guess she hasn't. She's got some big book deal now though, so I guess she's been saving it for that."

"You don't think that's a bit strange?" I sat on the bed, pulling my robe tight around me. "That she's never once spoken out about the night she escaped the killer?"

"Not really. It must have been pretty gnarly. I mean, all they found of Nicole was hair and teeth…"

"Ugh, don't." I stared out of the window at the pseudo-sleepy town. "I guess I wouldn't want to talk about it either. Not in public anyway." A shout echoed up the stairs. "Sorry, Mads, I've got to go; Dad's taking me to see my gran in the hospital."

"I thought she went home?"

"She did but she has some kind of infection now, so she was readmitted last night. Poor Gramps must be exhausted. I think we'll be back late. Let me know if you manage to quiz your moms, though."

"I will. Oh – there's another memorial tonight. For Shay and Kacey. The police department has lifted curfew until it's over. Do you think you can come?"

"I can see if Dad will swing by with me later? I don't

know, though. It seems kind of … scary to be going out after dark." I'd wanted to say "irresponsible", but I also didn't want to piss off one of my only friends.

"OK. Well, hopefully see you there. Oh, and, Paige?"

"Yeah?"

"I think you're good for my brother." Her words tumbled out in a rush. "He's … himself around you. See you later!"

Madison hung up the phone as I picked up my jaw.

What did she mean by that? Did Carter *like* me?

"Paige! Move it!" Dad shouted up the stairs. I pushed Madison's comment to one side and ran down to the car. I'd think about that later.

"Sorry," I panted, climbing into the pick-up. I still wasn't used to the size of it, but big cars seemed the norm around here, not like Mum's tiny red Fiesta back in Manchester. Every second person in Shorehaven drove a beast. "What time is visiting again?"

"Eleven. We have time, don't worry." I clicked my seat belt in and sat back. "We can go in for an hour and then take Gramps for lunch before going back in for afternoon visiting hours."

"OK." I wrapped my arms around the bag in my lap. I'd packed a couple of textbooks but snuck the diary in too. I had no idea when I'd read it though – it was so conspicuous-looking, I'd have to hide it inside my chemistry book or something.

Shorehaven fell away and I was surprised to see we were taking the road that led out to Devil's Den. I started to say as much but quickly remembered I had never told my parents I'd been there that night. I fiddled with the radio instead, settling on a station playing Taylor Swift.

"Nice try, P," Dad said, checking his mirrors, "but I'm too tired to listen to you tell me why I should be a Swiftie based on this song in particular." I opened my mouth to argue but he was right. Busted. "Find me an old people station, please. I don't want to listen to anything from this millennium."

"Fine." I messed with the dial as we hit the highway and finally a song I recognized filled the speakers. "'Waterfalls'?"

"Now you're talking. Song of the day by TLC." He started singing along but I froze.

"What did you say?"

"What? TLC? It stands for the band's names, Tionne, Lisa…"

"No, the other thing. Song of the day."

Dad didn't reply, but I swear the blood drained from his face.

"Put what you want on," he said. "I need to concentrate on the road anyway."

"I'm going to snooze," I said, silence unfolding between us as my brain whirred. Song of the day – was that a common thing? I'd never heard him say it before. I'd known that he and Mum hadn't told me everything about the house since the night Gramps warned him to keep me out of the basement. For some reason I'd never really thought about him knowing Nicole, but of course he would have. It was a small town – everyone knew each other, even if it was only a little bit.

Just how well had he known her?

I closed my eyes as we passed the entrance to Devil's Den and feigned sleep, my head spinning, but before I knew it someone was actually shaking me awake.

"Wakey wakey." Dad's voice cut through the sleep fog. He seemed anxious but otherwise back to normal. I shook off the strange feeling I'd had before, it was obviously just the sleep deprivation. "You ready?"

"Yeah, sorry." I undid my seat belt and stretched, popping the door handle open. I shouldered my bag and climbed out, following Dad from the parking lot to the modern hospital building. We checked in at a pastel-coloured desk and a smiling, pastel-clad nurse took us through to see Gran. Even though I'd been warned, my heart sank when I saw her in the hospital bed.

"Paige," she croaked, holding out a frail hand. "You came. I'm sorry you had to skip school to see your old grandmother." She chuckled and I glanced sideways at Dad.

"She doesn't know," he hissed, "and she's on a lot of painkillers."

I thought she seemed cheerful.

"Hi, Gran," I said, taking her hand and sitting on the chair next to the bed. "How're you feeling?"

"Oh, just wonderful." The oxygen tube that fed into her nose and the cannula in her hand said otherwise. "They'll be letting me back home any day now."

"That's great, Mom." Dad sat down on the opposite side of the bed, and we chatted back and forth about the weather and the fact that Gran wanted to get home and tidy her garden before it turned frosty. Dad looked at me pointedly and I looked at the clock. We'd been there fifteen whole minutes and there was no sign of Gramps. "Paige, do you want to go get us a coffee?" He rummaged in his jeans and handed me a bunch of change. "And whatever else you find out there."

"Sure." I let go of Gran's hand gently. She'd nodded off. "I'll text if I find him," I whispered.

Dad nodded.

I left the hospital room and wandered down the hallway. It was different from the hospitals I'd been in at home. There, you walked into a ward full of beds, curtained for privacy but not private at all. People lived out some of the worst moments of their lives behind those curtains. Here you got a room with a door and a pastel-curtained window. Gran was lucky, considering.

"There you are." I spotted Gramps immediately, reading a newspaper in a space that was the designated

"Family Area" according to a pseudo-cheery sign on the wall. "All OK?"

"Hey, Paige." He smiled but it didn't reach his eyes. He looked drained. "I'm just having a break. Saw you coming in so figured I'd leave you both with Gran for a little while."

"It would've been good to know that. We've been worried about you too, you know," I chided him gently. "Let me just tell Dad you're here, and then I'll buy you a questionable cup of coffee."

"Sounds good." He folded the paper carefully as I fired off a text and approached the vending machine.

"What's your poison?"

"I haven't tried the hot cocoa yet, let's give that a whirl."

"You got it." I placed some unfamiliar coins in the slot and pushed the button. A little beige cup shot out and began to fill with a sweet-smelling brown liquid. "So, why are you really in here?"

"I'm just tired, honey."

"You weren't catching up on the case?" I eyed the newspaper pointedly as I handed him the molten plastic cup. "Dad said Gran doesn't know what's been happening." I repeated the process at the machine and waited for my own cup of lava to trickle out.

"No, she doesn't." Gramps put the cup on a coffee table and shook his hand out, a gesture so similar to something my dad did that it made me smile a little. "The whole ordeal back in '95 upset her enough. She's too fragile to hear it's all happening right now, especially with you guys living in the Jackson house."

"What do you mean?" I took my own cup and sat opposite him. The plastic scalded my fingertips, so I put it down quickly, blowing on my hand. Gramps took a deep breath.

"Bad things happened in that house." He paused and I let the silence hang. I wasn't about to interrupt. "Not just the fallout of poor Nicole going missing, but before that. The Jacksons always seemed like pillars of the community, but on the force, you find out things."

"I thought Gran was friends with them, though?" My mind flashed back to the pentagram I'd found in the basement. What did he mean by bad things?

"She was. We both were, to an extent, but they were church friends. Your gran has always been the churchgoer in the family. Jake and I joined her for Sunday services, everyone in town went to those, from the high and mighty Astors to the Vickers and the Browns. But your gran helped with the clothing drives, the bake sales, all that stuff. She knew the Jacksons that way, especially Hilda, Nicole's mom. We didn't socialize with them outside of that, but we'd see young Nicole always there, helping out. She didn't get to mix with people her own age much from what I could tell."

I leaned forward. "Gramps." I kept my voice low in case

one of the overly cheerful nurses walked in. "Why is there a pentagram painted on the basement floor?"

His tired face dropped.

"You weren't supposed to see that. Do your parents know you've been down there?"

I shook my head. "No. I haven't wanted to worry them, with all of this going on."

"Well, the Jacksons called that a devil trap. A demon trap, in other words. It was used to cleanse evil spirits."

"That ... doesn't seem like a bad thing?" I tried to wrap my head around what I was hearing. Weird, yes, but bad? People cleansed their spaces with sage and crystals all the time, my social media was full of it.

"Have you heard of the Satanic Panic, Paige?"

"I know a little. I read that some people think the Shorehaven Ripper was trying to punish 'sinners'" – I made little inverted commas with my fingers – "but I also know that's a bullsh— I mean, that's a ridiculous excuse that my feminist brain has several issues with."

To my surprise, Gramps smirked. "You're right, it was a bullshit excuse. Those girls didn't deserve to be killed whether they were sinners or angels."

"So what does the Satanic Panic have to do with it?"

"What you have to understand is that back then, the world seemed smaller. There was no internet, very little cheap travel. We had grown up and lived in a small town that had small-town ideals and small-town problems. It was a predominantly white-Christian neighbourhood, still is, I guess, and that was the most important aspect of life for some people. When the internet started to loom and young people could find out about, well, whatever they wanted, some people didn't see that as a good thing. They got scared. They hated change, hated that one day their 'safe' little neighbourhood might not look the way they wanted it to. So, people began to create their own narrative. *Different* was bad."

"And let me guess – to some people 'bad' meant 'Satanic'?"

"Yep. It seems irrational to us now; to be honest, it did to most of us then too, but there had been so many cases around the country over the years. It just got to Shorehaven a little late."

"What are you saying, Gramps? That these girls were killed to punish them for being different?"

"Maybe…" He shrugged. "Or they were leading good Christian boys astray. Something to that effect. There was one massive thing they all had in common, though. Something that was never published in the press."

"What was that?"

He sighed deeply and picked up his cocoa. "Their parents all took them for exorcisms. Exorcisms that the Jacksons carried out in your basement."

23

"They did *what*?" Madison gaped at me, almost losing her grip on the giant Frappuccino in her hand.

"Exorcisms," I hissed. Dad had caved and agreed to bring me to the memorial on the way home from the hospital, but it didn't start for another half-hour, so we were in Grounded. He'd graciously gone to sit in a corner, but I could feel him watching me. "Apparently it was a thing in their church. Like, people knew it was happening and just let it. Encouraged it, even."

"Jesus." Carter shook his head. He was wearing a baseball cap today, hiding beneath its peak. He didn't want to talk to anyone after being taken in for questioning and I didn't blame him.

"I don't think Jesus had anything to do with it," I said. Madison almost choked on her drink.

"So you think the Jacksons had something to do with

the murders? But that wouldn't make sense for what is happening now, would it? They're both dead." Carter toyed with his water. "What do you think they did to the girls? When they exorcised them?"

"I don't know. Gramps wouldn't tell me any more. I think he only told me out of sheer exhaustion, he's probably not thinking straight."

"How is your grandma?" Carter asked kindly.

"OK, I guess. Hopped up on painkillers, but she should be back home in a few days."

"That's good." Madison chewed on her straw. "Hey, you don't think The Moms ever had anything bad happen to them, do you?"

"No." Carter shook his head. "I hope not, anyway. They didn't come out until after all of this happened, did they? And they'd moved away to college. I reckon they spent most of their time here trying to appear as 'normal' as possible."

"That's really sad, but it makes a good point," I mused, blowing on my caramel macchiato. It was cold out there tonight and I needed to wash the taste of hospital cocoa out of my mouth. "Why were those girls specifically chosen to have exorcisms? Like, what were they doing that was so bad people assumed they were possessed?"

"Sex, drugs, rock and roll?" Madison said and Carter raised a sparse eyebrow. "I'm only half-joking. We know Nicole had sex with CJ, maybe her parents found out about it after all."

"And her diary makes it clear they wouldn't have approved of her even being friends with Tiffany, right? So maybe the other girls were like Tiff. People the Jacksons would have *disapproved* of."

"Let's see." Madison sat up a little straighter and discreetly wiped a bit of cream off her top lip. "Hey, Justin," she said as he appeared next to me. "Are you going to the memorial?"

"Can't," he grunted, gesturing to the packed coffee shop. He collected a tray full of empty cups that had already been on our table when we arrived. "It's chaos in here and Whitney ditched again. I'll watch out the window instead. How're you guys holding up? I'm sorry about your friends."

Madison wilted slightly. "Thank you. We're not bad, I guess." She hesitated. "Does it ever get easier?"

Justin sighed and perched on the arm of our sofa. "I never knew my Aunt Phoebe, but I know how much my grandmother suffered after what happened to her. They were like chalk and cheese by all accounts, but I think that made it even worse for her. In time she seemed to remember the good things more than the bad, but honestly? I don't know if you ever get over something like that."

"What was she like? Do you know?" I kept my voice gentle, hoping I wasn't prying too much.

Justin smiled. "A wild card according to my parents.

She was obsessed with Alanis Morissette, even sang with a local band occasionally. Mom digs the photos out every year but my dad – she was his sister – finds it too hard to look at them. She looked intimidatingly cool."

"She sounds it." I smiled at him, and he stood up, all business again.

"Best get back to work. Drop those cups off at the counter on your way out, will you?"

"Sure." I barely finished the word and he had gone.

Madison turned on me, her eyes wide. "See?" she said. "Sang in a band and listened to blasphemous soft rock. Enough to get her an exorcism?"

"Probably," I said, finishing my coffee. "But do we really think the Jacksons were murderers? The other parents knew what was happening too. In fact, today Gramps specifically mentioned the Astors attending the same church as them. I bet Phoebe was down in my basement at least once. I wonder if Justin knows that little fact about his grandparents?"

"I doubt it. Most exorcisms during the Satanic Panic were essentially torture; you wouldn't exactly advertise if you'd done it, would you? And there's a fine line between torture and murder, right?" Carter said. I could barely hear him, his head was ducked so low. The coffee shop had started to empty out.

"Maybe."

"They might not have killed them on purpose,"

Madison pointed out. "It could all be a massive cover-up." She took a noisy slurp of the end of her drink and stood up, holding out a hand for Carter. He glared at her but took it. He was unsteady on his feet today. "His steroids are wearing off," Madison explained. "Makes him tired."

"Madison." The word was pure warning and I left them to it, dropping my cup at the counter and approaching my dad instead.

"Hey, Dad. Are you coming?"

"Yeah. Everything OK?" His eyes followed Carter as he walked slowly to the counter "Carter looks a little worse for wear."

"I think he's just tired."

"Kid's had a lot on. We all have." He checked the blue-strapped watch on his wrist. "I promised your mom I'd have you home for eight and we'd bring a pizza. You think this will go on for long?"

"I doubt it. The last one didn't." I followed him to the glass door, and he held it open, the bell tinkling. Madison and Carter were behind us.

"Good. I'm going to hang back, let you see your friends. Meet me right here when it's over or I'm sending out a search party, you hear me?"

"Loud and clear," I agreed.

"Um, I might stay here too," Carter mumbled, looking at the floor. "If that's OK with you, Mr Carmichael?" He looked at his sister. "I can't handle seeing everyone."

"Fine with me, kid, as long as you don't call me Mr Carmichael again. It's Jake."

"Thank you," he whispered. Madison leaned over and gave him a quick hug.

"It'll blow over. We'll be back before you know it."

The crowd swallowed us up as Madison led me over to the front of the stage. The other cheerleaders were all there holding those little plastic candles. Madison passed me one and exchanged hugs with what felt like a hundred people, immediately melting into tears at the sight of her friends. I hung back, watching the guys close ranks around Shay's boyfriend and surreptitiously pass a small silver hipflask between themselves. Josh stood at the other side of the group, closest to the stage and he caught my eye, nodding solemnly. I didn't think I'd ever seen him smile.

"You want some, new girl?" Hunter broke ranks and came to stand next to me. His breath reeked of alcohol and he was unsteady on his feet.

"I'm fine, thank you." I tried to sound polite, but his face furrowed in drunk fury.

"We not good enough for you, English girl?" He leaned towards me and each word he spat brought tears to my eyes. "Who do you think you are——"

"Hunter, dude. Cut it out." Josh appeared and placed himself between us, a restraining hand on Hunter's chest. "Sorry." He turned to look at me as he beckoned a couple

236

of the bigger guys over. "He's not a good drinker at the best of times, but today…"

"Hey, I get it." Hunter stood next to me quietly as his friends approached to take him away. "His girlfriend just died. I can't begin to imagine."

"Yeah." Josh's shoulders visibly sagged as his father appeared onstage. It was like Groundhog Day: Josh's mom was even polishing off a glass of wine offstage, just as she had on Sunday night. "Here we go," he muttered.

"Ladies and gentlemen, friends and family of Shay Kalani and Kacey Molloy. Welcome." Chase Vickers' voice boomed over Main Street. I twisted my head towards Grounded to make sure Dad and Carter were still there. Dad raised a hand and I turned back to the stage. He must be watching me like a hawk. "It is with great sadness that we gather here tonight, to remember the bright lights that were snuffed out too soon."

Josh snorted softly next to me. Not a fan of his dad? Interesting. I hadn't picked up on that last time we met.

Chase continued his speech as I let my attention drift. The street was packed. I recognized some faces from school and Officer Tatum stood next to Tiffany at the bottom of the stairs. She looked pristine as usual, and I wondered if she would speak today.

"In the spirit of overcoming these heinous acts, Westpoint High will reopen tomorrow. What's more, the homecoming football game and dance will go ahead as planned. Tomorrow's football game will be dedicated to the memories of Shay Kalani and Kacey Molloy." A roar went up from Hunter as he punched the air but not everyone seemed happy about it.

"Does that mean curfew is lifted?" a woman called from behind me.

"Have you caught whoever did this?" Another yell from the back of the crowd, a deep voice this time. Chase held his hands up.

"The police department and I are more than happy to have these events go ahead as usual," he explained, his tone one of a teacher patiently trying to explain something to a child. "Several leads are being followed and our detectives are on top of it. Of course, there will be an increased police presence at both events. We want people to feel safe. Now, take care on your drives home and see you all at tomorrow's game."

Mutters broke out around us as Chase descended the stage. Tiffany was stony-faced as he leaned to whisper in her ear. She nodded, scanning the crowd.

"That's my cue," said Josh. "Sorry again about Hunter."

"Don't mention it. See you at school, I guess."

"Yeah, see ya." I watched Josh weave through the crowd to his mum, whose face flooded with relief as she clutched his arms. He said something to her and her posture changed suddenly, her back straight and tall as she scanned the crowd. Josh turned and pointed in my direction before catching my eye and beckoning me over.

Oh God. Was I about to meet Nicole's Tiff?

Panic surged through me as my brain tried to decide what to do. I could pretend I hadn't seen him ... head back over to Carter and my dad ... look for Madison...

Josh caught my eye again.

Shit. I had no choice.

The road had cleared quickly so I waved at them and crossed the gap between us. All I had to do was pretend I'd never read the diary. Easy, right?

"Paige, hey!" Josh smiled at me, the first smile I'd seen since we met. "I wanted you to meet my mom. Mom, this is Paige, the girl I was telling you about."

Telling her about me?

"Paige." Tiffany held out a delicate hand and I shook it, feeling the bands of several rings beneath my fingers. She didn't grip hold of me like her husband had; instead her soft skin was a whisper on my own. "So nice to meet you. How are you enjoying Shorehaven?"

"It's ... different. Very nice, though," I rushed to add. She had snapped straight back into beauty queen mode. There was no nervous mother now. She must be used to hiding her real feelings.

"Wonderful. Well, I hope the locals are treating you well." She smiled at her son and I could swear he flushed a little.

"Everyone has been lovely," I agreed, silently praying that someone would come and rescue me before she asked me what it was like living in her dead best-friend's house.

"Paige Carmichael! Great to see you again," Chase Vickers boomed from behind me. Thanks, universe. Not quite what I was looking for. I braced myself for another crushing handshake, but instead he nudged between his wife and son and wrapped his arms around their shoulders. "Tiff, Paige is Jake's kid. He married the English girl and ran off to the UK." He didn't wait for his wife to answer but carried on. "Tell your dad we'd love to see him at the town council meetings. He's a computer guy, right? Can always do with a few more of those."

"Will do!" I smiled.

"Great. Enjoy the big game tomorrow." He looked down at his wife. "We should go, I have a seven a.m. tomorrow."

"Of course," she said, her smooth smile still in place. "Nice to meet you, Paige."

"And you." I looked at Josh as his parents started the walk to City Hall. "See you at school."

"Yeah, see you in homeroom." He followed them, turning around to give me one last wave.

Well. That was intense.

"Paige!" A voice called over. I turned to see Madison waving at me and manoeuvred through the crowd to my side.

"I wasn't expecting all of that," she said. She sniffed and pressed the corner of each eye. "It was nice, though."

"Yeah," I agreed, but I was distracted. I was still watching the Vickers family walk away. "Mads, was Chase Vickers on your list yesterday?"

"What?" She followed my gaze. "Well, yeah, but he couldn't be CJ. Josh's mom and dad have been dating since she was our age."

"Exactly." I waited for a second and her eyes widened. She gripped my arm and turned around.

"Wait… You mean what if Nicole couldn't tell her best friend who she was dating, because Tiffany was dating the same person?"

I nodded.

"I think Chase could be CJ."

241

24

"Are you ready for this?" Carter asked as I climbed into the twins' car. He was dressed head to toe in black, red and white: Westpoint High's school colours. A large "W" with a bear bursting through it decorated his baseball cap.

"Uh, I think so." I waved to Mum. She was not happy about school reopening, or the fact that I wanted to drive in with the twins, but she'd relented eventually.

"Red suits you." Madison gave me the onceover in the rear-view mirror. She was driving today. "You look cute."

"Not as cute as you. You look like something out of a teen movie."

"Thanks." She flicked her ponytail, the curls cascading down her back, red ribbons twisted through it. A "W" was painted on her cheekbone, and she was dressed in her cheerleading outfit. "I'll paint your face when we get out of the car."

"Er, great." I looked down at my outfit, thankful I'd been able to find my black jeans and the only red top I had. Luckily it was a slouchy knitted jumper – one that required little effort but made me look vaguely put together. "So what should I expect today?"

"Honestly, I don't know." Madison sighed. "The pep rally usually hypes everyone up, but I don't think anyone's up for it. Everything is 'in memory' of Shay and Kacey, but it all feels a bit off. I kind of wish they'd cancelled the whole thing."

"What?" Carter said, his voice hoarse. "Madison Garcia-Moore wants homecoming to be cancelled? You've been looking forward to this since we started school."

"I know. But it's meant to be all, I dunno, joyful. And this is not." She slowed the car and pulled into the parking lot, finding a space as far from the back entrance of the football field as she could. She plastered a grin on her face. "But the show must go on, right?"

"If you say so," Carter grumbled. We exited the car and I realized this would be the first time he saw his friends since he was taken in for questioning. I wondered if anyone else knew about it yet.

"Hey." I fell into step beside him as we watched Madison bounce away, her pleated skirt and ponytail swinging in time. "How are you feeling?"

"Like I want to go back to bed." He ducked his head, avoiding a group in head-to-toe red, hair sprayed to match. "For several reasons, but mainly so I don't have to be here."

243

"Do you want to stick together? It sounds like Madison will be busy for most of the day."

"Yeah." He smiled, adjusting the bag strap on his shoulder. When he dropped his hand, it grazed mine and my cheeks grew warm. Carter's eyes widened slightly, and he cleared his throat, but he didn't apologize. "Yeah," he repeated. "That would be good."

We walked across to the main entrance. It was early but it looked like everyone was here already. Students and teachers alike were dressed in the school colours. Some had cute little "W"s on their cheeks like Madison, but others had gone full bear face. "Wow," I said. "People take this stuff seriously."

"Oh, yeah." Carter burst out laughing as a cry of, "Bears!" was hollered from up near the entrance, followed by a round of cheers. "It's the highlight of some people's year. Alumni come back from all over for this game. That's why it's called homecoming."

"Now that makes sense; I always wondered why it was called homecoming. I have to say, my dad is pretty excited about watching the football game tonight. He used to play a bit for the Manchester Titans, but it's a pretty niche hobby in the UK. I know he's desperate to see a home game." We walked past a couple of girls balanced precariously on a step ladder, both trying to hang one side of a banner that would presumably drape over the entrance. The image of Tiffany Vickers in her prom dress suddenly flashed into my mind and my body shuddered, like someone had walked over my grave. Carter glanced at me from under his cap. Had he been talking to me?

"You OK?" he asked as we entered the school. "You're shivering."

"I'm fine, I should've brought a coat, that's all." I brushed the feeling off and refocused on him, ignoring the looks we were getting as we walked to Carter's locker. "Sorry, what were you saying?"

"Just that I miss it too." My face must have been completely blank because he turned to face me in front of his locker and spoke with exaggerated slowness. "Football. I miss it."

"Sorry. Wait, what? You played football?"

Carter looked affronted. "What? You don't believe me?"

As if on cue, the crowd in the corridor parted and cheers went up as part of the football team walked through. "It's not that, just … look at them," I stuttered. Hunter was in the centre, bleary-eyed and serious-looking. He was flanked by a tall black guy and a couple of stocky white dudes. They all had black stripes painted across their cheeks and wore black jerseys, their names and numbers emblazoned on the back in red and white.

I felt like I'd fallen asleep and woken up in Riverdale.

"So if you weren't ill … would you be doing that?" I asked as they passed. Luckily Hunter hadn't clocked Carter.

"Maybe." He shrugged, turning the dial on his locker

as the crowd knitted back together. "I had to quit before the end of last year, so I probably wouldn't have made it back on the team, even if I was better." He shoved his bag inside, pulled out a couple of books and slipped a pen into his tracksuit bottoms. "I haven't missed the training, but I do miss the games."

"You must be looking forward to tonight, then?" We headed to my locker next. I hadn't actually used it yet, so I pulled out my phone and opened up the notes app. I copied my locker combination, twisting the dial to each number before I heard a click. "I'm in!" I cheered. I popped open the little red door and paused.

There was something already in there.

"Paige? Are you sure you're OK? That's the second time you've gone pale in—" I took a step over so he could see inside the locker. "No. Is that what I think it is?"

"I think so." I reached out to touch the thick parchment nervously.

It was another letter.

"I can't," I said, slamming the locker shut and leaning on it. My breath started to come too fast, and I put every ounce of my energy into trying not to cry.

"Paige, you have to see what it says."

"Why?" My voice came out harsher than intended. "If it wasn't enough that some freak is sending me letters at home, now I have to deal with it here too?"

"It might be important." Carter looked at me

246

imploringly. "Look at the other notes. They wanted you to find the diary, to see the basement. *Why?*"

"I don't know!" I wanted to scream. It was all too much. Too much change, too much death, too much *responsibility*.

"Yeah, I don't know what they know, but it's too weird that you start getting notes and this all starts up again. You must be the key, Paige."

"Let me at those faces!" Madison appeared from nowhere, a block of face paint in one hand. "Wait, are you OK?" Panic crossed her features. "What's happening?"

"Nothing," I said, but way too quickly. I wouldn't have believed me.

"Carter?" Madison looked at her brother and he sighed.

"C'mon, Paige. Show her."

"Show me what?" Madison said, looking between us as I pushed myself off the locker. "Guys, come on. You're scaring me."

I opened the locker door and Madison peered over my shoulder.

It was still there.

"Oh, shit," she whispered, glancing around furtively. No one was paying us the slightest bit of attention. "Why didn't you tell us in the car?"

"I didn't get it at home," I mumbled. I could almost feel the blood that drained from Madison's face. "It was in my locker."

"What?" She crowded in closer. "Have you opened it yet?"

"No," I said. The three of us stared at the envelope in silence. Sweat broke out on my lower back as I contemplated it. "OK. Just keep a lookout."

I handled the envelope as though it might explode at any second. It was the same as the others, my name scrawled thickly across the front. I flipped it over as Madison and Carter covered my back, blocking me from the hallway. I tore open the seal and slipped out a piece of parchment paper, just the same as all the others.

"What does it say?" Madison breathed. I unfolded the note.

Hello, Paige.

Apologies for bothering you at school, but I thought your parents would be a little more cautious now there have been three deaths. If I had a teenage daughter, I sure would be keeping a close eye on her at the moment.

Keep sleuthing – and, Paige, can you stop the next murder?

Or are you going to fail me?

"This guy is sick," Carter breathed as he scanned the letter over my shoulder. Madison's phone beeped. "What the hell—"

"Wait," I cut him off. "This says three deaths. That's not right."

Madison turned her phone around, tears in her eyes. "Yes, it is. Look what's just been put in the group chat."

I stared at the open news article on her phone in disbelief. "Third body discovered in Devil's Den."

"No," I whispered, looking back at the letter.

Carter looked at me carefully, as if I wouldn't like what he was about to say.

"What?" I demanded.

"Paige, the letter writer, the killer … they're the same person, aren't they?"

25

Despite the breaking news, school carried on as normal. Chase Vickers had been true to his word about an increased police presence, but the sight of so many strangers on school grounds made me uneasy.

"So we just go to lessons now?" I asked Carter and Madison as we left homeroom.

"To class? I guess so," Madison replied as we pushed our way through the throng in the hall. I pulled up the screenshot of my timetable.

"Um, what do you guys have now?"

"English," they chimed in unison.

"Oh, thank god, me too. Room 403?"

"Yeah, Ms Lee. She's nice." Carter still had his head dipped, though the attention had been somewhat pulled away from him with the announcement of a third body.

"This is all so surreal. I can't believe they haven't sent

us home," Madison complained as we started up a flight of stairs. "Did you hear what Josh was saying in homeroom?"

"No?" I gripped the strap of the tote bag I'd brought from my locker. Madison glanced around, but the other kids on the stairs were too engrossed in their own conversations to bother with ours.

"Loads of people have been taken in for questioning over the last few days. It wasn't just you, Carter, even though the cops made out like you were on the FBI's most-wanted list. Apparently, Hunter was in yesterday and that's why he was so drunk at the memorial. He'd spent the morning at the police precinct where they practically told him he had murdered Shay."

"Jeez," I whispered. "So who else have they questioned?"

"All Shay and Kacey's male classmates, plus any other guys vaguely close to our age from town," Madison said. I followed them both into an almost empty room 403 and we huddled at the back. "I'd expect the cheerleaders to be next, since they were both part of the squad, but I think they're convinced it was a biological male." Madison tensed her arm pointedly, her well-honed muscles flexing. "They don't think a female would be *strong* enough."

"So they have absolutely no idea who they're looking for. Great." I watched the door as people dribbled in. Josh entered with one of the other cheerleaders, Kyla maybe? I was still struggling with names. Her face was tear-stained and he guided her to a chair at the front. He caught my eye as he sat down and nodded in our general direction. "Hey, was Josh questioned too?"

"For, like, five seconds, by the sounds of it," Madison said. "Daddy intervened pretty quickly. I heard the same about Justin. Granddaddy Astor had him out of there in no time."

"Sounds about right," Carter said, stretching his long legs out beneath the tiny desk. He had barely said a word since we'd left homeroom. "They're total nepo babies."

"Oof, someone's grouchy," Madison whispered as the teacher entered the room and everyone stopped talking.

"Good morning, class." Her voice was gentle and she was older than I had expected, a small Mother-Earth figure in a long sweeping skirt and cardigan. "I know this week has been rough, but let's try to lose ourselves in some poetry, what do you say?"

There was no answer.

"Great," she continued, unfazed. "Let's turn to page thirty-nine of your anthologies."

A hushed rustle of pages filled the room. I opened my tote bag and blinked in surprise. The diary was still inside – I'd shoved it in with the textbook before we went to the hospital yesterday. I'd meant to leave it at home. I ignored it and opened the school textbook instead. The poem was "Do Not Go Gentle Into That Good Night" by Dylan Thomas, and I tried my best to concentrate on it, but it didn't seem the most appropriate piece of writing to study after the murders. Wasn't the whole meaning of it that you should fight death? My eyes lost focus after I read the line: "Rage, rage against the dying of the light" for the third time and I knew my attention was shot. I bet those girls did rage, I bet they fought until their last breaths. The thought was unbearable – we couldn't let it happen again. There must be something else in that diary. There *had* to be – otherwise why had the letter writer chosen me? There must be some kind of clue in there, something that could stop it.

"OK, class. Let's call it a day." Ms Lee perched on the desk at the front of the room, apparently oblivious to the poem she had just assigned. "I can tell today is a write-off for most of us. But we have thirty-five minutes of this class left, so can I suggest you use it wisely? No phones, please, but read, meditate, do some overdue homework, whatever you like. Just do it quietly."

A sigh of relief echoed around the room and people began whispering and closing their books. I felt Madison's eyes on me.

"Read it." She nodded at my bag – she'd seen the diary.

I nodded back, looking over at Carter. His arms were folded on the desk, and he had rested his sleeping head on them. Dark circles stretched like bruises beneath his eyes.

I pulled out the diary and started to read.

Song of the Day: "Creep" (Radiohead)

Dear Diary,

Yeah, I know – such an angsty song of the day. I feel horrible and I'm desperate to talk to someone about how much I miss CJ, but I can't. I feel like I'm skulking around and lying to everyone. So, yep, I'm a total creep right now.

I've been so sick this week! I must have a virus or something. I've been dizzy and can't keep food down, which is not like me at all. I tried not to miss any school, but I was so sick yesterday morning that I had to spend the day in bed. Mom and Pop were less than sympathetic – they hate when I'm sick, like it's a sign of weakness or something. So this morning I dragged my ass into school, even though I still felt like death.

Tiffany cornered me at recess today. If I'm truthful, I've been avoiding her since my night with CJ. It hasn't been too difficult, she's so wrapped up in running for Homecoming Queen that she's been busy anyway, but I miss her. I want to tell her what happened <u>so bad</u> but it was just too special. I don't want anything to spoil it. Tiffany is my best friend but sometimes she just doesn't understand where I'm coming from. This was so ... sacred. Special. I love her but it was between me and CJ. The best secret.

I think I should probably call the doctor tomorrow. Mom keeps giving me vitamin drinks, but I spent the whole of lunch vomiting in the girl's bathroom after I got a whiff of the food in the dining hall. I must have food poisoning or something.

I'm off to bed now. I haven't felt this sick in a long time - thank god tomorrow is Saturday. Maybe Mom will take pity and let me sleep in.

Ha, right.

Write soon,

Nicole

P.S. Tiff told me OJ was found innocent, the jury announced it today! Whhhhat???

"Oh my god," I breathed. I glanced at Carter – his eyelids fluttered delicately and his breathing had deepened. Fast asleep. Today must be a bad day.

"What is it?" Madison leaned in, trying to read over my shoulder. She whispered the words as she scanned the pages, and my thoughts began to knot together. Looking at the date of the entry after her night with CJ and this one, the reason she was sick seemed so obvious to me. Nicole was brought up in such a strict Christian family, though. Like exorcism strict. She'd even said that she was withdrawn from sex education at school. She was secretly rebellious but clearly so naïve. "Oh my god," Madison finally repeated.

"Right?" I said, turning to look at her. "Nicole was pregnant."

"She was what?" Carter yawned over lunch. He'd slept through the rest of English, and we'd all been in different places for our next class, so this was our first chance to catch him up.

"I know. It makes it so much worse, doesn't it?" Madison stabbed at a tomato and nibbled unenthusiastically. "God, I can never eat before events."

"Do you think the killer knew that she was pregnant?" I asked, pushing my fries around. I didn't have much of an appetite myself.

"I don't know," Carter said. He hadn't even pretended to be hungry and sipped from his water bottle instead. "I guess if he was choosing girls that the Jacksons were doing exorcisms on then that would put her in danger? From what we know about how they treated 'sinners', Nicole would have gone straight to the top of their list. She'd committed the holy grail of sins."

"You think they would do that to their own daughter?" I asked.

"I don't think they were particularly sane about the whole thing," Carter said. "I mean, they were doing at-home exorcisms in their basement."

"That's true. Poor Nicole," I said, patting the diary through my tote bag. "Poor all of them."

Madison suddenly sat up straight. "Do you think the same thing is happening now?" Her eyes filled with tears. "Do you think … Shay and Kacey … you think they had to go through all that too?"

My blood ran cold. I hadn't thought about it. "I hope not. The Jacksons are both dead, so unless someone else has carried on their sick little tradition it's probably just a copycat killer." I stopped. "Not just, I didn't mean that."

"I know," Madison said.

"Is there any more news on the third body?"

"No, I don't think so." Madison scrolled through her phone to make sure and shook her head. "Nothing. Everyone in the cheer group chat is accounted for, though, thank god."

"That's good. I wonder who—"

"Hey, guys!" A Chinese girl with excellent red and black winged eyeliner bounced over to the table and dropped a pile of books with a bang. She wore a uniform to match Madison's and leaned down to give the twins a hug. "How are we holding up?"

"We're OK. Iris, have you met Paige? She's our new neighbour."

"Hi, Paige." She bent over and shook my hand so formally I couldn't help but laugh. "Great hair, by the way. Are the twins looking after you?"

"Of course we are." Carter smiled at me, and Iris raised her perfectly groomed brows. "What's up, Iris?"

"Just dropping these off." She produced a couple of envelopes from the pile of books on the table. "Mom said the rest of the results will take a few weeks, but I told her you wanted the basics for the science project. The rest will get emailed to you at some point."

"Iris, you legend!" Madison snatched the envelopes from her and stared at them. "Thank you so much."

"No worries. There won't be any accidental incest on *my* watch." Iris winked and picked her books up again. "See you at the pep rally."

"Yeah, see you soon." Madison was still staring at the envelopes. "I can't believe we really have DNA results in here." She looked up at her brother. "We might have siblings, Carter. How wild is that?"

"I'm still not on board," he muttered. "You know there will only be results if people have submitted their DNA to the same company, right? It won't show you the whole picture." He'd grown paler as the day had gone on, and I had a sneaking suspicion the only reason he hadn't gone home was so he could keep an eye on his sister. Maybe me too. The thought gave me a warm feeling.

"It's better than nothing." Madison held out an envelope to me, glaring at her brother. "Come on, Paige, open yours with me. I know *you'll* lend me some moral support."

"I predict a blank page," I joked. "Remember, only children only in my family." I ripped open the envelope and removed the printout. The line at the top read: *Garcia-Moore, Madison*. "Hey, I have the wrong one."

"What? Are you sure?"

Carter took the paper from her and pointed at the page. "This has my name on. Which means Paige is right, they're mixed up." He handed it to me as Madison took the one in my hands.

"This can't be right," I said. Letters and numbers swam before my eyes as I tried to make sense of what I was seeing. There was one result on the page.

Dominic Smith
27 years, California, USA
Shared DNA: **1,724 cM** across **47 segments**
Unweighted shared DNA: **1,724 cM**
Longest segment: **106 cM**

Possible DNA relationships
This table shows the percentage of the time people

sharing 1,724 cM have the following relationships.

Percent	Relationship
100%	Grandparent
	Grandchild
	Half sibling
	Aunt/uncle
	Niece/nephew

"I…" My mouth had gone completely dry. I took a swig from my water bottle and tried again. "This can't be right," I repeated. "What am I looking at?"

"Let's see." Madison eased the paper from my hands to study it. "Well, you don't have any nephews or nieces, right?"

"No."

"And definitely no grandchildren… What about your grandparents? Were any of them not biologically related to you?"

"I… No? I don't think so?" I realized I had no idea. I'd just always assumed that they were.

"OK, so that could be one solution," Madison said, running a finger down the list. "You said your parents are only children, so unless *they* have siblings they don't know about, it's got to be this one." She put the page on the table and pointed at two words.

Half-sibling.

"No," I said. "My parents have been together forever. A

half-sibling means this…" – I checked the page – "*Dominic* guy is only related to one of them, doesn't it?"

"Yeah…" Madison let the word trail off. I knew she was thinking the same thing as I was.

Did one of my parents have an affair?

"Wait, let me think about this." I took a deep breath. "It says he's twenty-seven, right?" My chest was tight as I tried to do the maths on my fingers. "So he was born in, what? The late nineties?"

Madison tapped some numbers into the calculator app on her phone. "Yep, '96. So your parents were, what? Eighteen, nineteen?"

"Yeah, around that. Dad's a year older. But they only met in '97. That's when Mum came over from the UK for university."

"Shit," Carter breathed.

"Shit is right," I said, anger building in my chest. "One of my parents had a kid and never told me."

26

Madison had to leave for her warm-up, so after lunch I blindly followed Carter towards the auditorium. I had written and deleted what felt like a thousand messages to my mum and dad, but I hadn't sent any. I couldn't get my head around the piece of paper in my pocket.

"It could be a mistake, right?" I asked Carter. He sighed. It wasn't the first time I'd asked him.

"Sure it could," he reassured me. "And it could still be an aunt or uncle you don't know about. But you won't know until you talk to your parents."

"But what if they've kept it secret from each other?" I twisted my hands around the handle of my tote until I had rope-burn. This was too big, too much to deal with on top of everything else. "What if I go home and drop this huge bombshell and it destroys our family? I don't think I could handle that."

"Come here." Carter removed my hands from the bag strap and pulled me out of the flow of bodies towards the side of the corridor.

He didn't let go of my hands.

"Deep breaths," he said, not breaking eye contact.

"I don't need to – I just want—"

"Deep. Breaths," he repeated, squeezing my hands.

I closed my eyes and complied, the heat from his hands spreading through my body. We stayed that way for a few seconds, and I found myself hoping that he wouldn't let go.

"Better?" he asked.

"I think so." Neither of us moved. "Thanks. It's a mistake; it must be. I should talk to them about it later, though."

"Good idea, you'll just dwell on it otherwise." The corridor was almost empty now and Carter pushed himself off the wall, hesitating before brushing a curl from my face, his fingers trailing sparks where they touched my cheek. "There, perfect." His voice was hoarse. "Um, we should go."

For a second, I forgot my own name.

"Come on." He led the way and I followed, numb. So many different feelings had coursed through my body in the last half hour that I felt dizzy. He didn't catch my hand again, but his fingers brushed mine more than once before we got to the auditorium. "It's about to start," he whispered, nudging me in front of him. "There, on the end of that bench, we can squeeze in. Go!"

I slipped through the door and slid on to the end of the bench he'd pointed at, smiling apologetically at the girl next to me. She rolled her eyes and shuffled up so Carter could cram himself in next to me, so close that I let out an involuntary gasp of air. The girl next to me didn't look amused, but Carter did. He grinned at me from beneath his Westpoint Bears cap, and I could see a red flush creeping up his neck, making him look healthier than I'd ever seen him.

"Before we begin today's pep rally, I have an announcement." Principal Goldberg spoke into the microphone and the crowd hushed at once. "As you may have heard, a third body was found in the early hours of this morning." A few whispers broke out and guilt flooded my body. How could I be thinking about imaginary siblings and how soft Carter's lips might be when all of this was going on? People were dying. "The young woman has been identified as Whitney Fox, a local college student." Chatter fully erupted now.

"She was a senior last year," Carter whispered. "She was wild, always in trouble for drinking, sometimes drugs from what I remember. I'd say she definitely fits the 'sinner' criteria. Not that she deserved anything close to this," he quickly added.

"I know you don't mean that, don't worry."

Principal Goldberg cleared his throat into the microphone. "Whitney was an ex-pupil of Westpoint High and as such I would like to acknowledge her passing with a moment of silence." Heads bowed around me and I followed suit. Carter's fingers brushed the back of my hand and as I looked down he held his palm out, glancing sideways at me. I slipped my hand into his, the warmth of it already familiar.

Screw it. People were dying. If I liked Carter and he liked me, we had to grab any fleeting chance of happiness.

"Thank you," Principal Goldberg's voice boomed as he gestured to the cheerleaders. Madison and the others rose gingerly and approached the front of the auditorium, clasping hands. They were joined by a girl with a perky blonde ponytail and the kind of healthy bronze glow I had to get from a bottle. "Now over to Anne Hargrove, the head of your homecoming committee!"

The announcement fell flat and a smattering of applause echoed in the large room. Anne took her place behind the microphone as the cheerleaders huddled to one side. My eyes were drawn to the portraits that hung on the far wall and I studied them, wondering sadly if the most recent victims would be added to the grim gallery.

"Hello, Westpoint High!" The perky blonde tried her best to sound cheerful, but her voice broke on the last word. She audibly sighed. "I know this doesn't seem right," she said, twisting her fingers in the hem of a red T-shirt that said: "I'm not Bossy, I'm The Boss" on it. "It doesn't feel like we should be planning to get all dressed up and dance the night away, but the show must go on, right? A lot of people have worked really hard to make the dance tomorrow night happen, and it would be great to see as many of you as possible there. Tickets are still available, and the committee has decided that all proceeds will go toward some kind of permanent memorial for our sadly departed friends." This sparked a round of whispers and Anne seemed to gain confidence. "In addition to this, the cheer squad, football team and homecoming committee want to dedicate the game tonight and the dance tomorrow to the memories of Shay Kalani, Kacey Molloy and Whitney Fox." A whoop echoed out from the back of the hall and the crowd warmed up a little, clapping and cheering. I tapped the back of the hand Carter was holding instead of clapping and he looked at me.

"I didn't want to let go," I whispered. His grin widened and I bit my lip. I can't believe I just said that. I focused my attention back on Blondie.

"Finally, a reminder that due to school being closed, the voting for the homecoming court was moved online. If you haven't yet voted, please do so before six p.m. today, when voting will close. The homecoming court will be announced at tonight's game. Thank you. Now, over to your cheer squad, the Westpoint Honey Bears!"

The Honey Bears. Oh … wow. That was an interesting squad name. No one else was fazed though, and a wave of applause filled the auditorium as Anne took her seat.

Madison approached the microphone and I glanced at Carter.

"She's got this," he whispered.

I hoped so.

"Thank you." Madison moved back from the mic and cleared her throat as the applause died down. "Thanks." She took a deep breath and stood up straight. "This week has seen the unthinkable happen in our school community. As a squad, we had serious thoughts about coming up here without Shay and Kacey, because it didn't feel right. They were our friends, our sisters. We felt lost and scared, like most of us have this week. But if you knew Shay and Kacey, you knew they were fighters. Those girls were two of the toughest people you could ever meet and, man, would they be pissed if we didn't cheer our team on tonight." There was laughter as Principal Goldberg shook his head from the side of the auditorium. "Sorry, sir!" Madison laughed along with the others. "But you know I'm right." The ice was well and truly broken as he relented and nodded in agreement.

I squeezed Carter's hand as we watched the Honey Bears try to get the crowd riled up. They led chants and did some frankly mind-blowing stunts where some of the girls backflipped, got thrown in the air and stood on people's hands and shoulders. No wonder Madison was so muscular. The male cheerleaders were visibly strong too and their coordination was like nothing I'd ever seen before.

This wasn't a group of girls bouncing around with pompoms like I'd thought, they were real athletes. How did they make their bodies do that kind of stuff?

My worries drifted to the back of my mind as I watched them. I joined in with the chants a couple of times, but it was undoubtedly subdued. It must be raucous on a good day. I clearly thought that too soon, as seconds later the cheer squad introduced the Westpoint High Bears and people started to get to their feet as the football team burst through the doors, followed by some poor soul in a giant bear outfit who ran around giving people high fives.

"You are kidding me!" I laughed out loud as Carter visibly cringed.

"Yeah. I've never seen it from this side before. It's a bit hero-worship-y, isn't it?"

"Yes." I laughed again, trying and failing to imagine him up there waving and flexing at the crowd. "Yes, it is. But it's kind of fun!"

We stood with the rest of the auditorium and Carter let go of my hand so he could clap and whoop to cheer his old teammates on. I clapped politely but the distraction had worn off and I was back to thinking about the letter in my pocket. As the excitement around me started to die down, I tried to rehearse a speech in my head, something I could say to my parents that wouldn't start World War Three.

"Excuse me," the girl next to me said loudly. She was standing up and it clearly wasn't the first time she'd asked.

"Oh, sorry." Carter had disappeared, so I grabbed my tote bag and shuffled out. The football team milled around the front now, accepting pats on the back and well wishes for tonight's game. I spotted Carter talking to Hunter and watched the two exchange a handshake that turned into one of those bro hugs that guys give each other, slapping each other on the back. I was glad they seemed to have cleared the air.

"Hey, Paige." I turned to see Josh standing behind me. His face was flushed and he looked slightly awkward in his jersey. "Was that your first pep rally?"

"It was indeed." I smiled, feeling incredibly British. "We don't have *anything* like that at home."

"No?" He laughed nervously and raked a hand through his short brown hair. "So what do the English do before a football game?"

"Drink, mostly." I caught Carter's eye over Josh's shoulder and he waved, heading over.

Josh laughed. "That's what we do after one. Actually, I was going to ask if—"

"Hey, man, good luck out there tonight." Carter slapped Josh on the shoulder, interrupting him. "You'll nail those amateurs."

"Yeah, we will. I was just going to see whether…" Carter threaded his fingers through mine and Josh paused. "Oh. I guess I'll see you guys at the game, then?" He ran the words together and left without waiting for an answer, his head down.

"Oh, shit." Carter looked at our hands. "Did he just ask you out?"

"What? No, I..." Realization dawned on me, and I knew my face had turned bright, flaming red. Josh, ask me out? I had hardly spoken to him. "Oh, no. I think maybe he was going to?"

"C'mon, let's get you home." Carter chuckled and shook his head, pulling me along. "Only here for a week and breaking hearts already."

Madison was staying behind after school to practise for the game, so it was just the two of us on the drive home. We drove in silence, Carter obviously in need of some rest, but it was a nice silence. Comfortable. I felt like I'd known him for a lot longer than a week.

"Straight to your door." Carter grinned as he pulled up at the end of my drive. He was pale again.

"Thanks. Are you going to rest?"

"Yeah, naptime for me. Rock and roll. I'll give you a call if I'm feeling well enough to go to the game, is that OK? I think I'll be fine, but I can nap like it's my college major."

"Yeah, sure." I smiled at him. "I ... had a good time this afternoon, hanging out with you."

"Me too." He smiled. "Listen, Paige, I get if this is all too much for you. You've been here five minutes, don't feel like you need to do whatever this is." He waved a hand between us. "I'm happy to stay friends; you're under no obligation to—"

I cut him off with a kiss on the cheek.

"One thing you'll learn about me," I said, "is that I don't like being told what to do."

He kissed me back, properly this time. I closed my eyes. His lips were as soft as they looked.

"But, Paige, I mean it." He pulled back and sighed, though he took hold of my hand. "I might die. I know I said my prognosis was good, but there's no guarantee this treatment is going to work the way it should. I've made friends with other kids at the hospital who aren't here any more and—"

"And I might be next on the killer's list," I interrupted him, though his words had shaken me a little. "Doesn't that kind of make it the best time to do this?"

He brushed my hair away and leaned in to kiss me again. "God, you're persuasive."

A loud bang on the glass made us both jump.

"Paige Carmichael, get inside this minute." My mum glared at us through the glass.

"Oh, god," I groaned, guilt and annoyance fighting for dominance in my body. "Sorry." I started to get out of the car.

"Thank you, Carter," Mum carried on, her voice curt. "I think you should be going now."

"Yes, ma'am." He started the engine and turned to me with a grimace. "Good luck," he whispered.

I closed the door behind me and walked up the

driveway as Carter pulled away. Mum marched ahead so I followed behind her, silently fuming.

"I cannot believe you, Paige." Mum flung the door open and waited for me to walk past her. "We've been here for five minutes and already you're associating yourself with—"

"With who?" I felt my confusion and anger all start to boil together in one as she slammed the door. Dad called from the kitchen, but I ignored him. "With the nice guy from down the street?"

"He is a murder suspect, Paige!" Mum threw her arms out in exasperation. "Did you forget that when you were snogging in his car?"

"He is not a suspect; everyone was questioned. And at least I was just *snogging* him," I yelled, pulling the DNA test from my pocket and throwing it at her. It fluttered to the floor in a pathetic show of un-cooperation. "There won't be any secret babies from *me*."

"What are you talking about?" Mum went to collect the paper and called out to my Dad. "Jake, can you get out here and talk some sense into your daughter?"

The doorbell rang.

"Jesus, what are you both playing at?" Dad appeared in the doorway, his eyes wide. Mum and I rarely argued. The doorbell chimed again. "Is someone going to get that or what?"

"Fine!" I yanked the door open, half-expecting to see

272

Carter with an apology, but my anger wilted quickly. A tall, tanned woman with strawberry-blonde hair stood on the porch. She was dressed casually, in cropped jeans and a thick, oversized cardigan. A small diamond stud glinted in her nose.

"Is this the Carmichael house?"

"Yes." I waited for her to say more, but she just looked down at her feet. She was strangely familiar-looking and wore Birkenstock sandals, even though it was almost November. "Erm, are you OK?"

"Who is it, Paige?" Dad came to stand behind me and the woman finally looked up, her nerves obvious. I heard him gasp and twisted to face him as realization dawned on me too.

"Dad?" I croaked.

"Hi, CJ," Nicole Jackson said gently. "It's been a while."

27

There was a dead girl in my living room.

"Nicole, I... I don't know what to say," my dad stuttered.

"Technically I'm not called Nicole any more ... oh, never mind. Let's not complicate things any more than they are."

"Not Nicole..." Dad was pale and slack jawed. He looked like he was leaning on the fireplace mantel, but I'm pretty sure it was holding him up. I felt pretty slack-jawed myself. Jake was short for Jacob, but so was Coby, apparently. It had been a private nickname between them, an in-joke. Coby Jake. Things started slotting into place – song of the day, my parents' reluctance to tell me the whole story about the house. Nicole, the Shorehaven Ripper's final victim, was alive. The girl whose diary I was reading was suddenly sitting on my sofa.

And my dad was CJ.

"I know it must be like seeing a ghost," Nicole said gently, her voice barely audible over Mum banging cupboard doors in the kitchen. She was perched on the other end of the sofa from me. "I'm sorry for that, I really am. But I had to do it."

"For the baby, right?" It was the first time I'd spoken, and she looked at me curiously.

"How did you know?" Nicole said.

Dad cleared his throat. "Baby?" He looked sick.

"Sit down, Dad," I helped him into an armchair as Mum reappeared with a bottle of Bourbon and four glasses. I raised my eyebrows.

"You're almost eighteen, you can have one drink. Manchester rules apply tonight." She sank on to the floor and cracked the metal lid from the bottle, looking at no one but making sure each measure was perfectly level. "Paige."

I grabbed two of the glasses and gave one to Nicole, who cradled it in beringed hands. I put Dad's directly under his nose.

"Drink," Mum demanded.

Dad took a swig and burst into a cough, his eyes clearing a little. "God, I hate Bourbon."

"I know." Mum glowered at him, drinking her own like it was water. "So, Nicole, without sounding incredibly rude, we – and everyone else in Shorehaven – thought you were dead."

"I know." Nicole placed her untouched glass on the floor. I picked up mine as I sat back on the sofa and gave it an experimental sniff. The smell was enough to turn my stomach, but holding it gave my hands something to do. Nicole sighed. "I really am sorry. It must be a lot, but I had my reasons at the time…" She trailed off, glancing around the room. "This wasn't a happy place to grow up. My parents were … strict."

"So you faked your own death?" Dad was incredulous. "Nicole, people mourned you. *I* mourned you. I know we hadn't spoken since I went back to college, but your death scarred me. I thought I'd never get over it, until I met Sarah. Not just that, but this town has kept your memory alive. It's—"

"Sick? Yeah." Nicole's lower lip wobbled, and she took a deep breath. "But like your daughter said, I wasn't just doing it for me."

"So this is accurate." Mum pulled the DNA test results from her blazer pocket. I'd never seen hurt like that in her eyes before. "Paige has a brother."

"Yes." Nicole's voice was small as she hung her head.

Dad finished his glass of Bourbon. "What … how?" he asked. He looked desperately at Mum. "Sarah, I swear I didn't know. If I did I—"

Mum held up a hand, cutting him off. "I know. I know you didn't." Her voice was thick with tears. "But just stop. We need to hear this. Nicole, please carry on."

"Thank you."

"Don't thank me." Mum laughed, though it was hollow and flat. She drained her own drink and poured another. "Just explain."

I took a sip and regretted it immediately as the liquid fire hit my stomach and threatened to come up again. I put the glass down next to my bag and picked that up instead.

"I think I might be able to help explain." I pulled the diary out and handed it to Nicole. "I found this, in the upstairs bathroom. That's my room now."

"Oh my god, my diary…" She ran one hand over the leather cover. "Coby, do you remember this? You gave it to me for my birthday."

"Yeah, I do." I'd never seen my dad look so ill. "Nicole, I… If I'd have known we had a … a *child*…"

"I know. But you didn't because I didn't tell you." She held up the diary. "Have you read this?"

"Er." I squirmed in my seat. "Well, yes, but I thought you were dead! And when I started getting the notes, and the murders started I…" I did what? I couldn't finish the sentence. "It seemed like a good idea at the time," I finished weakly.

"Wait." Mum put her glass down. "Diary? Notes? What the hell is going on, Paige?"

I exhaled and pulled out the folder where I'd been keeping the letters, spreading them out on the sofa. "I started getting these as soon as we moved in. They're …

harmless, I think?" No point scaring them all too much this evening. "Just someone messing with me. But they wanted me to look for your stuff. To find out things about this house."

"Oh my god." Mum got to her feet and started pacing the long expanse of the living room. "I knew moving here was a bad idea. I knew it!"

"Sarah—" Dad tried but Mum cut him off.

"No!" Mum yelled before taking a deep breath and closing her eyes. "No. You can speak later. I've done enough for you, Jake. I moved here, despite reservations about this house. I agreed to keep the past from Paige, even though I knew – I knew! – it was going to come back and bite us on the arse." She looked around the living room. "I gave you the benefit of the doubt that it would all be fine, but it's not. It's far from fine, and right now I want to know why our daughter has been hiding things from us and then I want to know why Nicole ran away and left everyone to assume she'd been murdered. OK?"

"OK," Dad whispered.

Nicole looked at me and shrugged, picking up one of the letters. "You first, Paige."

Nice one.

"I've told you everything, really." I looked at my mum, but she had taken a seat at the dining table, her head in her hands. "The first letter arrived on the day we moved in. It asked me if I was ready to be a part of the house's history. It was weird but I thought it was some kind of prank, something to scare the new kid. But then the next one asked me if I knew what was in the walls. There had been this clanking noise in the fan in my bathroom and when I looked inside, I saw something." I nodded at the diary on Nicole's lap. "That's when I found your diary, and some other stuff."

"I should have taken it with me," she murmured, "but I wanted a clean break. I took the tiny amount of money I'd been squirrelling away from birthdays and some clothes I'd stolen from the Church clothing drives. I didn't want there to be any way to trace me back to Shorehaven."

"So the letters." Dad interrupted. "You still have no idea who is sending them?"

I shook my head. "Not a clue. The next one arrived after Gran and Gramps had been over, and it asked me about the basement. I'd already been down there because I heard what Gramps said to Dad."

"What did he say?" Nicole picked up another letter.

"Not to let you see what was in the basement." Dad groaned. "So I suppose you went straight down?"

I didn't answer.

"Is there still anything there?" Nicole asked, rubbing her wrists. Her tanned skin had paled slightly. "From my parents?"

"A couple of boxes of newspapers that I didn't get a chance to look in. And, er, a pentagram type thing?

Painted on the floor." I took a deep breath before I went all in. "I Googled it and apparently it's a demon trap?" Mum made a noise behind me.

"Yeah." Nicole looked as though she was going to be sick. She held her head up and looked at my dad. "That's why I had to leave. The things they did down there… They called them exorcisms, but it was pure torture. If they had found out I was pregnant, they would have killed me and the baby."

"Jesus." Dad raked a hand through his hair. "Nicole, I'm sorry. I knew they were strict, but I never in a million years…"

"Coby, stop. None of this is on you. I don't know if you remember, but I worked really hard to keep the two halves of my life separate. Home was … tough. But I dealt with it. The last thing I wanted to do was come back to this house, but I saw what was happening… Those girls being murdered… I had to. I need people to know what really happened."

I let everything sink in, but I still had one question. I took a deep breath, wondering if I had the nerve to ask.

Fuck it.

"Nicole, do you think your parents killed those girls in 1995?" I felt Mum's arms wrap around me from behind as she perched on the arm of the sofa. I squeezed her arm. Poor Mum.

"No." Nicole put the letters down and drained the

glass of Bourbon at her feet. "Shit, that's strong," she wheezed. She took a deep breath. "They were too righteous to kill anyone, I mean, that would have been an actual sin. But they'd wholesale bought into all the Satanic Panic bullshit, so when it seemed to arrive on our doorstep, they felt like they were doing the Lord's work." She shook her head. "Those poor girls did nothing but live their lives. They were young women finding their feet in the world, experimenting, making mistakes…" Nicole stopped and wiped a tear from her face with the wrist of her cardigan and Mum released me and got up. "I wanted to do the same, so badly. So I played along at home, said my prayers, went to church, everything they wanted. But when I could I went out, changed my clothes, kissed boys. I used to sneak out when my parents were in bed and my best friend would collect me on the next street over. My parents didn't expect it of me, so they never suspected."

"Here." Mum handed Nicole a box of tissues and refilled her glass. "You were so young. You must have been so scared when you found out you were going to be a mum."

"Terrified." She took the tissues but handed the glass back. "Thanks, but I can't. I'm driving."

Mum took the bottle over to Dad and topped his glass up. When she sat on the arm of his chair, he gripped her hand like a drowning man grabbing at a life preserver.

Mum reached an arm around him and squeezed tight, kissing the top of his head. "We'll be OK, we've got this," she whispered before addressing Nicole again. "Where are you staying?"

"I don't know yet. I just flew in from San Francisco and hired a car at the airport, then drove straight here before I lost my nerve. I'm sure I'll get a motel somewhere, I bet Shorehaven isn't exactly tourist central at the moment."

"Stay here," Mum said. I almost downed the rest of *my* Bourbon in shock.

"What? No, I—"

"Nicole, someone is killing people and it's homecoming weekend. You won't find anywhere decent to stay tonight." Mum sighed. "Plus, we appear to be family, as weird as this whole thing is. Jake might be too shell-shocked to talk about his son, but I'd like to hear about him over a few more drinks. I bet Paige would too."

I nodded, realizing I was desperate to know about him. My brother. I never really thought about having a sibling. He was older than me; he might be married, have kids. I could be an auntie.

"I… That's so kind. Thank you." Tears rolled down Nicole's freckled cheeks again and she dabbed them away. "I can have that drink after all." She laughed weakly, taking a sip.

"Do you want to sleep in my, er, your room?" I asked nervously as Dad pulled my mum to her feet and wrapped her in a hug. Nicole smiled at them and for the first time I noticed a silver wedding band on her ring finger.

"No, thank you." She said it politely, but I was sure she was suppressing a shudder. She must have such bad memories of this place. "The sofa or something will be fine."

"We have a couple of spare rooms," Mum started as Dad disappeared out into the hallway. "But of course you know that. Sorry."

"Anywhere is fine," she said. "Honestly, this is so generous. I'll be gone first thing."

"Paige, where's the air bed? We can use that."

"In my room. Do you want me to—"

"Nope, I'll go," Mum said as she walked to the door a little unsteadily. "I need to check on your dad, anyway."

Nicole and I sat in silence.

"Nicole, can I ask another question?"

"Sure. About Dominic?"

"Who? Oh – Dominic." I looked at the crumpled page that now lay on the floor. "That's his name."

"Yeah."

Dominic. I liked it.

"No, not yet anyway." I tucked my hair behind my shoulders. "I wanted to ask – why did you really come back?"

Nicole narrowed her eyes slightly. "What do you mean?"

"Well, everyone thought you were dead. You sound like you have a nice life. So why come out of hiding now?"

Nicole downed her drink.

"Because it's happening again. I've been beating myself up about it since I saw the first murder on the news."

"Why?"

"Because if someone is copying what happened and they're following the same pattern, then two people will go missing tomorrow night. But that's not what really happened; I was never a victim. I just let the world believe I was. Some innocent girl could be in trouble because the killer is trying to repeat something that didn't actually happen."

"You mean your murder."

"I mean more than that, but I can't tell you yet. Tomorrow, maybe." She pointed to my glass. "Are you drinking that?"

28

I snuck upstairs with my phone as soon as I was able to. It had died hours ago, and I knew I'd missed most, if not all of the football game. I really hoped Carter had made it and just assumed Mum was too angry to let me go. I was desperate to talk to him and Madison. Nicole hadn't mentioned anything else, but I guess she'd dropped enough bombshells on my parents that evening. I'd left them talking about Dominic with the remains of a take-out and a fresh bottle of wine. Alcohol seemed to be helping.

I plugged my phone in and waited for the screen to light up, tapping my foot impatiently. It stayed irritatingly dark, so I grabbed the roll of packing tape I'd found downstairs and started to stick the notes to the wall. No need to hide them now.

My phone buzzed on the bedside table.

"Finally," I breathed, throwing myself down on the bed. I scrolled through the notifications. Missed calls and texts from the twins: Madison's were all from earlier but Carter's last text was only ten minutes ago. I checked the time – almost eight – and assumed Madison must be mid-cheerleader stuff, so I called Carter.

"Hey!" he pretty much yelled down the phone. "Give me a second, it's busy here!"

"OK." I stayed on the line and listened to the chatter of the crowd. Despite everything that had happened tonight, I was kind of gutted I'd missed the big game. The crowd noise dulled slightly as Carter came back on.

"Are you OK? We were worried about you after your mom went nuclear."

"Define OK." I let out a sigh that was far more dramatic than I'd intended. "Sorry – yes, I'm fine, we just had some … family drama."

"About the DNA test? I'm sorry."

"Kind of. Are you sitting comfortably?" I heard him shuffle around and tried to picture where he was. In the parking lot, maybe?

"I am now. Spill."

I filled him in on everything that had happened since he dropped me off, ignoring his gasps and countless interruptions. I could barely believe the words coming out of my own mouth. Nicole was alive. Dad was CJ. They had a son.

"Jeez, Paige," Carter said. "Give me a second here. How are you dealing with this?"

"I don't know if I am yet," I answered truthfully. "It's … a lot. Actually, I'm not sure that I should have told you any of that, should I? Promise you'll only tell Madison."

"I promise," he said. "But wait—"

"No, you wait, I'm not at the best bit yet."

"The best bit?" He sounded dubious.

"The most important bit, then." I lowered my voice without meaning to. "Carter, I think she's hiding something."

"Nicole is? What else could she be hiding?"

"I don't know." I chewed my lip. "She said she was here to stop the killer but that there was more to it. I think she's here for some other reason."

"Such as?"

I sighed. "I don't know." I looked up at the notes on the wall. I hadn't quite put the leads together yet, but the picture of Tiffany in her homecoming dress kept flashing in front of my eyes.

"Paige?"

"Sorry, my head's all over the place. By the way, I showed them the notes."

"You did?" I could hear him pacing, his breathing a little more laboured.

"Sorry, you must be freezing. Do you want me to call when you're home?"

"No, no, it's fine. I'm just heading back to see the homecoming court get announced. So you showed your parents?"

"And Nicole."

"And?"

"They weren't happy but agreed it was probably some kind of prank, for now. I'm not sure, though. I think whatever Nicole is keeping secret ties in with the letters somehow."

"You do? But doesn't she live all the way in San Francisco? It couldn't have been her sending them, could it?"

"No." I paused. "I don't know. Sorry, Carter. I need to think about this. Something's not quite connecting yet."

"Let me know when it does." Carter sounded distracted and I could hear someone testing a microphone in the background. "Listen, they're about to announce. Do you want us to call over on the way home?"

"No." I thought of the drunk trio downstairs. "Probably best if you don't. Let me find out what Nicole is planning to do tomorrow, and I'll let you know."

"OK." A cheer went up from the crowd on the other side of the phone. "Speak to you later?"

"Yeah, speak soon."

"Oh, and, Paige – have you seen the news?"

"What? No, why?" Please don't let it be another body. "What's happened?"

"Just watch it and I'll speak to you later."

I clicked my phone shut and stared at the blank screen. My head was banging and so full of new information that it felt like it might burst, and then a text pinged through from Carter, a link to a local news report. I swiped the screen to open it again and saw that I had missed a live video conference at five p.m. I turned up the volume. A handsome man with amazing teeth appeared on screen, dressed in a suit and tie. He stood on the steps outside City Hall.

"This is Cooper Darnell, coming to you live from Shorehaven City Hall, where the mayor and the police department have called a news conference. We have no information yet but … one second. Yes, it looks like Chief Detective Winchester is about to make a statement."

The camera panned away from the news anchor and refocused on an unfamiliar man in a formal police uniform. A wooden lectern had been erected on the steps of City Hall. The backdrop was stunning, the stately building decorated with black and orange Halloween fabric draped from the balustrades. Several police officers stood on the steps to the left and I wasn't surprised to see the mayor among them.

"Good evening." Detective Winchester's voice was deep, gruff almost. *"Today at eleven a.m., we received a tip-off from a member of the public. Consequently, we took a suspect into custody which eventually led to an arrest. Evidence at the suspect's place of*

289

work has shown possible links to the murders and we are working with the county sheriff's office to gain access to similar evidence found at Devil's Den." He cleared his throat. *"In light of this, we would like to lift the darkness falls curfew with immediate effect, so our students at Westpoint High may enjoy tonight's homecoming football game against the Hamden Hornets. We will keep you updated on any further developments. Thank you."*

With that he stepped away from the podium. Cameras flashed and several reporters clamoured at the bottom of the stairs, shooting questions and thrusting their microphones in the air. Chief Detective Winchester calmly ignored them all and followed the mayor and other officers into the building, closing the doors behind them.

"Wow," I whispered, thinking of Nicole rushing across the country and ruining her life for no reason. They'd caught someone. It was over.

I scrolled through the article, taking in the updates. It was mostly speculation and details of the arrest were vague. Evidence was mentioned several times without ever saying what it was. When I reached the top of the article, I refreshed the screen in case there were any more updates. The screen buffered for a second before filling with a photograph and the caption: "Local man arrested over murder of co-worker".

Oh god. A familiar face stared out at me.

Justin Astor.

My heart pounded as I thought of his reaction at

Ackerman's Antiques that very first night. I'd found a necklace in the mailbox just after – had I been on his original list? Had he scoped girls out at Grounded and then attacked them? It made sense – Shay and Kacey had both been around there at the first memorial and the third victim, Whitney must have been the co-worker who never showed up the other evening. My body flooded with a mixture of emotions, but the overriding one was relief. They'd caught the killer. I carried on reading and was still doom-scrolling when a message appeared at the top of my screen, a photograph and the caption: "She did it!"

I opened the message. Madison beamed out from the screen. She was still wearing her cheerleading uniform, but now there was a sash over the top of it and a large bouquet of flowers draped from her arms. A sparkling crown on her head told me all I needed to know.

Madison was homecoming queen.

I studied her face. The smile was practised but didn't go all the way to her eyes. I didn't blame her. After what had happened to her friends, being crowned queen must seem surreal. Insignificant, even.

My phone buzzed again, another message from Carter.

Carter 20:41
I know it's short notice, but I need a date for the dance tomorrow.

I bit back a smile, swallowing down my feeling of unease over, well, everything, and replied with one word.

> **Paige** 20:41
> Oh?

Three little dots danced at the bottom of the screen for what seemed like a lifetime. My eyelids grew heavy, like someone had sewn tiny lead weights into them. I was beyond tired. Maybe I should just close my eyes for a minute.

My phone buzzed and I pried my blurry eyes open, taking a second to slide my contacts out.

> **Carter** 20:42
> Paige Carmichael, would you like to go to homecoming with me? I promise I won't make you dance.

My face broke into a grin so ridiculous I was glad there was no one there to witness it. I typed out the next message through a happy yawn.

> **Paige** 20:43
> I don't think I have any other plans...

Carter 20:43
Is that the British way of saying yes?

Paige 20:43
Yes. I'd love to. Sorry, I'm half-asleep. Talk in the morning?

Carter 20:43
You bet.

Paige 20:44
Goodnight, Carter. Tell Mads well done.

Carter 20:44
Night, Paige.

I closed my eyes and drifted off with a smile on my face.

29

"Hello?" I tiptoed down the hallway and past my parents' room, nervous in my own house. I hadn't set an alarm and it was only the blazing sunlight through my window that had roused me. A good omen for tonight, I hoped. Mum and Dad's door was closed and the house was quiet, so I assumed the grown-ups were still in bed, especially after the amount they'd drunk last night. I was also half-convinced I'd dreamed the whole thing. "Anyone up?" I tried again.

Not a sound.

The smell of coffee tickled my nostrils. So someone was awake, after all. I followed the curve of the stairs, and the basement door caught my eye.

It was open.

"Hello?" I raised my voice as I tiptoed to the bottom of the stairs, scanning the room for a makeshift weapon, but the hallway was sparse, the only furniture being the small table covered in junk mail. I eyed the distance to the kitchen, deciding I could make a run for it, when the door swung open further and Nicole appeared, a steaming mug in her hand.

"Oh, Paige!" She winced, the coffee in her cup sloshing dangerously as she backed up. "You scared me."

"You scared me," I countered. It was just as surreal to see her in the daylight. She looked completely … normal. Her loose white T-shirt hung casually from one shoulder, tucked into faded blue jeans that had rips at the knees. If she was wearing make-up it was light, showing off her freckles and the fine lines that crinkled at the corners of her green eyes. Her strawberry-blonde hair was cut in a long bob and hung in loose waves down to her collarbone. Leather and gold bracelets decorated her wrists and a toe ring sparkled on her bare feet. She was the picture of California cool, a long way from the confused, nervous girl who had written in the diary. It felt weird that she'd be such a big part of my life now.

"I was just…" She gestured to the basement stairs and shuddered, closing the door. "I don't know what I was doing. Revisiting trauma, I guess." She glanced down at her mug. "I made coffee, I hope you don't mind?"

"No, of course not." What else was I supposed to say? I ignored the basement and headed to the kitchen instead. "Is there any left?"

"Yeah, I made a pot." Nicole followed me, her bare feet tapping a hollow beat on the kitchen tiles. "I was never allowed to drink coffee in this house," she mused, perching on a stool at the island. "What's that?" she asked, pointing at the plastic bag in my hand.

"Oh." I blushed, pushing it towards her. "It's yours. It was in the air vent, with your diary." I watched her peer inside.

"Wow," she whispered. "I'd forgotten about this stuff. I used to hide all sorts in that air vent – Tiffany's idea."

"I listened to the mixtape," I admitted. "I can't believe my dad was the one who made it for you."

"Song of the Day." She shook her head, turning the cassette case over in her hand. "I still do that, you know. Pick a song of the day. It's so cheesy but music is like therapy sometimes." I found a glass in the dishwasher and filled it with ice and vanilla syrup as she looked through the rest of her stuff. The kitchen fell quiet. "This is my favourite room, you know," she said, breaking the silence. "It looks nothing like it did in 1995."

"You can have a look around the rest of the house if you like?" Mum appeared at the door, wrapped in a fluffy robe. I grabbed a mug and poured her some coffee, emptying the rest into my glass and leaving it to cool. I handed her the cup. "Thanks, honey," she mumbled.

"Thank you, but I think I've seen enough." Nicole smiled at Mum and I marvelled over the strength of these two women. You wouldn't blame them for hating each other, but they seemed to have formed an easy bond.

"Is Dad up?" I asked, busying myself by changing the coffee filter and putting on a fresh pot. The machine bubbled and hissed as I grabbed my glass and a long-handled spoon and joined them at the island.

"He's out running." Mum sipped her coffee. "I don't know how he does it. I need a vat of this before I can function, especially after we drank half of Shorehaven last night." She grimaced at the memory. "Thank god it's Saturday."

"What are you doing today, Nicole?" I asked, hoping my voice sounded casual.

"First I need to find a hotel." Mum opened her mouth to argue, but Nicole placed her mug down and shook her head. "Thank you, but no." I got the feeling they'd already had this conversation. "I can't stay here again, it's too hard. I just … have some stuff to do. I've been selfish for long enough. I should have come clean years ago but my mom and pop…" She trailed off. "I wanted to wait until they were dead."

We sat in silence, digesting that for a moment. I was immensely grateful for my parents right then. I couldn't imagine how Nicole must feel, about to own up to almost thirty years of lies.

"So." Nicole injected fake brightness into her voice, throwing the attention back to me. "What are you doing today, Paige? It's homecoming, right?"

"That's right." Mum drained her cup and pointed to the machine. "Top me up, Paige." I slid off my stool, grabbed the new pot and filled her empty mug. "We saw the news last night. The curfew has been lifted, they have that boy from the coffee shop in custody and a little birdie tells me you have a date."

"What? Who told you that?" I offered the pot to Nicole, who accepted a refill too.

"Emma texted me this morning." Mum blew on her coffee and sighed. "I'm sorry about how I reacted last night. I was just worried about you. But Carter seems like a nice kid, and he deserves a little happiness. I'm glad you're making friends here."

"Thanks, Mum," I mumbled, stirring the last splinters of ice into my coffee before taking a gulp. "There is one pretty big problem, though."

"You don't have a dress."

"Bingo."

"That we can solve. Emma has recommended The Dress Studio on Main Street – it might not have the perfect one, but we can try it. Apparently homecoming is a little less formal than prom. And Mia has booked you an appointment at her hair salon for a blow dry. Seems they're both fully Team Paige."

"That's so nice of them." My eyes filled up a little. "And thanks, Mum." Despite everything, excitement began to fizz inside of me. I was going to my first ever school dance.

With a really cute guy.

"Can we swap errands?" Nicole let out a flat laugh and Mum patted her arm. I should leave them alone for a bit.

"I'll go get showered," I said, draining my coffee and pulling a face. All the vanilla syrup had gathered at the bottom. Happened every time. "What time is the hair appointment? Should I wash it first?"

"Nope, you've got the full works. It's at one but we should look at dresses first."

"Give me an hour."

"That one's nice on you." Mum held the curtain open as I looked in the mirror. I kicked out the skirt and frowned.

"It's so heavy," I complained, pulling at the strapless neckline. "It feels like it's going to fall down. And it's too long. Madison said everyone was wearing short dresses."

"Well, you've tried most of them now. I'm afraid it's either choose one or go in your jeans."

"I have one left." I eyed the last dress warily. "Fingers crossed." Mum closed the curtain and I shimmied off the ballgown. The dresses had been so over the top, but Mum had insisted. I'd never gone to my leaver's ball at school, so this was all new to me.

I reached for the last gown. It was a gorgeous delicate blue and so far out of my comfort zone it was ridiculous, but it *was* beautiful. The top half was a chiffon halter neck, gathered in tiny pintucks up to a high throat that dropped away under the arms, so it would leave the skin of my back bare. A beaded band at the waist held together layers and layers of soft tulle that formed a short skirt that was full but not princess poufy. I unzipped the top of the skirt and stepped into it, fastened the neck and zipped it back up. It felt much more secure than it looked and when I turned back to the mirror I gasped.

"Is that a good noise or a bad one?" Mum called. I peeked my head out through the curtains.

"I think this is the one."

"Really? Oh, thank god. Come out, then."

I pushed the heavy drapes to one side and twirled as I stepped out into the shop. The older lady behind the counter slid her glasses down her nose for a better look and smiled at me.

"Oh, Paige," Mum said, and I could hear tears in her voice, the big softy. "You look beautiful."

"That colour is stunning on you," the shop lady said. "I think you've picked a winner. How does it fit?"

"Like it was made for me, actually." I craned my neck so I could look at the back in the mirror. "I don't think it needs any tweaks."

"Let me see." She came over, a soft tape measure around her neck, and started tugging at the waist and bust. "You're right." She looked at Mum. "Would you like me to ring it up? It's a sample so I can take twenty per cent off for you."

"Perfect," Mum said.

The shop assistant removed the tag and they walked to the till while I disappeared back into the changing room. I emerged in my boring jeans and cardigan and joined them at the counter, where the woman zipped my dress into a garment bag.

"Thank you," I said as she handed it back to me. I couldn't help smiling at the thought of Carter seeing me in it later.

"Come on, princess." Mum held open the door for me. "Next stop, hair."

Mia's salon was only a few stores down from The Dress Studio. When we entered, the place was buzzing; I was surprised they could fit me in on a Saturday. Mia spotted us at the reception desk and waved but she didn't come over. I was kind of relieved – I wasn't ready to get the third degree about being Carter's date tonight. Mum took a seat in the waiting area and pulled a magazine from the table as I followed a small woman with tightly braided cornrows to a sink.

"I'm Shonda," she said as I sat down, and she ran a hand through my curls. "Gorgeous. I wouldn't change a thing, but you're going to homecoming I guess?"

"Yeah."

"OK, doll, tell me about the dress and let me do the rest."

I described the high neck and bare back and relaxed as

she started to rinse my hair. The hum of the warm water allowed a million thoughts to fight for space in my brain, but I forced them out, choosing instead to think about the dance. Would Carter be wearing a suit? A tuxedo, even? He'd look good in a tux. What was Madison's dress like? I hadn't spoken to her since yesterday and I wondered if Carter had caught her up on everything else. I wondered how she felt about the dance, considering two of her closest friends wouldn't be there.

I wondered how she felt about me being her brother's *date*. Actually, knowing Madison, it had probably been her idea.

"I'll just put this on and we can head over there." Shonda wrapped a towel around my head and helped me get up. I followed her to a seat next to the window and pulled my phone out of my pocket. She started to towel dry my hair as I fired off a text to Madison, my nerves suddenly getting the better of me. She'd still want to be friends, right?

My phone immediately beeped in response and I opened it to see a photo of her dress laid out on her bed, the sash and crown on top of it. The dress was a bright flash of red on her white duvet: short, silky and strappy. The colour was going to look gorgeous on her tanned skin. A second photo came through, this one of a navy suit and shirt laid out on a checked bedspread. This was accompanied by the caption: *Your date is almost ready.*

So she knew, then. I took a deep breath and typed out another message.

> **Paige** 13:09
> Is it weird that I'm Carter's date?

Madison started to call my phone.

"Sorry, Shonda, can I answer?"

"Sure you can. You've got two minutes before the dryer goes on."

"Thank you." She combed through my hair and scrunched it like a pro as I answered. "Hey," I said cautiously. "You OK?"

"It is *not* weird that you're Carter's date," she said. "In fact, I'm kind of delighted. I haven't seen him smiling this much in a while." My cheeks went pink in the mirror. "You're coming with us tonight, right? Josh got some big fancy car from his dad, so we have space. We're meeting a bunch of people at Iris's house to pre-game and then all going to the dance together."

"Josh?"

Madison sighed. "Yeah. I wasn't going to go with a date, but he was crowned homecoming king and he asked me after the game. I felt kind of bad; I think something's going on with him. Please? We can take cheesy photos — the whole nine yards."

"Are you sure? I can just meet you there?"

"Nonsense. The Moms will have a fit if they don't get photos of you and Carter together before the dance. They're pretty stoked to see him happy too. So, be at mine by six?"

"Sounds good." I caught Shonda's warning eye in the mirror. "Gotta go, I'm getting my hair done at your mom's salon."

"Oh, I can't wait to see! Mine was done at an ungodly hour this morning. I'm essentially half-hairspray right now. Oh, wait one sec." There was a noise like she had covered the mouthpiece and I could hear muffled talking.

"Mads, I really have to—"

"What colour is your dress?" she asked.

"Oh, er, like a light blue."

"Nice." She whispered in the background again. "OK, see you later!"

"Bye." I looked at Shonda in the mirror. "Sorry."

"Don't apologize. Just close your eyes and relax. I'm going to make you look a million dollars." I did what she said and drifted off as Shonda dried my hair. The pull and tug of the brush was soothing and when she shut off the dryer, I opened my eyes to find my usually bouncy curls had been transformed into long, sleek waves. I grinned at her in the mirror.

"That is gorgeous," I said, running a hand over it.

"I'm not done yet," she said, dropping a handful of

sparkling grips on to the little counter in front of me. I watched as she pinned back one side, letting the deep part drape over my face. I looked like a Hollywood starlet. "There. This should suit the high neck but keep the focus on the open back. If you want to loosen it up later just take out these grips."

"Thanks, Shonda. I love it." I grinned at her as she removed the little black cape I'd been wearing. I got ready to show Mum when a movement outside caught my eye.

"You look stunning, Paige." I looked up to see Mia and my mum smiling at me in the mirror. My face had gone a strange shade of grey. "Wait — what is it?" Mia asked. "If you don't like it, we can do something else?"

"No," I whispered, my throat suddenly dry. "It's not that." I pointed out of the window. A crowd stood in front of the coffee shop, gathered around the entrance as a figure emerged with their head down.

"No," Mia breathed. "He should be in custody."

"I heard he made bail." Shonda joined us at the window. "You forget how rich that boy's granddaddy is."

"How is that right, after what he did to those girls?" Mia frowned. Mum squeezed my shoulder as I typed out a text to Madison and Carter.

> Paige 13:53
> They've let Justin go.

30

Hushed whispers greeted me as I trailed down the main staircase, the skirt of my dress bouncing. I didn't descend all the way but waited until Mum and Dad stopped whispering and looked up. "Well?"

"Oh, Paige." Mum smiled up at me. "It really is perfect. You look stunning." I let out a nervous laugh as my dad stared at me. Mum nudged him. "Doesn't she, Jake?"

"Beautiful," he said, his voice hoarse. "Definitely not my little pea any more."

"I'll always be your *petit pois*," I said as I navigated the final steps and gave him a hug. "Promise." I held him at arm's length and looked between him and Mum. "Is something wrong? What's happened?"

Mum rubbed my dad's arm. "Tell her, Jake."

"It's your gran," Dad said, his voice thick. "She never regained consciousness this afternoon."

"What?" My whole body turned cold. "Is she—"

"No!" Mum interrupted. "God, no. She's still with us." Relief flooded through me. Jesus. "There have just been some complications with the infection. The doctors are going to put her into an induced coma, allow her body to recover. She's in good hands, though," Mum reassured me.

"I didn't want to ruin your night," Dad said, his eyes wet. "Sorry, P."

"Don't be daft; I want to know." My poor dad, what a week he'd had since coming home.

"We've been talking and I'm going to drive your dad over to the hospital. We checked on Nicole earlier – she's at the Motel Six, so she won't need to stay here, but I will be home later to hear all about your evening."

"No, I can come too," I said. "I'll get changed and—"

"Not a chance," Dad said. "It's homecoming and you are going to have a blast. Mom's going to drive me over and I'll get a room out there, near the hospital. You can both come and join me in the morning."

"But, Dad, I—"

"No arguments." He shook his head firmly. "Please just go and have fun for me, OK?"

"OK," I lied. Fun? I couldn't feel more hollow.

"Let's get you down to the twins' house for photos before we go." Mum steered me gently towards the door and I followed on autopilot. My whole body was numb as

I collected my small silver clutch bag and emerged into the cool evening. I shivered. "Do you need a coat?"

I looked down at my dress. "No, nothing I have matches. Besides, we'll be indoors like ninety-nine per cent of the evening."

"Just don't catch your death… Don't get a cold." Mum changed the subject quickly. "You got the keys, Jake?"

"Yeah." He followed us on to the porch and we walked down to the twins' house in silence. I regretted not having a shawl or something immediately – there was a real cold snap in the air. I glanced at Dad's drawn face and wondered what was going through his head. How exactly was I supposed to have fun tonight?

"Wow, Paige!" Mum pointed to the Garcia-Moore driveway, where a huge Hummer with blacked-out windows was parked on the drive. "Looks like your ride is here!"

We walked past the car and I rang the doorbell, craning my neck to look at the massive balloon arch that surrounded the front door. "School colours," I noted, glancing at Dad. "Homecoming's kind of a big deal, then, huh?"

He cracked a smile. "Homecoming's a big deal!" He tutted in mock-disgust. "You are so English," he said as Carter opened the door. I stopped listening.

Carter looked beautiful.

"Hey!" He grinned at me and hastily invited my parents in.

308

They exchanged a glance but left us alone at the front door as he closed it behind us. "That colour is just… Wow," he said, his eyes taking in my dress. "You look amazing."

"So do you. Your hair!" It was the first time I'd seen him without a hat and was surprised to see there had been hair beneath it the whole time.

"Yeah," he said, awkwardly running a hand across the short brown buzz cut. "This isn't what I really look like, but it finally started growing back on this new chemo. It itches so bad, though."

"Well, I think it suits you," I said, still grinning up at him as Madison sashayed into the room. Her red dress was stunning, each drape of the silk masterfully hinting at her athletic figure without being too revealing. Her hair was set in pin-up girl waves, similar to my own, and the thin spaghetti straps showed off her naturally tanned skin. I felt like a little kid playing dress up in comparison.

"Paige, you goddess!" she squealed, looking between me and her brother. "*Hermosa!* You two are disgusting," she said happily.

"Madison, you look amazing," I said as she grabbed my hand and dragged me into the kitchen.

"The dress is a winner, hey? Come on, get into the kitchen for photos. We have a schedule to keep to!" My low-heeled sandals clicked on the tiles and I marvelled at Madison's ability to walk in her strappy black heels. She really did look unbelievable.

"Thanks." She lowered her voice and let Carter go ahead of us. "I'm like five inches taller than Josh in these shoes, I'm dreading the photos. I am definitely taking my Chucks for later."

"You'll be fine!" I laughed, thanking Mia as she thrust a glass of something fizzy into my hand and wandered back over to Mum and Emma. "Alcohol?" I asked.

"I wish…" Madison said. "Just good old sparkling grape juice."

"Oh." I took a sip and wrinkled my nose as the thick, perfumy taste coated my tongue. "Wow, we don't have this at home."

"No?" She laughed. "So what would you be drinking instead?"

"Prosecco!" I sighed, surrendering myself to the grape juice. "But this is nice too."

"Liar," she said with a smile. "Come on, let's keep the parentals happy and then we can get out of here."

"Hey, Paige." Dad beckoned me over. He was standing with Josh and Carter by the back door. "You never told me you knew Chase's son. I was just telling him we played for the Bears together for a couple of years."

"Oh, yeah. Sorry, I didn't think." I smiled at Josh. He looked handsome in a tailored suit, but his face was as serious as ever. The jacket was made from a lush forest green velvet and it brought out the golden flecks in his eyes. "I like your suit."

310

"Thanks. You, er, you look great – really pretty." He stumbled over his words and Carter caught my eye over Josh's head. Awkward.

"Not as good as the homecoming queen." I shifted the attention over to Madison, who was busily arranging a glittery gold backdrop at the other side of the kitchen. "Is that for photos? It's so cool!"

"Yep. Mads is as extra as they come. Wait until we get to the photobooth at school!" Carter grinned. "Josh will have to pry her away from it."

"Come on." Madison clapped her hands. "Photo time! We have to be at Iris's house for the pre-party in thirty minutes, people, let's go!"

I allowed my worries to take a back seat while Madison directed us like we were doing a shoot for *Teen Vogue* or something. I plastered a smile on my face and tried to forget about everything that had happened over the last few days, which was much easier when Carter slid his fingers through mine. I cringed a little at the cheesy couple photos, but Madison insisted, and our parents thought it was adorable, so we went along with it. I kept catching myself glancing at him, butterflies in my stomach.

"That's a wrap!" Madison called, clapping her hands. "Be ready to leave in two minutes!" The adults laughed as she disappeared upstairs. Even Josh had relaxed slightly. He waved a key fob in the air as Madison reappeared, a white sash draped across her dress.

"Your carriage awaits, Queenie," he said. "I know it's totally OTT, but Dad insisted."

"Are you joking?" Carter slapped him on the shoulder. "It's awesome, you gotta let me drive it later."

"Come on, come on!" Madison straightened the sash and held out the crown to Mia. "Mama, can you fix this in my hair?"

"Of course, *mi amor*," she said as Emma snapped candid photos of mother and daughter. She really did look like royalty. "There. You are perfect."

"Thanks, Mama. Enjoy your date night."

"Now who are we waiting for?" Carter yelled from the driveway. I followed him out to see all three guys, my dad included, swooning over the Hummer. At least he was distracted for five minutes.

"Men!" Mum rolled her eyes next to me. "Such a mystery."

"Which is why I married a woman," Emma joked as Mum laughed. "Paige, I just wanted to say you look beautiful. Despite everything this week, Carter is the most … well, the most *Carter* he's been since his diagnosis. So, thank you."

I felt my cheeks warm up. "He's a good guy," I said. "A really good guy." Emma nodded.

"We know."

"Are you ready?" Madison said as she and Mia joined us outside. Carter and Josh waited by the car, ready to open doors for their dates.

"Ready as I'll ever be," I said. Mum gave me a hug.

"I'll see you tonight and I'll text updates. Have the best time."

"And be careful." Dad gave me a hug and glanced over at Carter. "Look after my girl."

"Yessir!" He opened the rear door for me. I kissed Mum and Dad and climbed into the Hummer, rolling the window down.

"Give Gran and Gramps big hugs from me please, and tell them I'll see them tomorrow."

"Will do!" Mum waved. "Have fun, sweetie."

I sat back in the buttery leather seat as Carter climbed in next to me. Madison was already fiddling with her crown in the passenger seat mirror and Josh was typing into his phone, a frown on his face. He placed it back into his pocket.

"Everything OK, Josh?" I asked.

"Yeah, fine. Let's go." Josh beeped the horn and reversed out of the driveway. It wasn't only our parents watching us, but a few little kids and their parents had gathered on their lawns, waving as we drove past. I waved back, grinning at their excited little faces. How stinking cute was that. We were off Ocean View in no time, driving towards Shorehaven. My excitement built as I wondered how the night would pan out.

"Smile!" Madison held her phone up to snap a selfie and Carter and I pressed our heads together in the back. I opened my bag to do the same and went to grab my phone but all I saw was a key, my purse and lipstick and a little tube of emergency eyelash glue. My heart started to race.

"Guys, has anyone seen my phone?"

"What?" Madison twisted around. "You don't have it?"

"No. I thought I did." I felt around the seat and lifted the layers of my dress in case it had slipped between the tulle and the leather. "It's not here."

"Did you leave it at our house?" Carter asked, patting around in the footwell.

"No, I didn't use it." I wracked my brain. "I must have left it charging at home."

"You can use mine if you want to check in on your gran," Carter said quietly. "Is that what you're worried about?"

"Yeah. Thanks." I leaned back into the seat. "But my mum won't know that. What if she tries to call me?"

"Let's go back and get it, then," Carter said.

Madison groaned. "Here, just text your mom off my cell and tell her," she said, passing it over. "We're already running late."

"Madison, have some empathy," Carter snapped. Josh glanced at him uncomfortably in the rear view. "Josh, do you mind? We haven't gone far."

"Sure," he said quietly. "It'll take two minutes; we'll be on time," he promised Madison. She muttered to herself but didn't argue as Josh turned the car around and in less than a minute pulled up at the end of my drive. My parents' car was gone already, they must have headed straight off.

"Sorry, Mads," I said, opening the door. "I'll be super-fast, I promise." I jumped out and trotted up the drive, leaving the front door open behind me. I ran to the stairs, kicking my shoes off so I could take them two at a time. I was out of breath when I got to my room, but the first thing I saw was my charger dangling from the plug to the floor. There was no phone at the end of it.

"Shit." I started to fling stuff around, burrowing through the bedclothes, checking the bathroom. I couldn't see it anywhere.

I ran downstairs, wondering if I'd left it in the hallway on the way out.

"Hey."

I jumped, my heart racing as I saw Madison standing in the entrance hall.

"Hey, I'm sorry, I can't find it." I rushed past her. "Just let me check the kitchen and if not, I'll just borrow yours."

"Let me help you," she insisted, appearing in the doorway. "Hey, listen, I'm sorry for being a dick. I'm just nervous, you kn—" There was a loud crack and her face froze before suddenly going slack. Her knees buckled.

"Madison?" I raced to her, but she hit the ground with a slap before I could reach her, her head bouncing off the tiled floor. Blood started to ooze from a wound on the back of her head. The back of her head? That didn't make sense. "Madison?" I called, shaking her gently. "Madison!"

"Looking for this?" My blood ran cold. Someone stood over us. I glanced up slowly and saw my mobile phone in his left hand, a bloody tyre iron in the other. "Sorry," he said, dropping my phone to the floor. "I had to take it." He stamped on it with the heel of a polished black shoe and raised the tyre iron over his head before bringing it down again.

31

I wasn't sure what I noticed first, the blinding pain in my head or the thick dust in my nose and mouth. I sucked in a lungful of dirt and a fit of coughing wracked my body before I could even summon the energy to open my eyes. I blinked carefully, the movement sending bolts of lightning through my head, and my vision filled with grey. I was lying face down on something cold and when I tried to push myself up, I realized I couldn't move my arms. They were stuck. No, not stuck.

Bound.

"You're awake." The voice came from my right, and I scrunched my body in half, trying my best to use my non-existent core muscles to help me sit up. The room was dimly lit but even that hurt my eyes and I was rapidly becoming aware of something sticky and wet pulsing down my left temple.

"What's going on?" I slurred, my tongue swollen in my mouth. I tried to decipher the other shapes in the gloom as the room was coming into focus. Even though I couldn't see my attacker, I knew he was there, and now I could make out two other potential bodies in the room, one sitting in a chair and the other slumped under the open tread stairs.

We were in my basement.

"Josh," I wheezed, "why are you doing this?"

He took a step closer, and I could see him more clearly. His jacket was smeared with dust and something else I didn't want to think about. Madison's crumpled face flashed before my eyes and I gasped.

"She's alive," he said, reading my mind. "For now, anyway." A flash of red became obvious then and I saw that the lump beneath the stairs was Madison.

"You don't have to do this," I said, gaining a little more focus with every passing second. I finally managed to push myself up to sitting, but my arms were tied firmly behind my back, so my balance was off. Josh. I hadn't seen it, hadn't even suspected him. Was he really the killer after what had happened to his mum?

"You have no idea what I have to do." He sighed. I couldn't see a weapon but that meant nothing. "I tried to help you, you know."

"What are you talking about?"

"The letters!" he said, exasperated. "I wanted you to figure it all out before something like this happened!"

"That was you?" His eyes were wide now, and he looked scared, like a deer caught in headlights. My head was pounding, blood rushing in my ears. "I don't understand."

"I do," a voice croaked from the centre of the room. I blinked hard and focused on the shape. A chair was positioned in the very centre of the demon trap, a female figure tied into it.

"Nicole," I breathed. "I thought you were at a motel." Nicole was in the chair. Madison was by the stairs.

Where the hell was Carter?

"I was, but he found me. I'm so sorry, Paige. I should have never come. I just wanted to see Tiffany, tell her I was coming clean. She deserved that much at least."

"Why?" My head was swimming as I finally realized what had been nagging me about Tiffany. She hadn't just been a good friend. She'd been a good liar. "Wait. Did Tiffany *know* about you? That you weren't really dead?"

Nicole nodded, a sob coming from deep in her chest. Josh snarled at her.

"Do you want to explain how you ruined my mother's life? Or should I?" Nicole's shoulders heaved as twenty-eight years of guilt flooded out. "Fine, just shut up with the crying. I'll do it." Josh paced along the basement floor, following the white lines.

"Josh, whatever happened, we can fix it," I tried. My breath was coming in little shallow gasps, but I tried to focus on something in the room, something static. I could not lose my head now.

"Oh, right!" he shouted, turning to face me. "I wanted you to help me! I told you to find the diary, didn't I? My mom was always telling me Nicole hid her stuff in the walls, so I hoped you'd find it when your family started renovating. I thought you might read it, figure out that my mom and Nicole were close, that she knew about Nicole's plan. But you didn't, so here we are. My mom never got the chance to come clean and then all of this started up again." He took a deep breath and peeled his jacket off, throwing it into a corner. "You have no idea the pain I've endured listening to my alcoholic mother cry and wail about her fucked-up life since I was old enough to understand. My mother has been telling me about Nicole and her secrets for so long it's almost like she was part of the family, but since she only did it after a Valium and a couple of bottles of wine, she could pretend she'd never told me anything."

"I never wrote about our plan in the diary. I didn't want anyone to find us." Nicole started to sob again, and Josh let out a roar.

"I told you to SHUT UP!" he screamed. Nicole sucked in a deep shaking breath and stayed quiet. "Good, now maybe I can think."

I watched as he continued to pace. I needed to get out of there. Call my parents … the police … find Carter. I closed my eyes for a second. Where was Carter? I couldn't cope if Josh had hurt him too. *Come on, think, Paige.* I needed to stall for time while I figured out what my wrists were tied with – if I knew that, maybe I could figure out how to get loose. My ankles were free, but between the blow to my head and the fact I was trussed up, there was no way I would be able to take Josh out. Plus, he was strong and I really wasn't.

"Why don't you tell me about it?" I said, slyly rubbing my wrists together. I felt a flat, sharp edge bite into my skin. A zip-tie, it had to be.

"Did you know it wasn't just Nicole who ran away?" Josh stopped pacing and looked at me. "Oh, no. She managed to convince her best friend to go with her. My *mom*. They made some kind of pact that they were going to run away together, leave and let everyone think that they'd been victims of the Shorehaven Ripper. How sick is that? But Mom knew my grandparents would have died from the grief, so when it came down to it, she got cold feet. Nicole was adamant though, and convinced that her batshit parents would lock her in the basement if they found out she was pregnant. She'd convinced herself that they would do one of their exorcisms on her and she'd lose the baby and, from what I know, she was probably right. So Nicole came up with a plan. Mom would get ready for the dance as normal – she was queen too, you know? – but she would never show up. Tiffany Brown and her best friend would

321

go 'missing' on their way to homecoming, kidnapped by the serial killer that was stalking Shorehaven. In reality, she and Nicole stole a car and drove it up to Devil's Den, all to plant evidence that would 'prove' Nicole had been there."

"Evidence?" I was only half-listening to him, thinking back to all the videos I'd seen about escaping zip-ties. I think I was supposed to force my arms apart really hard, but I couldn't do that while Josh was watching me, so I kept him talking instead. "I'm not sure what you mean."

"Well, they never found all of the bodies, did they? There were one or two more, er, *obvious* body parts that identified the other girls, but all they found of Nicole was a couple of teeth and some strands of hair."

"So they pulled her hair out?"

"When they got up to Devil's Den, Mom pulled two of Nicole's *teeth* out with a pair of plyers." Bile rose at the thought of the desperate amateur surgery. "They left them up there, where the other bodies had been found. So, all that blood you see on Mom in that famous picture really was Nicole's, it just didn't get there the way people were led to believe. Instead, she left Nicole with the stolen car and walked back from Devil's Den to the school dance in bare feet, to make the whole kidnap thing more believable. They hoped that everyone would be so distracted by the amazing escape of the homecoming queen that it would give Nicole a head start, time to get away before people began looking for her."

"We never spoke again," Nicole sobbed, "but your mom kept the secret all this time. She was the best friend I ever had."

"Holy shit," I said. I couldn't help it.

"She didn't quite keep it, though, did she? Imagine hearing all this from your sobbing mother at nine years old. That was the first time she told me that her whole life had been a lie." He sounded angry but sad too. "She – *we* – have lived with the fact that she's escaped the Shorehaven Ripper her whole life, and none of it is true."

No wonder she drinks.

"It sounds like Nicole was so scared for herself and her baby she'd do anything." I tried to reason with Josh as he started to pace again. He kept glancing between a still-unconscious Madison and me, like he was trying to decide what to do. "And it sounds like your mom really was a good friend."

"Which made her a shitty mother," he snapped.

I closed my eyes and took a deep breath. "I am so sorry, Josh, I really am," I said, "but all this – killing all of those girls, your *friends* … you didn't have to do that. You don't have to carry on." Josh opened his mouth to reply, but a voice came from behind me instead, the vague scent of coffee coming with it.

"Oh, Josh didn't do any of that," the voice said. "That was all me."

32

I craned my neck around. A dark figure was silhouetted in a doorway behind me. I realized now that it must lead out to the empty pool area in the back garden. I hadn't even known it was there. "Hello, Paige. I've been visiting you for a while now, you've mainly been asleep, though."

Goosebumps prickled over my body as I realized what that meant. The lights on my stairs, the figure in my room. I hadn't imagined it.

Adrenaline coursed through me as I pushed myself to my feet and ran for the stairs, but I knew it was a bad idea as soon as I started to move. My bare feet slipped on the floor and with nothing to break my fall, I tumbled over in slow motion, my hip crashing painfully into the hard concrete. I cried out as stars burst before my eyes. I dragged myself over to Madison. I might not be able to get out, but at least I could check if she was OK.

"Well, that was pathetic." The figure entered the basement and closed the door behind him, a glint of black metal in his hand. "I thought you said she was clever. Oh, well. We can make this quick. Well done, Joshua."

"Thanks, Dad," he mumbled.

Dad.

Chase Vickers shrugged off his tailored grey jacket and handed it to Josh. He didn't put the gun down, instead transferring it from one hand to the other in a smooth, practised gesture before sliding it into a holster at his waist. I swallowed hard, praying that Carter had got away somehow. That help would be here at any second.

He had a gun. A *gun*.

"Come on, Mads," I muttered, shaking her as inconspicuously as possible. A small groan escaped Madison's lips and I almost sobbed in relief. She was still alive. I glanced up. Chase was now standing over a seemingly unconscious Nicole, waving a steaming cup of take-out coffee under her nose.

"Wakey wakey," he sing-songed and a shiver ran down my bare back. "Come on, Nicole, let's have a chat." On the last word he grabbed Nicole's hair with his free hand and thrust the entire scalding cup into her face.

Nicole screamed like nothing I'd ever heard before.

"Oh, so you are with us!" he crowed, taking a step back as Nicole's screams faded. "Don't be so rude. Your parents certainly didn't bring you up that way, did they? Speaking of your parents," – Chase drained the end of the coffee and scrunched the cup, tossing it on to the floor – "this was one of their tricks, wasn't it? Only they used hot water, from what I remember, and of course they didn't mark anyone's face, but I got an extra coffee on the way over here. I wanted to be *awake* for the evening."

He was criminally insane.

"Paige?" Madison mumbled. I shushed her and tried to take hold of her hand, but it was too difficult.

"Just play dead," I said, wincing at the word. Madison's shoulders went slack, and I wasn't sure whether she'd followed my orders or actually passed out. Chase went back to the doorway and opened a holdall I hadn't spotted before. It was black leather, a bit like an old-fashioned doctor's bag, and when he opened it, I could hear clinking.

"Usually I wait until I've had the rest of my fun for this bit," he said as he rummaged around, "but I want to *hurt* you, Nicole. Really make you scream." He selected a shining silver scalpel and examined it in the dim light. Acid filled my mouth and I forced myself to take deep breaths. We needed to get out of here. "You've fucked up my plans not once but twice, and I am getting a little fed up with you." He wagged the scalpel at her like he was scolding a naughty puppy.

"Do whatever you want to me," Nicole croaked, her voice already thick with pain, "but let the kids go. Please."

"Oh, I can't do that!" He laughed. He put the scalpel

326

down and started to remove his golden cufflinks, clicking his fingers for Josh who ran to him, holding out a hand to collect them. "You see, when you pulled your little stunt all those years ago, you ruined my mission. I had a plan. I was helping the church clear this town of sinning little bitches like you." He folded up his sleeves in precise, crisp movements. "It didn't fix all of Shorehaven's problems, but it sure was a good start."

"Wait," I said, cursing myself, but I couldn't help it. Things were finally lining up. "You knew Tiffany was lying? About being the final victim?"

"Of course. Just like I knew Nicole must still be alive somewhere."

"Because *you* didn't attack them. Because *you* were the original Shorehaven Ripper."

Chase glanced at Josh. "Seriously? You thought that this girl could figure it out? What a waste of time those letters were. Not only did they fail, but now I know I can't trust you. Going behind my back like that. Pathetic," he spat as Josh cowered away from him. "Get out of my sight; go and watch the door or something. Be useful." He huffed as Josh crept past him, head down, and left the basement. "You kids really are getting stupider," Chase continued. "Of *course* I'm the Shorehaven Ripper. But I never made those last two kills, because they didn't really happen, did they?" He addressed Nicole again. "Thanks to you and my darling wife, I had to stop. Tiffany felt so guilty

327

about lying to the police that she told me everything after homecoming. We got married after graduation because I realized I had an opportunity – I could stop killing and let everyone think the spree was over. They could blame it on an outsider as the town healed and I covered my tracks. Of course, Tiffany suspected me eventually; it's hard to hide some things when you live together for so long, but we had enough dirt on each other to form an unspoken truce. I've waited a lifetime to finish what I started and these two are going to be this year's grand finale." Chase picked up the scalpel and waved it in our direction, his voice lowered to a growl. "I'll finally get to gut the homecoming queen."

Madison started to sob quietly.

"Chase, please," Nicole begged. "You can stop. We won't tell a soul. I shouldn't have gone to see Tiff, I know that now, but this isn't the answer."

"Of course it is. And, no, you shouldn't have gone to see her, look where that's got you." He approached her with the scalpel and calmly sliced open the front of her white T-shirt, exposing her sternum. "But Tiff knows not to talk. She's used to keeping other people's secrets. Plus, we have a million-dollar book deal to think about. If you come back on the scene that's going to disappear, isn't it? Nobody will want Tiff's story any more."

"Fuck you," Nicole said, spitting at him.

Chase's face hardened, his smiley façade completely gone now. "You little psycho." He pulled her head back and lowered the scalpel, pressing the sharp blade into the thin skin over her breastbone. Nicole screamed in pain as blood flooded down her chest. "Oh, shit, this is messy!" he crowed, heading back to his bag for a towel. The level of preparation made me feel sick. "Bitches don't bleed this much when they're dead." My breath came in fast gulps as I started to sob too, but then it occurred to me.

He was distracted. *Really* distracted.

I drew in the deepest breath I could and sat up straight. Nicole screamed again.

Now.

I tensed my arms as hard as I possibly could and tried to snap my wrists apart. Nothing happened but the zip-tie bit into my wrists painfully. That wasn't right. I thought hard and slowly moved into a kneeling position while Chase turned away for his towel. I lifted my bound arms as high as I could get them and slammed them back down on to my rear. That was it. The zip-tie didn't break but I swear I felt it loosen. Madison looked at me out of the corner of her eye and I could see her tense her arms too, so I tried to tell her to wait. She nodded and we waited for Chase to start carving the next letter. Nicole wailed again, and when he reached for the towel I nodded.

Blinding white pain shot up my arm.

Vomit filled my mouth and I choked it back down, the pain in my wrist unbearable as Madison crammed her hand over my mouth to stop me from screaming. I'd

broken something, I could feel it hanging loose and …
wait. I looked down, my eyes fuzzy with pain. My right
hand dangled uselessly but it was in front of me… Madison
had been able to cover my mouth… We'd done it. I tried
to ignore the pain, but it was overwhelming, a white-hot
poker pressing on every nerve of my hand.

"He's busy," Madison hissed and I saw that Chase had
gone back to his bag at the other end of the basement.
She quietly slid off her heels as Nicole groaned, her back
still to us. I had a feeling she was being loud on purpose,
drowning out our voices. We couldn't waste it. "We have
one chance. I'm going to charge him for the gun, and I
want you to run for the stairs. Can you do that?"

I shook my head, the back of my throat burning. "No,"
I slurred, the pain slowly fading as shock took over. "It's
too dangerous."

"I'm stronger than you," she said simply. "And I'm
worried about Carter. Where is he? You need to get out
and run to the closest house, call the cops."

"What about Josh?" I asked.

"Take that." She pointed next to the boxes of newspapers,
and I saw the bloody tyre iron that Josh must have discarded
earlier. Chase was busy looking for something, which
worried me, but we might not get this chance again. "When
I say go," Madison hissed, "you go."

"OK." I tried not to think about my useless arm, or the
sound Josh's skull would make if I cracked his head open.

Instead I took long, deep breaths. I inched towards the tyre iron and picked it up with my uninjured hand, standing up when Madison gave the signal. We both rose to our feet in silence, a couple of princesses rising from the depths of hell, and when Chase started to turn, Madison screamed at the top of her lungs.

"NOW!"

I ran blindly towards the steps, trusting that Chase would be too distracted by Madison racing towards him to worry about me running upstairs.

I didn't expect the gunshot.

I dropped to the ground at the bottom of the staircase, the sharp treads smashing into my ribs as my survival instincts took over. I looked through the gap but tried to keep my head low, ears ringing, trying to figure out where the sound had come from. Madison's body was sprawled out on the floor, a pool of red, and Nicole's head hung back at a concerning angle. Oh god oh god oh god.

We were going to die.

A gurgling noise caught my attention, and I risked a glance at Chase.

The mayor of Shorehaven had fallen to his knees and his hands were pressed to a large red stain that was spreading across his white shirt. His face was slack with disbelief as he stared at the basement door, fumbling for the weapon at his waist. I held my breath as he managed to lift it from its holster but it slid through his bloody fingers. There was a muffled clatter as it hit the floor and a figure entered the basement.

"Don't fuck with my best friend," Tiffany Vickers snarled. She emerged from the shadows, her tiny frame shaking as she held a gun at arm's length, the barrel aimed at her husband. Chase let out a strangled rasp as he made a desperate lunge for the gun he had dropped.

"No!" Madison sprang up from the floor and dived at him, swiping it into the shadows as Chase's fingers brushed against it. I ran after her without thinking, dragging her away from his grasping hands as another loud gunshot filled the room. We dropped to the floor in a tangle of limbs and I screamed as my wrist shattered beneath me. "Paige, Paige!" Madison grabbed my shoulders, looking for a bullet wound.

"It's my wrist," I tried to say, but my tongue was so thick in my mouth that only a groan came out. Madison's eyes widened in alarm so I shook my head. "I'm OK," I tried again, raising my head to nod towards Chase. "Look."

The stain on his shirt had spread thanks to the second bullet wound and his body buckled beneath him. Mayor Chase Vickers crumpled unceremoniously to the floor, red foam trickling from the corner of his mouth as his final breaths rattled out. Tiffany lowered her arm as she looked down at her husband. Her captor.

"It's finally over," she murmured.

332

33

407 Ocean View swarmed with uniformed police officers.

I watched it all from the open back of the ambulance. The shock, combined with the drugs I'd been given, was making me groggy and I was fighting sleep, but I was waiting for Madison to come back with news. I needed to know what had happened to Carter to stop my brain conjuring up worst-case scenarios. A sob filled my throat. He had to be OK. I concentrated on the cannula in my good hand instead, the liquid from the IV burning cold in my veins. A burly paramedic had already strapped up my broken wrist and tended to the gash on my temple, promising me it could have been worse.

What the fuck did he know?

"Paige!" Madison poked her head around the open door.

"Please tell me you found Carter?"

"Not yet…" She held her chin up and I could tell she

was trying not to panic, but her face was tearstained. "The police are still looking. They'll find him."

"Do you think Chase might have—"

"Hold that thought." Carter appeared from behind the open doors and my heart finally left my mouth, sinking back to its rightful place as Madison threw herself at him in a hug. He was paler than I'd ever seen him. Dried blood trailed down his neck and pooled in the collar of his shirt, but he was here. He was OK. "I'm so sorry I couldn't help you. I thought something was off and tried to follow Josh into the house but he was so much stronger than me. He knocked me out … put me in the trunk… I'm so glad you're OK. I'd never have forgiven myself… I thought I'd lost you both." Madison started to sob and he squeezed her tight before joining me in the ambulance. "How're you feeling?" He asked, gently brushing the tangles of hair from my forehead.

"High," I admitted, nodding to the IV that was delivering painkillers directly into my veins. "But that's a good thing. I think I'll be sore tomorrow, but that's not important right now. I am so happy you're OK."

"You know me." He kissed me gently. "If there's one thing I'm pretty good at, it's staying alive."

"Have you seen the moms, Carter?" Madison asked. "Do they know you're OK?"

"Yeah. Look." Mia was shouting at Officer Tatum and the young man looked terrified. She made a shooing motion at him before heading our way, her face like thunder. She joined us in silence, draping a thick woollen blanket over Madison's bare shoulders then passed another over to Carter, who gently did the same to me.

"Paige, your parents are almost here," she finally said as she started fussing over Carter, beckoning a paramedic over to double check his head. "We're going to stay with you until they get here."

"Thank you." I wasn't about to argue with her and there was no way I wanted to be alone. A flurry of activity around the side of the house caught our attention as two paramedics wheeled out a gurney. Whoever was on it was in a body bag. "He's dead?"

"Looks like it," Madison said. We watched as Josh and Tiffany were escorted around the side of the house. Despite them both being in handcuffs, Tiffany had her arms wrapped tightly around her son. Her face was a mask. "She saved us."

"Yeah, she did." I didn't know what to make of it all yet. I needed time. I needed my mum and dad. We watched in silence as Josh and Tiffany were separated and placed into different police cars, when the final body was wheeled out.

Nicole.

"Is she dead?" My voice came out weirdly flat as she was placed into the back of another ambulance.

"No," Mia said, "I heard a cop say her injuries are

superficial, thank god. She'll recover, physically anyway. She's one tough cookie. A bit like you guys." She hugged Madison tight as I let my head rest on Carter's shoulder and finally closed my eyes.

Tiffany's words echoed in my head. It was finally over. Maybe this time we could really start again.

EPILOGUE

"Three … two … one … happy holidays!"

Mum hugged me tight and we cheered as Dad switched on the Christmas tree lights. Even though it was already December twenty-third, we had only just found time to decorate and the three of us had been at it all day. I craned my head back to see the star on the top of the ten-foot tree. It filled the entrance hall and I couldn't love it more. The tiny bulbs sparkled in the dusky evening light and every bough had been decorated with an ornament from back home. I could almost imagine that nothing bad had ever happened in this house.

Almost.

"What time does everyone arrive?" Dad asked for the hundredth time.

"The Garcia-Moores will be here any minute and Dominic and his partner are due in around an hour." Mum said.

337

She placed her hands on his shoulders. "You've got this, Jake." She turned to look at me. "*We've* got this."

The doorbell rang.

"Paige, get the door. Jake, help me get drinks in the kitchen," Mum ordered. Dad winked at me as he followed her.

"Happy Christmas!" Madison cheered as I pulled the door open, gritting my teeth as my wrist ached. I tried to refocus on Madison as she bounded past me, her arms full of beautifully wrapped gifts. I exchanged hugs with the moms and pointed them to the makeshift bar. Carter entered behind them and wasted no time wrapping his arms around me. He carried the crisp smell of snow.

"Hello, gorgeous," I said, standing on tiptoes to kiss his freezing nose.

"How's your wrist? Getting used to the cast being off?"

"Still sore," I admitted, "but feeling stronger."

Carter pressed his cold lips against my earlobe. "Poor thing. Do you need me to take your mind off it?"

"Get a room," Madison groaned directly in my other ear so I could do nothing but laugh and shrug out of Carter's embrace.

"Sorry, Mads. Here, give me your coats and we can go and snag a glass of champagne. Manchester rules in this house at Christmas."

"I *love* Manchester rules." Madison shrugged off her coat and disappeared in search of a drink. "Oh, Moms!"

"I don't know why she thinks they'll agree." Carter slid off his gloves and put them in his coat pocket. "They said no at Thanksgiving."

"Madison is the most persistent person I know. They have to give in eventually." I took Carter's coat and hung them both up on the rack. "Anyway…" I twined my arms around his neck again. "How did the scan go?"

"Fine, thanks. No results until after New Year's though, so I'll have a nice case of scanxiety for the next two weeks."

"I hope it's good news," I murmured.

"Me too. It would be nice if my last treatment was actually my last one."

"It would," I agreed, playing with the long hair at the nape of his neck. "But if it's not, I'm here. We all are."

"I know." He kissed me again and I felt all our worries drift away, for a little while at least. It was Christmas. We could worry about the house not selling and Carter's potential relapse another day. He pulled away and tugged at my hand instead. "Come on, we'd better join them before Madison drives everyone— Ouch!"

"What is it?" My heart started to pound. "Are you OK?"

"I'm fine." He dropped my hand and rubbed his hip, straightening the console table by the front door. "Ugh, sorry, I keep forgetting your mom moved that table." A pile of junk mail slipped on to the floor.

"Don't worry, I do too. I'll bin this stuff." I leaned down to pick up the flyers and a thick, cream envelope peeked out at me.

My blood ran cold.

"Carter, get in here!" Madison appeared at the door, a glass of champagne in her hand. "The moms said we can have a drink. This is *unprecedented*!"

"No way!" Carter's face lit up. "Wait – you played the cancer card, didn't you?"

"Mayyyyyybe..." Madison ducked back into the kitchen, calling over her shoulder. "Come on!"

"Amazing!" He shook his head. "Come on, I want to have my first ever glass of champagne with my girlfriend."

"I'll be there in a sec." I watched him disappear and pulled the envelope from the pile with shaking hands. My name was carved into the front with black ink. I ripped open the seal, slid out the thick, folded paper and held my breath as I started to read.

Hello, Paige.

ACKNOWLEDGEMENTS

My first thank you this time must go to you, lovely reader. Without you I wouldn't be writing my twisted little books and having the time of my life doing it. Thank you for spending your hard-earned cash on my words and coming out to meet me at events. You are awesome.

A huge thank you to team *Signed Sealed Dead*. Yasmin Morrissey for first draft wisdom and always letting me follow my instincts on a story; Jenny Glencross for a thoughtful line edit; Sarah Dutton for her wonderful copyediting skills; Tierney Holm for proofreading; Jamie Gregory for gorgeous cover and interior design; Harriet Dunlea for being Number One organizer and Polly Lyall Grant for everything in between. Thank you as always to my super-agent Stephanie Thwaites, Grace Robinson and all the team at Curtis Brown.

In my first published novel, I thanked all the hospital

staff I met during 2016. I was thirty-two when I was diagnosed with breast cancer and it's take a long time to get to a place where I could write about it in some way. Though the character of Carter has leukaemia, a lot of his thoughts and feelings are ones that I had during my treatment (and still sometimes do). Over the last year I have been fortunate enough to attend some online meetings of a book club organized by Cathy Cook, a Teenage Cancer Trust Youth Support Co-ordinator. Not only does the club quiz me on why I choose to kill off certain characters, they also really helped me nail down Carter's emotions and coping mechanisms. Talking to you all about how it feels to go through treatment was so helpful and cathartic in a way I didn't know I needed. Thank you all, I hope I've done you proud. You're all rockstars.

Rosie and Kat, thank you for all the encouragement while we were all trying to draft. To the Discord group – you're awesome. Thanks for letting me in the terrible reviews gang. Finally, to Karen McManus – thank you for your kindness and support – and an AMAZING cover quote.

Thank you to Alison Weatherby, the first reader of my first (very English) draft. You did a great job "Uncle Sam-ing the shit out of it" (her words, not mine).

Thank you to the Winchester brothers. 2023 was the year I watched *Supernatural* from start to finish and the reason for the thing in Paige's basement :)

Thank you to all of my family and friends who are so supportive. I love seeing pictures when you find my books in the wild – it never gets old! Thank you to my lovely writer friends for being so much fun, I look forward to our gatherings so much. Georgia – can't wait until I have a whole shelf of books by you. Vampire Falls 4Eva! Mum and Dad, I love you so much, thanks for being so proud of me and for babysitting the dog when I'm off gallivanting. You're the best. Loli – thank you for the cuddles and walks. You keep me sane and make me laugh every day. I know you can read this.

Luke – you legend. Thank you for being you and being part of everything, from A&E runs to champagne celebrations. I'm so proud to have you as my better half and I look forward to boring you with many more weird ideas over an MPA. I love you xxx

OTHER SPINE-CHILLING BOOKS BY CYNTHIA MURPHY